I0610424

Catching Fox

By Aimee McNeil

Catching Fox

Limitless Publishing, LLC
Kailua, HI 96734
www.limitlesspublishing.com

Formatting: Limitless Publishing

ISBN-13: 978-1-64034-986-5

Dedication

To my daughter, Taylor.
So strong and beautiful.

In life there will always be some,
who will try to knock us down.
It is up to us to pick ourselves up,
and keep moving forward,
Because in the end, you are the only one,
who can truly get in your way.
Follow your dreams and be true to yourself.
I love you forever and always,
To the moon and back.
xox

Prologue

Adalynne sat on her wooden swing, twisting her new white shoes into the dirt beneath her feet. Tears dripped from her cheeks and she watched as they disappeared into the fabric of her dress, leaving tiny dark spots on the material. The ropes of the swing creaked loudly with every sway as she gently pushed it back and forth.

"Why are you crying?"

Adalynne looked up through a veil of perfect blonde curls. A boy close to her age was standing in the line of trees backing onto her property. His voice was so quiet that she thought at first it might have been the breeze. His unkempt dark hair fell over his eyes in dark waves. His knees were visible through his ripped pants and his shirt was adorned with a monster truck with its tongue hanging out. It was a sight that brought a smile to her lips despite her tears.

Adalynne wiped her face with the back on her hand and studied the boy. "Where did you come from?" she asked, looking around to see if anyone else was in his company.

"I live through that way." He pointed into the dense trees behind them. "I heard you crying while I was playing in the woods," the boy explained, looking nervous.

"It's my birthday today and I wanted to wear my favorite dress with pink and blue stripes but my mom made me wear this yellow dress and it scratches my skin," she confessed sadly.

Adalynne slipped off the swing and closed the distance between them. The boy took a hesitant step back with her approach. "What's your name?" she asked curiously. He didn't answer her question but instead looked behind him, anxious and ready to flee. "Don't go," she pleaded.

The boy stood frozen, watching her intently. Adalynne moved slowly out of fear she would scare him away. She had never seen eyes like his. The color green they exhibited was vibrant and breathtaking, putting the foliage around them to shame. It made her think of her bright green crayon that she had used earlier to color the leaves of her trees. He was so beautiful and quiet she thought he might be her imagination. She smiled big and bright, letting him know she wanted to be his friend.

When she was close enough she reached out and took his hand to confirm he was real. His hand trembled beneath her fingers as she held it gently. "My name is Adalynne," she said softly. He looked back at her with wide eyes. Not even a hint of a smile on his lips. "It's my mother's name too." She found herself talking out of fear he would leave if she didn't keep his interest. "It's probably why she wants me to be just like her." Though he remained quiet he seemed to be interested in her words. "Sometimes I wonder if I had another name it would be different and I wouldn't have to wear uncomfortable clothes, and she would just let me be me and have fun."

"You want a different name?" he whispered. He seemed puzzled by her, as if she were a strange creature that mysteriously washed up on shore, his curiosity keeping him captivated.

"Yes! I would love another name." Adalynne reached out and took his other hand in hers as well. He looked down at his hands tightly clasped in hers.

"What would you want your name to be?" he asked.

Adalynne giggled. "Hmmm…" She pondered the thought. The idea of picking her own name excited her. She watched a bee hover over some nearby flowers and her smile deepened. "Bee," she responded happily. "Because then I could wear stripes all the time and play in the flowers whenever I wanted."

He smiled back at her then. It was simply beautiful. "What would you choose?" she asked happily, her tears forgotten now. He shrugged his shoulders and slowly tried to pull his hand from hers but Adalynne was scared to let him go. There was something different about this boy that drew her to him. "How about…" Adalynne thought about what was befitting of the boy in front of her. She remembered when she was playing in her backyard and saw a fox peeking through the trees. It left as quickly as it came without a sound. She never told her mother for fear she wouldn't let her play outside anymore. "Fox?" He could be her secret fox.

Adalynne grew excited with her suggestion. "You remind me of a fox because you are quick, quiet and…beautiful." The smile fell from her lips. "You don't like it?"

"No…I do…I like it," he responded with a small smile, bringing her own back to life.

"I like you," she confessed.

"Adalynne!" She turned back toward her house when she heard her mother call her name. The boy pulled his hands from hers and retreated back into the woods as quiet as he came. It felt like he took a piece of her with him when he left. Her sadness returned as she walked toward her mother's call.

Chapter One

Two Years Later…

Adalynne giggled in excitement but Fox was quiet. They had snuck into her living room and Fox was nervous about being inside her house. "My parents aren't home. No one will know you were here." She reached over and took his hand. He squeezed back before he hesitantly sat down next to her on the piano bench. "I'm glad you'll be the first person I play this for. I've been practicing for a long time." Adalynne positioned her hands before she began, letting the music play through her. She felt so relaxed with Fox by her side. She flawlessly flowed through the notes. When she finished she looked over at him. His beautiful eyes shone with amazement and in that moment she knew she needed to give Fox the gift of music. She could see the wild fire burn in his eyes as he fell in love with it. She would never forget the moment it happened.

Adalynne showed him where to place his hands on the keys and gave him the names of all the notes he played. She found her lesson books from when she started playing and was amazed how he absorbed everything she gave him. They were so entranced in their lesson that they didn't notice the footsteps coming their way until they neared. Fox flew from the piano seat and hid before Carmen, her housekeeper, came into the room.

"Hey there, Addie Girl, I thought you might be hungry with all that practicing. I put a few extra on the plate just in case." She winked at Adalynne before turning on her heel. "Oh and you can tell that young man he doesn't need to hide on my account. He's more than welcome as far as I'm concerned," she called behind her with a chuckle.

"Thank you, Carmen!" Adalynne replied. When she looked around for Fox she found him looking down at the plate of cookies Carmen had set on the coffee table. She always thought it was funny how he looked at food like it was treasure.

"They're still warm," he commented as he stared down at them.

"Go ahead. I'm not hungry." Adalynne smiled. He gave her a smile before he ate the entire plate of oatmeal cookies.

Chapter Two

Two Years Later…

Fox was waiting for her when she got to their meeting place in the woods. He seemed sadder than usual when she approached him, biting his nails like he did when he was upset about something. When he noticed her approach his sullen expression turned into a smile. "Carmen made the banana muffins you like." Adalynne smiled excitedly.

"Sounds good. I'm hungry," Fox said, eyeing the basket.

"You're always hungry." She rolled her eyes and passed him one of the muffins Carmen had packed. They spread out the blanket then lay down on their backs to look up at the sky. Being with Fox was the most natural thing in the world. This is where she felt at home most of all.

"What's wrong?" Adalynne asked after an unusual stretch of silence.

"Dad lost his latest job. He's been really mad lately," Fox whispered. He was always edgy when he talked about his father.

"Are you scared?" Adalynne whispered back, turning on her side so she could look at him. His eyes found hers and held them. She didn't like it when he was upset and it seemed far too often. Fox never did feel comfortable talking about himself. It was always hard for her to manage a clear picture of what bothered him so deeply. She never pushed for information for fear that he would leave. She thought of her own father who she had seen upset on a few occasions but it never made her feel scared. Even her mother, who was always upset about something and Adalynne had been on the receiving end of her anger many times, had never made her feel scared.

"Yes." His beautiful green eyes were Adalynne's favorite color. She moved closer and wrapped her arm around his chest, snuggling close. He lay very still as she held him.

"Why do you never talk about your mother?" Adalynne let the question slip from her lips before she could stop herself. Her question lingered in the air without a response from him and she wanted to take it back. She could feel his heart racing under her touch.

"She died when I was little," he said quietly after a long stretch of silence. They didn't raise their voices more than a whisper, as if they were having a forbidden conversation. Though they were far from anyone and everything, the reason they picked this place as their own was it was their escape. Adalynne didn't say anything for worry she would say the wrong thing. She only waited with the hope that he would continue talking. "I don't remember her much but she liked to sing. I can remember her singing me to sleep."

"That's a nice memory to have," she said softly, saddened by his confession.

"It made me feel safe." He reached up and returned Adalynne's embrace for the first time since she met him. They laid there for a long time holding each other until the day grew old and they knew they had to return to their separate lives.

***

It was dark and she had been asleep until a sound against her window woke her from her dreams. She crawled out of bed and peered down to see what had caused the sound. Her eyes fell on Fox, standing below. She pulled open her window and a gentle breeze blew in around her, encircling her in her curtains.

"What are you doing here?" Adalynne whispered, looking around to make sure his presence was unnoticed by anyone else.

"Can I come up?" His voice sounded different and it scared her. She could tell he had been crying. She nodded in response and he immediately began to climb the tree that grew tall outside her room. She reached out to take his hand as he neared, helping him through her window. When he was inside she noticed the blood on his face. She touched his swollen lip to reveal the blood was now dry. He flinched slightly at her touch but did not pull away.

"You can sit on my bed." She motioned toward it before disappearing in her bathroom adjoining her room to retrieve a wet face cloth. She tried to clean his injured face without disturbing the cut. She didn't realize she was crying until Fox reached up and wiped a tear away from her face.

They crawled into bed together. Adalynne pulled the blanket up tightly around them. She didn't want him to be sad anymore. Wrapping her arm around him, she quietly sang. She wanted him to feel safe with her and to know she would always be there for him. She hoped he would remember how he felt when his mother was still with him, so she sang until his breathing slowed and he was fast asleep. He stayed with her that night, curled up beside her in bed.

The next morning when Adalynne woke, she got up quietly to let Fox continue sleeping. He hadn't moved since he had fallen asleep. He looked more peaceful than she had ever seen him, despite his swollen lip. Her parents always left early for work and Carmen always let her sleep in, so she wasn't worried anyone would find him in her room. As she watched him she picked up her drawing book and colored pencils to draw a picture.

"Hi," Fox said when he woke a short while later. Adalynne looked up to see his eyes open. It looked funny to see him in her pink frilly bed, surrounded by lacy curtains that hung from the framed poster bed.

"Hi," she responded with a smile. "Do you feel okay?"

Fox sat up and rubbed his eyes. "Yeah."

"I drew a picture of us." She held up her picture she was working on.

He grinned. "I like it."

Adalynne turned the picture back toward her and smiled at her creation. The picture she drew was of a fox and a bee with hearts all around them. "I like it too."

Chapter Three

Two Years Later...

"I packed lunch today too since you haven't been coming home until late," Carmen, called out to Adalynne after she ran through the kitchen, grabbing the basket on her way.

"Thanks, Carmen, you're the best," Adalynne hollered over her shoulder as she made her way to the garage to grab some nails. She remembered they were getting low yesterday. She hurried through the trees quickly, eager to get to the camp before Fox. Lately he was always there first and hard at work when she got there. When she arrived he was already there as usual, sawing away at pieces of wood. They only had a handsaw because they were in the middle of the forest. Their progress was slow but steady as the summer days passed. After all their hard work it was finally taking shape and the excitement of what they built swirled in her stomach.

"Morning." Adalynne smiled when he noticed

her arrival. They worked for hours that day doing the finishing touches on the roof. When the sun began its descent from the sky in the late afternoon they sat inside, exhausted from the work.

"It's perfect." Adalynne leaned back against the wall. Fox followed suit and leaned back beside her but flinched slightly when his back met the wall.

"Again?" She reached for the sleeve of his shirt, pulling it up to expose the marks on his shoulder. "Oh my god, Fox. You have to tell someone. It happens so often now." Her concern for him was strong with her words.

"No. I can handle it. You can't say anything, Bee. You promised me." His green eyes turned on her, the fear of what would happen ran deep. She only nodded, unable to form any words upon her lips. His fear felt as if it were hers. She only wished she knew how to help him. She was tired of feeling helpless when he was in pain. She hated his father for hurting him so much but he refused to let her tell anyone who could help. No matter how many times his father hit him he never spoke ill of him. She didn't understand why he protected his father when he did nothing but hurt Fox. Adalynne didn't know what she was supposed to do and she was stuck doing nothing at all.

"I brought something for you, so you will remember me when you go away," Fox said, reaching for his sweater.

"I could never forget you." Adalynne smiled sadly. She was still haunted by the marks upon his skin.

Fox turned around, handing her a small box.

"What's this?" she asked, studying the box he placed in her hand.

"Open it." He smiled encouragingly.

She pulled the lid off to reveal a chain with a small bee charm. "I love it! Thank you. Can you put it on me?" When Fox clasped it around her neck it fell perfectly in view. She reached up and touched the small charm and smiled. "Can I give you something?" she asked after she admired the necklace.

"Sure." He smiled.

"I want to give you a kiss," she told him. The smile fell from his lips as he stared at her. She couldn't read his expression as he stared at her. "Um…I heard that your first kiss is special and you never forget it so I want it to be with you." She leaned closer to him but Fox remained perfectly still. "Okay?" He didn't speak but only gave her a slight nod in response. She looked at his lips, the way they curved into the perfect shape. Her stomach felt as if she swallowed fireworks. She leaned in until she could feel his uneven breath upon her face and she closed her eyes before pressing her lips to his.

Chapter Four

Five Years Later…

On the first day of school Adalynne planned to surprise Fox. It was the beginning of senior year and she was riddled with excitement. She had envisioned the whole scenario in her mind over and over about his reaction with her arrival. She had struggled with keeping the secret over the summer every time he slipped into her bedroom window late at night. Things were different now that they were getting older. There were not so many days spent in the woods but rather nights curled up in bed together. She always left her window open for him because most nights he would come. Sometimes they talked and others they just lay together. On those nights with him beside her she slept well; on the nights that he did not come she was too worried to sleep.

She loved the nights she could wrap her arms around him and become intoxicated with all the new feelings he stirred within her. He was more than just the boy Adalynne loved. She was falling deeper into exciting unknown territory. She often wondered if he was on the same path or if he still saw her as the little girl with scraped knees and endless questions.

One of the stipulations for attending the public school was no school bus. Her father had arranged a car service to take her to and from school and unfortunately the driver had strict orders to drop her off at the front entrance. Adalynne exited the car quickly, noticing the car was drawing much attention. She avoided the stares of the many students that scattered the school yard and began her search for Fox. It wasn't long before she saw his lean form sauntering through the sea of people. He was her oldest friend and she had known him for many years but this was the first time she had seen him in a public environment and not in the shelter of their secret world. He had a confidence and power to him that seemed strange to her. She didn't draw his attention immediately. Instead, she familiarized herself with the side of him that was new to her. His jeans rode low on his lean hips and his loose fitted shirt could not hide the well-formed chest beneath. He was always taller than her but surrounded by all these other people his presence seemed so much larger and demanding. His disheveled dark hair fell over his eyes and begged for her fingers to run through it. He was always the most beautiful thing to her. Her heart swelled watching him. He didn't notice her as he approached a group of people she could only assume were his friends. She watched how at ease he seemed to be with them and the way they were drawn to the powerful presence he exuded.

A girl broke away from the group. She had long straight brown hair and a very short skirt which revealed beautiful long legs. She wrapped her arms around Fox's waist and pressed her body against his. A smile formed upon his lips as he welcomed her embrace and leaned in to kiss her readied lips. Adalynne's heart shattered as she struggled to breathe. She stood staring at them kissing as her heart beat raged above any noise around her. She stood staring in a state of shock until someone in the group noticed her. He must have said something to the group because everyone's eyes swung her way. Fox's eyes met hers.

His expression gave nothing away before he dismissed her, turning his attention back to his friends. They all laughed at something he said and her world crumbled. The haunting realization of his disregard crushed her. Adalynne turned abruptly and hurried into the building before anyone saw her tears. She felt like an idiot for not realizing that maybe the reason he had kept their relationship a secret for all those years was because he was embarrassed or didn't see her as important enough to be a part of his real life.

Adalynne had loved him from the moment he showed up in her backyard and she held his trembling hand within hers. The feelings she had for him over the years spoke of so many promises of what they could share together. She had given her heart completely to him and now she was left with nothing but the shattered remains.

Over the next few months as Adalynne adjusted

to life at her new school she was painfully aware that Fox was avoiding her in every way. Not once did he attempt to talk to her. He went so far as to deny he knew her, leaving her to pretend he was a stranger to her as well. She had fought so hard to get her parents to agree to let her make the change to public school; she was not about to let them know it had been a mistake. Fox never came to her window again after that day. She lay awake night after night with the hope he would come back to her and explain this whole horrible situation but she was only left with disappointment. Sometimes she found herself walking by him in the school yard just to feel close for a brief moment but his scent would only stir her broken heart. When he sensed her nearness, his posture would noticeably stiffen like he couldn't stand being close to her. It became too much to bear so eventually she avoided him altogether. All she had of him was her memories and the occasional glance from a distance. Her Fox was no longer hers.

Adalynne tried to engage in life around her and make the most of the situation. Making friends was easier than she expected and life began to find some normalcy despite the circumstances. Soon she fell into a pattern with her new friends. Her mother luckily approved of Molly and Brooke because of their reputable parents. Adalynne didn't care much about where they came from but their friendship was a comfort to her and she enjoyed their company. Molly was the gossip queen and loved to talk about everything and everyone but she had a big heart and never intentionally caused any harm.

She had naturally curly strawberry blonde hair she insisted on straightening until no one would even fathom that a curl ever existed upon her head. Brooke was short, barely reaching five feet, with shoulder length brown hair and thick framed glasses that complemented her features beautifully. She was completely obsessed with boys and clothes, full of sweetness, and was always the first to lend a hand. They made her adjustment bearable and she was grateful to have met them.

It also took some time to get used to attention from boys. It was new, exciting, and somewhat uneasy at the same time for Adalynne. Coming from an all-girls school, she wasn't used to hanging out with the male population on a regular basis. She quickly realized how sheltered she had been as she transitioned to her new school. Collin was one of the first boys who made an effort to get to know Adalynne. As far as Molly was concerned, he was as good as it got.

Collin was tall, muscular, and liked by the entire school population. Adalynne appreciated his company and enjoyed getting to know him. He had a charm people found irresistible and Adalynne was no exception. It was also nice to have the distraction. It soon became a regular occurrence to find themselves in the company of Collin and the other football players. Molly and Brooke loved the new turn of events.

"He is so crushing on you," Molly breathed excitedly in her ear as she pulled Adalynne aside. They were standing with Collin and a few of his friends in the hallway before classes started.

Adalynne looked up toward Collin. He winked in return and Adalynne could feel her blush warm her face.

"Really?" Adalynne had noticed his subtle touches and the way he always found an excuse to spend time with her but she didn't trust her feelings lately. She had been completely wrong when it came to Fox.

"Maybe he will ask you to the winter formal...I bet he will. You guys would make a beautiful couple." Adalynne looked at Collin and wondered what it would be like. Her whole life she only considered one person to give her heart to but everything had changed and maybe it was time she tried to change with it.

Molly had been right, it was only days later that Collin asked her to the winter formal. She had gone with Molly and Brooke to buy the dress for the evening. She felt exposed and daring but she wanted to dress to impress. She had to admit she did love the way the dress hugged her curves and the fabric flowed weightlessly around her thighs. The material stopped just before her knee with a couple of slits that traveled further. She had gone to Brooke's house to get ready for the dance because she had a feeling her mother would not approve of her dress choice.

Collin had been wonderful and she was glad she agreed to go with him. When they arrived at the gym she remembered the excitement that coursed through her. It had been her first dance and she couldn't contain the delight that painted a ridiculous smile on her face.

"I know I already told you this but you look amazing," Collin gushed in her ear. The music was loud, making it hard to hear. After thanking him for his compliment she took a sip of the cold liquid in her glass. She was met with an unexpected taste of liquor in her mouth. The burning sensation watered her eyes.

"Wow," she said in response to the foul tasting drink.

"Good, huh?" he asked with a smile.

"Yeah, great. Thanks!" she said brightly, despite the fact that she didn't think she could stomach anymore. She let her eyes wander to the dance floor. Her stomach dropped when she noticed Fox across the room. His girlfriend was hanging off his arm with her tiny black dress and bright red heels. She tried to ignore them but it was like trying not to notice an elephant walk into the room; it was the only thing she could see. Her gaze kept navigating back to their affectionate interactions every time she averted her eyes. Anger and jealousy simmered low in her stomach, burning away all the initial excitement from earlier.

"Who are we looking at?" Molly asked, coming up behind her. "Oh…Damon Knight. That's trouble if I ever saw it. Did I tell you about the time he was arrested for breaking and entering? At least he's easy on the eyes. Such a waste of a good thing, don't you think?"

It was always strange hearing him called by his real name. Adalynne had only ever known him as Fox and never with this bad boy image. She wondered if she ever really knew him at all. The boy across the gym looked like her Fox but he was more of a stranger than anyone else.

"Yeah. Do you mind distracting Collin for me? I have to go dump this gross concoction he gave me and replace it with regular punch." Adalynne stuck her finger down her throat to emphasize how gross it was.

"Let me try it." Molly took a sip. "Harsh," she gasped, "gotcha covered." She smiled before heading toward Collin.

Adalynne weaved her way through the sea of people, deciding to take the long way to avoid Fox and his attachment. When she reached the punch table she discarded the glass Collin gave her and poured a new one.

"Nice dress." Adalynne's heart quickened at the familiar deep voice close to her ear. The nearness of him startled her. "Not your usual look, but I approve." There was cockiness to his voice that was foreign to her, making her heart twist painfully. She took a deep breath and turned to acknowledge him.

"Hello Fox. If there's one thing that I have learned this year is that people change and just so you know, I don't care for your approval." She hated the fact that he looked so beautiful. He wore a dark fitted buttoned shirt with jeans that fit him perfectly. Adalynne wanted him to acknowledge her for so long and now that he finally did, she wanted to run away. Wounds that she thought were beginning to heal were suddenly ripped wide open and she was completely vulnerable. She needed to get away from him to keep her composure, she already felt herself coming apart at the seams. All she could think of was wrapping her arms around him and searching those green eyes for any sign of her Fox.

"Bee?" he called, grabbing her wrist when she tried to walk past him. She looked down at his hand firmly gripping her wrist before looking up into his eyes. His touch felt better than she imagined it would after being apart for so long. It was like an electrical current that excited every part of her. Her body and soul screamed out for more but they were feelings she could no longer trust. She knew it was all just an illusion now. She pulled away and walked as fast as she could back to her friends. She tried not to look back but she couldn't help it. He stood where she left him staring back at her.

"What was that all about?" Brooke asked, noticing the exchange between them.

"Misunderstanding is all. Do you want to dance?" She pulled Brooke out on the dance floor before she even had time to answer and Molly soon followed. She tried to forget about Fox being there, about how she still craved his touch after what he had done to her. She needed to forget him. Dancing with the girls was a nice distraction and she could feel her forced smile turn genuine as the night carried on, though his presence was like a beacon in the dark room calling to her.

Soon a slow song followed the string of dance music and Collin requested a dance. He pulled her close to him, wrapping his arms around her waist. Adalynne leaned into him as they moved to the music; his hands slowly explored the curve of her back. She breathed in his musky cologne and tried

23

to lose herself in the moment. Collin was a good guy, handsome and athletic. He wanted her; she could feel it in the way his hands roamed her body and in the way his eyes always followed her in a room. She wanted to want him too. She pulled back and glanced up into his eyes, looking for a connection that would burn away any lingering doubts. Collin surprised her when he leaned in and claimed her lips in an unexpected kiss. It was slow and tentative as he waited for her to react. Her first instinct was to pull away but she decided to return it. It felt nice.

The kiss was suddenly cut short when Collin was ripped from her arms. She screamed when Fox punched Collin in the face, knocking Collin to the ground before he could even register what was happening. "What the fuck, man!" Collin's hand immediately went up to his mouth. His lip was dripping blood down his light blue shirt.

"Fox!" Adalynne yelled before she could stop herself. Collin shot her a confused look as she reached down to help him up but instead he launched himself toward Fox. The two of them battled it out until a teacher managed to break up the fight.

Adalynne couldn't get home from the dance fast enough. Molly and Brooke showered her with questions but she didn't feel like talking. She apologized and left with their questions still lingering in the air. She was grateful her driver was waiting outside and she crawled into the back of the car without having to give an explanation for her early departure. Fortunately her parents weren't home when the driver dropped her off. She ran directly to her room, locked her door, and collapsed on her bed.

She wasn't sure how long she laid there before she heard a noise outside. She was lost in her turmoil of thoughts. She looked up to see Fox had slipped in her open window and her heart began to race. She could see the dark bruise forming under his left eye and the realness of the night returned to her. He leaned against her window with his long legs stretched across her floor. He didn't move any further into the room as he watched her on the bed. Adalynne sat up and pulled a clip from her hair, letting a cascade of loose waves fall over her shoulders and down her back. She could feel the hot tears run down her cheeks but she made no move to wipe them away. She hated herself for wanting him there. Despite everything, his presence still brought her comfort.

"What happened?" she asked in a strained voice.

"I got in a fight," he replied with a small smile that curved the edges of his lips.

"No, not that." Adalynne sighed. "With us. Why do you hate me now?"

"I don't hate you, Bee. I could never hate you." His voice was strange to her, rough and tired.

"Well, you fooled me." She slid off the bed and leaned against the post at the foot of her bed.

Fox ran his fingers through his hair and looked away from her, avoiding her gaze. "I didn't want you to know that part of me. I panicked. I'm not a good person. When it was just you and me, you didn't know who I really was, just the parts I showed you."

"I like every part of you," she whispered.

"You wouldn't say that if you knew who I really am." He looked up at her with his eyes full of sorrow.

"You never told me you had a girlfriend." She couldn't hide the jealousy that slipped through with her words.

He shrugged his shoulders. "I didn't think it was important."

"Well, it was. When I saw you together I was mad because I wanted to be the one you kissed like that." Color flooded her cheeks at her confession. They had been close for so long, talked about everything, but this was the first time she confessed her feelings toward him. This is the first time she indicated she wanted more. They had shared many kisses over the years but they were innocent and without expectation. She wanted him to want her with the need she had for him.

Somewhere along their path, her feelings changed from their innocent childhood friendship to an attraction altogether different. The need to be physically close to him was overwhelming. Everything about his body called to her. The way he moved, the confidence of his actions, his tall muscular lean frame, the sound of his voice, his smell, the look in his eyes when he looked at her, they all taunted her with a desire she could not fulfill because she was scared he could never return those feelings.

"Don't say that. We can't be together like that. It would never work." He leaned his head back against the window pane and closed his eyes tight.

"Do you love her?" Adalynne whispered just loud enough for him to hear. It was a question that she wanted to ask but she was scared of what his answer might be.

"No," he answered without hesitation. Adalynne let out a breath she didn't know she was holding.

There was a long stretch of silence before Fox filled it. "You shouldn't wear clothes that are so revealing."

"Why?" Adalynne looked down at her plunging neckline. "You said you approved of it and besides, most of the girls there were wearing similar if not more revealing clothes."

"You aren't like the other girls. You are so much more beautiful than them. You don't need to draw attention to certain aspects to make yourself more appealing than you already are." He looked at her then, like he used to when their world was just the two of them. His green eyes seemed endless.

"Apparently I'm not appealing enough for you," she said as she reached back and unzipped her dress, letting it fall to the floor at her feet. "There, I'm not wearing it anymore. Is that better?"

She watched the look of shock on his face at her unexpected move. He just stared at her. "You're wrong. I think you are the most appealing thing I have ever seen."

Adalynne unclasped her bra, letting it meet the same fate as her dress.

"Don't." He tried to pull his gaze away. His voice was pained. "Please don't."

She didn't stop because she wanted him to see

her. She wanted him to be the first to ever see her naked, to know her body. She wanted him to be all of her firsts because he was the first one to claim her heart. Sliding her panties off, she stood before him completely bare. He didn't move as he took in her body, learning the way she curved. His eyes scorched and excited her. She didn't know where she was calling her bravery from. This was a bold move for her but she didn't know if this moment was all they had.

"You make it so hard for me to do the right thing." He stood then with a hunger in his eyes she had never seen before. He ran his fingers through his hair again, causing it to fall haphazardly around his perfectly chiseled face. He closed the distance quickly, wrapping his arms around her waist and pulling her against his body, crushing his lips against hers. They were urgent kisses, like he was scared the moment would end. His hands felt her bare flesh and he pulled her closer still. She met his kisses and touch with the same insistence. Grasping his shirt, she pulled it up to expose his perfectly formed stomach. The feel of her naked flesh against his was the most sensual, unreal experience she'd ever had. He pulled his shirt off the rest of the way with one quick motion and discarded it on the floor. She pressed her soft curves against his hard body, completely dizzy with need. Adalynne's hands found his belt and she undid it, pulling it from his pants. He immediately shed his pants and Adalynne was taken aback by how striking he really was as he stood before her naked.

"You don't know how long I have wanted to do

this," he panted against her neck, "to touch you like this." Adalynne was shocked by his confession. She had no words for the intensity of the moment, she wasn't even sure she was still able to speak.

Fox laid her back against her bed, leaning upon his arms he looked down at her. She ran her fingers through his hair as he took her breast in his mouth, teasing her nipple. She cried out in unexpected pleasure and she let him explore her. His hand traveled down the length of her body, slowly past her navel until he gently touched her wetness that welcomed him. His fingers against her body, touching her, pleasuring her, felt like an out of body experience with sensations that she did not know were possible. The feeling of bliss filled her so full that she was suddenly awash with an overwhelming sense of release that made her cry out. He leaned down over her trembling body.

Adalynne reached down to take him in her hand, feeling the length of him. "Don't," he pleaded, trying to stop her hand.

"Please," she begged before her insistent hand continued. She stroked him, discovering his body before he moaned and spilled his hot pleasure on her stomach.

It was Adalynne's first and only intimate experience. She cherished the memory because it was all he gave her. The next day at school he broke up with his girlfriend. Adalynne remembered watching the dramatic scene his girlfriend pulled in front of the school yard.

Things didn't change much for how they interacted at school or in public. He kept his distance from her and she didn't push him, respecting his wishes. Sometimes when he walked by her in the hall or in the schoolyard, he would purposely brush against her and sometimes even grab her hand for only a moment before he was gone. He never did come to stay with her at night again after that, even though she left her window wide open for him every night. When she woke in the morning to see her window closed tight she knew he had been there and it was enough for now. She wanted more but it was better than the cold shoulder he gave her before.

Chapter Five

Present Day…

"How long are you gonna make him wait?"

"What are you talking about?" Adalynne looked at her friend standing beside her. The sun shone in full glory down upon them, unwavering in its heat. It brought out the red in Katie's auburn hair as her wet curls glistened in the light. Her barely there bikini top was paired with cut off jean shorts. It was much the same as the other girls' outfits, including her own. It was the dress code for the event. They were hosting a car wash to raise money for their sorority house. Their house mother, Meghan, insisted they pull off the infamous sexy car wash because it was a guaranteed money maker. Adalynne looked down at the small triangles struggling to contain her assets and sighed. How Katie talked her into wearing this getup was beyond her.

"*Hello hottie*," Katie drew out appreciatively as she pointed toward Matthew. He was standing with a group of guys watching from the sidelines like starving animals. Adalynne swatted her hand down before he saw they were talking about him. Too late. Matthew waved back confidently, loving the attention.

"You're making his head swell even bigger." Adalynne complained. Katie and Adalynne had met the first day of initiation for the Roth Sorority, just over a month ago. It only took them a moment to hit off a friendship and they had been practically inseparable since. "His boner's been pointing at you since he got here and he's practically frothing at the mouth. He's just itching to get a taste of what you are hiding in those seriously short shorts."

"Katie, please." Adalynne widened her eyes in a silent *shut-your-mouth* look before grabbing her sponge out of the bucket of soapy hot water.

"Well?" Katie persisted.

Adalynne sighed. "It doesn't feel right yet...I don't know. I want it to be perfect. Besides we haven't even really had an official date." Adalynne trailed off as she rubbed her sponge over a black sports car she knew they had already washed earlier; apparently the owner was eager to support their 'cause.'

"Oh my god, Addie! You're still a virgin!" Katie blared, to Adalynne's horror. Adalynne could feel the color creep across her face as the girls around them shot her looks.

"Katie, seriously!" Adalynne begged her to be quiet.

"Sorry. It's just, how can *you* still be a..." Her words trailed off when Adalynne gave her a warning look. "That breaks the law of physics."

"That doesn't even begin to make sense." Adalynne sighed. This was the last place she wanted to talk about her sex life—there were a bunch of gossiping girls surrounding them.

"Waiting for Mister Right, huh? Well, if you ask me, Matthew looks pretty right. He is hot—look at how his muscles are formed in all the right places. It's sinful," Katie said staring at him, "but what do I know. I gave my virginity away ages ago. It was some guy at one of my sister's parties. It's funny I can't remember what his name was...Tom maybe. Anyway the whole time I couldn't wait for him to stop. I felt like I was going to throw up. He was shoving that thing around in there like he wasn't sure what direction he wanted to go. Afterward I had nightmares for weeks because I kept hearing his moaning in my ears like a zombie was going to attack me when I lay in bed at night. Seriously, he sounded like he was straight out of one of those cheesy zombie flicks. I was traumatized but eventually I moved on to others. All different variations of bad, mind you, but never as bad as my first. I figure I'll be forty by the time I find someone who knows what they're doing. I'm getting tired of having to get myself off." Katie pulled her sponge out of the bucket and slapped it on the car, taking her frustrations out.

A loud cheer erupted around them. Adalynne and Katie both turned to see Mary and Kimber playing the crowd with a make-out session against the front of the car. The owner had his phone trained on the scene while drooling at the action his car was getting. It was pretty much guaranteed this was ending up online. The second wash was definitely paying off for this man because he was getting his money's worth. The car looked expensive but he didn't seem fazed that two girls were lying down on the hood, grinding against each other. Adalynne didn't know them very well but she knew this wasn't the first time they had pulled this display to please a crowd of adoring men.

Adalynne took the opportunity for a break. The scene looked like it could go on for a while as the audience was waiting in hopeful anticipation clothes would soon come off. She was in desperate need of a drink. The sun was hot and she had lost count of how many cars she had scrubbed down. Katie followed close on her heels as they made their way into the convenience store next to the parking lot they had claimed for their fundraising efforts. Adalynne headed straight for the glass doors in the back of the store. Countless brands of beverages lined the shelves but she grabbed the most normal looking bottle of water she could see and immediately placed it against her neck. "Ah…feels good. It's so hot today."

"Tell me about it. I am sweating in places I didn't know I had." Katie grabbed her own beverage before heading to the checkout. A nervous looking young man sat on a stool behind the counter. He was on the thin side, with long brown hair that hung in his face. They dropped their purchases on the counter in front of him. A deep red crawled over his skin as he took in the barely dressed girls. "Great day for a car wash." His voice cracked.

"You enjoying the view?" Katie leaned over the counter in an attempt to emphasize her cleavage. The young guy's eyes widened, his edginess causing him to knock over a display of protein bars. They fell down and scattered at his feet. Katie had a curvy physique she was not afraid to use to her advantage. Adalynne, on the other hand, tended to be more conservative with her figure, but based on what she was currently wearing, one would never know it.

"Yes…ah…the drinks are on the house…you look hot. I mean you look like you need a drink." The boy stumbled through his words. He dropped down to pick up the bars without waiting for their reply.

"Thanks a bunch, sweetness." Katie beamed, leaning over the counter.

The main door opened. Adalynne turned to see Matthew walk in, his attentions focused on her. She couldn't help but smile. He was beautiful with his bleached blond hair and strong masculine features. "Addie, you look good enough to eat." His signature sly smile spread across his lips.

"Hey there, the show getting too hot for you out there?" Katie raised her brow.

"No such thing. I just wanted to see what Addie had planned tonight?" He turned back toward Adalynne with a sparkle in his eye. "Any plans?"

"Not that I know of, but I'm sure Meghan has something planned for us newbies." Adalynne rolled her eyes. Meghan was simply wicked when it came to exacting her power over the new sorority recruits. She couldn't help but appreciate how gorgeous Matthew was. He looked as if he walked off the cover of a magazine with his perfect lines and magnetic gray eyes. She marveled with the idea of spending time with him, wondering what would come of it. When she started school in a new town she promised herself she would date, meet new people, and enjoy everything this new adventure brought. A part of her reeled at his attention. This is what she wanted after all, a fresh start, but a much bigger part of her still mourned what she left behind when she came here. She just didn't know how to overcome it.

"Maybe I'll speak to Meghan to see if I can persuade her to let the girls out for a little fun tonight. Our house is having a small get together." His confidence was a stark contrast to the nervous boy behind the counter. Adalynne couldn't help but find the quality incredibly sexy.

"Sounds like fun. Hopefully your skills in persuasion are exceptional because Meghan seems to be the stubborn type." Adalynne smiled despite her hesitance. She didn't have much luck when it came to parties, in her experience.

"All my skills are exceptional." He winked before turning to leave. "Any time after ten. See you there." He turned back when he reached the door. "Oh and Adalynne, I do believe red is my new favorite color," he added before pushing the door open. He let his eyes roam the length of Adalynne's body before walking out the door. Adalynne was sure her cheeks turned the same color as her bathing suit after he left. She was grateful he wasn't there to see it.

"You are in so much trouble!" Katie could barely control the excitement in her voice as she warned Adalynne. "I have no idea how you can retain your self-control around him. I would let him do whatever he wanted to me and he could even moan like the walking dead all he wanted."

"Oh Katie." Adalynne shook her head with a smile.

"What?" Katie countered before they both erupted into a fit of laughter. "I'm just saying I think he knows his way around a woman's body."

***

True to his word, Matthew came through with his plan to persuade Meghan into letting them have the night to enjoy with no strings attached. It was strange not having a task to fulfill or duties to carry out for Meghan or the other senior girls of the house. Those girls took their position of power seriously. Meghan had taken a special interest in making her life miserable since Matthew started paying Adalynne so much attention. Katie had dug up some information and informed Adalynne it was because Meghan and Matthew had a history together and apparently she wasn't over him.

Since the moment she had arrived for her first year of university it had been a whirlwind of commotion. Other than the drama and demands the sorority provided, Adalynne also started a full schedule of classes she had no interest in, making it hard for her to focus. Her reason for attending this prestigious school was because generations of her family before her had attended and it was expected that she uphold the tradition. Her mother's main priority had always been maintaining appearances. There was never a discussion of which direction Adalynne wanted to steer her own future. It was decided for her long before she even considered what she wanted her career to be. Adalynne's father was a successful lawyer from a family that had established a name in the industry for many generations. Her mother was a therapist who worked with high profile clients. Although the grades came easily to her, neither one of these professions interested Adalynne.

Adalynne's love was the arts, preferably music. Unfortunately her mother viewed music as simply a pastime and not a suitable career choice. Even though she was not currently working toward her own goals, she was at least granted the freedom to be out of her mother's stifling grasp on a daily basis. Her heart was not with her in this new endeavor and it was slowly taking its toll on her. The course load was heavy, and without her passion to drive her, she found it hard to push herself. Her busy schedule allowed no time for music or painting. The few art supplies she had brought were still packed in a box in the bottom of her closet and it called to her now as she sat in her room organizing her latest assignment, surrounded by a sea of papers covering her bed.

Adalynne opened her closet and pulled out the heavy box. Ripping the tape from the top, she revealed the treasures waiting inside. It seemed like a lifetime ago when she packed this box as she ran her fingers over the tubes of paint. Adalynne's fingers came to rest on an old notepad from when she was a child. The cover was worn and practically falling off as she smoothed out the bent edges. Flipping through the pages was like stepping back through time. Memories swirled the emotions within her. She came to rest on one drawing she remembered very clearly. Running her fingers over the pencil lines, a smile graced her lips. It was the picture of a fox and bee she had drawn the first night Fox came to her room.

It had been four years since Adalynne first met Fox on her sixth birthday. They had seen each other many times since that day, always meeting secretly in the woods behind her house. Fox refused to venture too far from the cover of the trees for fear her parents would see him. He made her swear not to tell her parents about his visits and insisted that their friendship remain a secret. Adalynne was more than happy to oblige. Her mother had so many rules and she knew well enough by then if her mother found out about Fox it would be the last time she would see him.

In the summer they met almost every day in the secret meeting place they had discovered together— a small clearing in the woods where the sun would shine down on them and a few large rocks made perfect places to sit. During the school year their visits tended to be restricted to weekends. Much to Adalynne's dismay, she was homeschooled by a woman her mother hired to come to their home. Mrs. Clemont was dreadfully boring and never made anything exciting. Adalynne wanted to go to school with other children her age. Most of all she wanted to go to school with Fox and missed him desperately when he was gone for long periods of time. Even the playdates her mother arranged for her with other girls her age didn't ease her sadness. She would always find herself just waiting for his return.

Adalynne always asked their housekeeper, Carmen, to pack her a picnic to eat in the woods for lunch whenever she met Fox. She had told Carmen to pack extra just to be safe; never revealing it was because she was meeting Fox. Carmen just smiled at her with her friendly brown eyes and always packed special treats for two without question.

Unlike her mother, Carmen always gave Adalynne the freedom she craved to play and have fun. Carmen had a way of knowing things without having to be told that always amazed Adalynne. She adored Carmen, a constant in her life for as long as she could remember. Whenever Adalynne needed anything Carmen was the first person who came to mind. In her eyes Carmen was a part of her family.

The jarring sound of the door swinging open and banging against the wall jolted Adalynne from her thoughts.

"Party time!" Katie bounded into the room, slamming it closed behind her. "Isn't it lovely to be free of those demanding bitches for the evening?" Katie threw herself on her bed on the other side of the room. The springs of the mattress protested against her abuse.

"You just wait till you're the senior girl of the

house. You'll be worse than they are," Adalynne replied, closing up her box of paints and sliding it back in the closet.

"Of course. I will be the most demanding bitch. It will be my right, after all." She giggled delightfully at the thought of the shift in power. Adalynne sat down on the edge of her own bed.

There was an invisible line that ran through the center of the room showing the joining of two very different people. Katie's side of the room was eclectic with a mix of every color, pattern, and knickknack possible crammed into her side of the room, while Adalynne's side was bare. She never felt expressive in her room. In fact, since she had arrived she couldn't ignore a strong sense that this was not where she was supposed to be and it showed in her lack of interest in making the space hers.

"What are you wearing tonight?" Katie asked, half muffled into her pillow.

"Not sure. I was thinking of something black," Adalynne responded. She gathered up her papers and set them on her nightstand. Adalynne admired Katie's carefree, energy abundant, and always eccentric roommate. When Adalynne arrived at the Roth house on the first day she felt anything but excitement for what lay ahead. She didn't know how long she stood outside of the house after her driver dropped her off. Both her parents had to work and she insisted that they didn't have to take the day off to help her move. She couldn't bear to hear her mother's 'this is where you belong' speech again or she would lose her sanity.

She stared at the sorority house, unable to bring herself to walk up the front steps to the door of a life she did not want. She was assured her belongings had already arrived by her father, who had them delivered the day before but it provided little comfort. She felt like she was in someone else's life and wondered if she would ever be able to live her own.

She remembered when Katie walked up behind her, loaded with as many bags as she could carry.

"I was already in there for a tour. It's not that scary...well, that doesn't apply to some of the girls in it. I think it would be best to find out who not to cross quickly if we want to survive our first year."

Adalynne smiled at the spunky girl beside her with the wild curls and big brown eyes. "I'm Adalynne."

"I'm Katie and you look terrified." She beamed brightly back at Adalynne.

"I am," Adalynne admitted. "That obvious?"

"Let's stick together. It might improve our chances of getting out of here alive." Katie nudged her.

"Sounds good," Adalynne agreed, taking one of the many bags Katie was struggling with.

It was then that their bond began to form. It wasn't long before Katie found her way into Adalynne's heart. She was truly a wonderful friend.

Katie jumped off the bed. "Not black. Wear something more...alluring for your admirers." Katie threw open Adalynne's closet doors and rifled through her clothes.

"Oh yes, how could I be so thoughtless and not consider my many admirers?" Adalynne said sarcastically.

"Deny all you want but you are the new hot piece of meat on campus and all the boys are hungry. Just look at Matthew. He doesn't know what to do with himself," Katie said, pulling a red dress from her closet. "Wear this."

"Ugh. Let's just stay in and order pizza," Adalynne tried to entice Katie with her favorite food.

"Nice try but not a chance. Besides, it wouldn't be long before Matthew hunted you down. I'm pretty sure it was his idea to have this party just so he could get you in his house and put the moves on you. Oh…" Katie darted over to her own closet, permanently open due to the fact that the contents within were spilling out onto the floor. "Look at this!" She pulled out a multi-colored mini dress and did a little happy dance. "What do you think?" She looked up at Adalynne, wild with excitement.

"I think you are in for an exciting night with that dress." Adalynne couldn't help but smile and wonder if Katie's curvy body would even be covered in the small piece of fabric she held up.

"I know!" She squealed. "Bring it on."

***

The music from the Alpha house could be heard as soon as Adalynne and Katie walked out of the Roth house. Adalynne had caved to Katie's insistence about wearing the red dress. The fabric hung weightlessly around her thighs and then hugged her waist and barely covered her chest but it still seemed conservative next to Katie's attention grabbing dress. When Katie pulled the dress up to make sure she was decent on the top end she would reveal too much on the other end. Considering the fact that Katie was looking for attention, the dress would surely deliver.

Adalynne thought about the last time she had worn this dress. It had been two years ago. Adalynne's mother finally allowed her to attend public school after many years of begging and pleading. When Adalynne had turned twelve her mother sent her to an all-girls private school, resulting in most of the year being away from home. For those years she mourned the loss of her time with Fox. The summers did not fill the void after the passing of so much time. The changes in him were so drastic she felt robbed of the time they were supposed to have together. She was miserable and after much debate with her parents and without indicating the true reason for her sorrows she was permitted to experience public high school. There were many stipulations but Adalynne would have agreed to anything. She remembered the stories that Fox had told her and she wanted to experience that life with him. To share something with him that wasn't a secret. She wanted desperately to reconnect with the person who owned so much of her heart. She had worn it to the winter formal. It was the first time the lines of their friendship blurred into something else. The memory refused to fade.

Chapter Six

"You seem distracted." Katie words barely registered through Adalynne's thoughts. "Is this the big night? Is that what you're thinking about?"

"What do you mean?" Adalynne asked, shaking her mind of the memories that pulled her attention so deeply.

"You know...are you gonna give Matthew the big prize?" Katie wiggled her eyebrows and laughed.

Adalynne sighed. "Oh that...I don't know."

As they neared the Alpha house Adalynne couldn't believe a neighbor hadn't complained about the excessive noise pulsing from the structure. The front yard was already littered with plastic beer cups and the groups of people hanging out on the front porch were all screaming over each other in an attempt to be heard.

"Hey, it's Addie and Katie!" Someone amongst the group announced their arrival. The girls waved in response to no one in particular. The outside of the house was poorly maintained under the layer of mess from the party. The front step was in desperate need of repainting. A few of the spindles from the railing were broken and many missing. When the girls walked inside the sad condition continued as a theme throughout. It showed the wear and tear of many guys with no regard for upkeep. The walls were in desperate need of a good cleaning and painting, not to mention a few repairs. The furniture had seen better days. The sofas were worn, stained, and occupied by weight well beyond their limits with the amount of bodies wedged together.

Someone passed Adalynne a plastic cup of beer filled to the top, the froth spilled over the side, running over her fingers before splattering on the floor. Adalynne looked down to see the many other spills covering the wet floor and decided not to bother drawing attention to it. Apparently making a mess wasn't a concern and by the stickiness of the floor it hadn't been for some time. "Thank you." She smiled up at the guy who gave her the drink. She had met him before but couldn't remember his name. He had short brown hair, brown eyes, and an exaggerated square jaw. He looked every bit the athlete he was.

"No problem. You need anything, you just let me know," he said, placing his hand on her shoulder, letting his touch linger. Adalynne nodded with a tight smile. She tried to discreetly pull away from him. She didn't want to give the wrong impression. She could tell he was intoxicated and did not want to encourage anything other than friendly conversation. Luckily Katie saved her with her wonderful timing. She grabbed Adalynne's arm and shuffled her away into another room. "Best to stay away from that one; he obviously has a death wish if he is trying to move in on you. Matthew has made it pretty clear from what I hear that you are his." Katie smiled. "Isn't that romantic?"

"Umm...not really." Adalynne found herself surprisingly annoyed. "I mean he hasn't even asked me out on a proper date. I'm tired of people making decisions about me without consulting me." Adalynne almost shocked herself with her confession but the words were true. Her parents had decided what she was supposed to do with her life. Fox had decided she had to be a secret, and now Matthew was claiming her before he even officially asked her out. At least he was actually claiming her and not pretending not to know her by keeping her in the shadows. It could be considered an improvement from Fox. The thought of Fox saddened her.

"You okay?" Katie asked, leaning in with a sincere look of concern.

"Yep." Adalynne managed the best smile she could. She shook away the sorrow that always surfaced when she thought about her Fox and how much distance had grown between them.

Katie pulled her into the bathroom and closed the door behind them. It made the music slightly easier to talk over. "I don't only mean this moment. Since I met you on the first day you have been a fish out of water. I know you don't want to be here. I know your parents made you but that's not all of it. You're holding out on me. You have been walking around a shell of the person I know you are and you keep going no matter how miserable you are. I have seen hints of your potential. I can honestly say you're one of my most favorite people and I want to know why you're so lost so I can help you. You have to eventually talk to me about this, you can't avoid it forever. You can trust me, you know."

"I know." Adalynne closed her eyes and took a deep breath. She thought she was disguising her feelings better. "I fell in love with someone a long time ago. He didn't feel the same and I don't know how to stop loving him." Her confession came directly from her heart. Katie immediately wrapped her arms around her and squeezed tight. "I really want to move on but he is a part of me. I feel stuck."

"Wow! That must be some guy." Katie pondered for a moment. "I tell you what. Let's get drunk tonight. We're going to let loose, have some fun, and then tomorrow we're going to come up with a plan, Operation Make Addie Happy." Katie's conviction was touching and it made Adalynne smile.

"You're the best, Katie." Adalynne wrapped her arms around Katie. She knew her problem could not be solved so easily but she liked the enthusiasm behind Katie's expression.

"I know." She grinned triumphantly. "Now let's go have a good time."

It was amazing how good she felt after her confession. Katie was right. She needed a night of fun, to let loose and stop thinking about what was beyond her control. She tipped her glass up to her lips and drained the rest of the beer.

When they walked back out to the main area she noticed Matthew in the kitchen. He looked up and noticed her when she approached. His eyes followed her without fail. "You're in trouble." Katie elbowed her in the side with a chuckle.

"Red is definitely still my favorite color." His easy smile drew her in. Adalynne wanted to get lost in those eyes that greedily drank her in. "I'm glad you came."

"Me too. I thought you said you were having a *small* get together?" Adalynne raised her brows in question.

"It's *smallish*." Matthew shrugged playfully. "Can I get you ladies a drink?"

"Sure." Katie beamed. "It's like you read my mind."

Every time Adalynne finished one drink a new glass quickly replaced it and before long her mind was blissfully numb to the plaguing thoughts that had been tormenting her. Matthew stayed close to her side and occasionally leaned in to whisper in her ear or run his fingers down her back. It was exciting to be adored. It was easy to be in his presence and he certainly knew how to make a girl feel special.

She lost herself in the endless debates and laughter around them until one of Katie's favorite songs started blaring. Katie pulled her out on the makeshift dance floor before she even realized what was happening. "You look like you're having fun!" Katie yelled over her shoulder though she barely heard her. Adalynne smiled in response. She had to admit she was enjoying herself.

The music found its way into Adalynne's body

and soon they were dancing in the mass of people. All of the furniture in the living area had been removed and was currently on the front lawn. Most of the faces around her she recognized from campus, though there were also many new people. All of the Roth girls were accounted for and enjoying themselves. The usual drama in their day to day lives was forgotten and everyone just strived to have fun. At this point most of them were too intoxicated to remember much of anything.

Adalynne's blood was heated from the liquor. She found herself laughing with Katie and a few other girls from their house they hung out with regularly. Her earlier troubles were forgotten as she engaged in the festivities. She couldn't remember the last time she'd laughed so hard. She needed this more than she realized. Strong arms wrapped around her waist and she turned to see Matthew smiling down at her.

"Hey." She giggled at his unexpected arrival.

"Hey, come with me." He wound his fingers in hers and pulled her along. Adalynne stumbled occasionally as she followed close on his heels. In this moment she couldn't think of a reason not to follow. She needed to feel wanted, she was desperate for it. He led her down a long hallway until they reached the last door. He opened it and walked in, pulling her in against his chest before kicking the door closed.

"Did you wear red for me?" Matthew's voice rumbled against her neck as he pulled the strap off her shoulder. He didn't allow her to answer before he covered her mouth with his. She immediately thought of Fox's lips on hers, how wonderful they felt. With Fox she felt like he would never be able to kiss her enough to satisfy the need that burned for him. Matthew's kisses were different, too eager and strange. She found it hard to find a rhythm to his movements. She wondered if the alcohol streaming through her blood was the reason she did not feel the connection with him. She closed her eyes tightly, trying to push thoughts of Fox from her mind as Matthew found the zipper on the back.

"I may have gotten some inside information that it was your favorite color," she teased. But that had not been the reason at all for her wearing red. It was merely coincidence.

"I approve," he moaned before claiming her lips once again. His words immediately brought her back to the night of the winter formal she had shared with Fox. It frustrated her that she could not escape thoughts of him, especially in this moment. His hold on her was too strong. Even drunk the thoughts of Fox managed to find themselves front and center. She moved with Matthew as he directed her toward his bed. He pulled her dress down and greedily fondled her breasts while one hand slid up under her hem, pulling her panties aside.

"Wait!" She pushed back against his chest, forcing him to step backward before his fingers could slide into her. "Don't. I can't...this is too fast." The reason she couldn't let him enter her was because she had always pictured Fox as her first. He was the first boy to hold her hand, he first boy she gave her kiss to, he was the first to see her naked and touch her body, and she had wanted more than anything for him to be the first to have her completely. Part of her wanted to tell Matthew to keep going. To take it from her so Fox could never have it, maybe then she could move on. She knew he didn't deserve it after how he treated her, keeping her in his secret world where she could never really have him. But she would always remember this first like she did all the others and she wanted it to be with the intensity of feeling that only Fox had ever stirred in her. She stepped away from Matthew, who reluctantly let her go. She grabbed her dress and lifted it back up to cover her breasts as she sat down on the edge of the bed. She felt like a silly girl who was holding onto a dream that slipped through her fingers long ago.

"I can wait," he whispered almost painfully before he collapsed on his back on the bed. Lying back he rubbed his hands over his face with a sigh.

"Thank you," she whispered sadly before standing back up to zip her dress. Matthew stood up and helped return her dress to order, leaving a gentle kiss on her shoulder.

"You are worth the wait," he said before kissing her again on the lips. Adalynne had to stop the sob that almost escaped her. She didn't understand why she was thinking about Fox when Matthew was all the things she should want.

Adalynne didn't stay at the party after their intimate exchange. Matthew tried to encourage her to remain longer, even going so far as to pout and beg but she had too many thoughts running through her mind. She was suddenly exhausted and could not get herself motivated to step back into the party scene, still in full throttle. She noticed Katie dancing away with a guy named Steven on the dance floor. She was pulling all her signature moves of seduction, indicating she was really into him. Adalynne didn't want to intrude on her good time. Instead, she told one of their house girls to give Katie the message after she was gone. She wanted Katie to stay and enjoy the evening. She didn't want to be any more of a buzzkill than she already was.

On the walk back to the Roth house Adalynne brought her fingers up to her lips in memory of Matthew's kiss. She wished when Matthew kissed her she hadn't thought of Fox. She wished Matthew could sweep her off her feet and she could forget about the rest of the world. Matthew was wonderful, handsome, polite, and had a bright future ahead of him. He could quite literally be the embodiment of perfection. She even knew her parents would approve and that was not an easy feat. He was everything her mother always said she wanted Adalynne to find.

It could have been so easy to move on if she could have just let Fox go. Instead of reeling at the thought of a possible relationship with Matthew she was left with thoughts of when she shared her first kiss with Fox. Her feelings for Fox ran so deep and for so long it had become a part of who she was.

It was the summer before she left for boarding school. She was barely twelve at the time. Fox and she had been building a camp in their secret place in the woods. They had worked tirelessly every day and it had taken the majority of the summer. Every morning when her parents left for work, she would jump out of bed and grab the breakfast Carmen would pack for her. Fox managed to bring some wood but the greater part of it they cut themselves from the forest around them. Adalynne did not have any experience with building but Fox was confident and knew how to use tools. She was always impressed by what he was capable of. She held on tight to the memory, holding it close to her heart. It would always be hers. It was in their special place, staring into those bottomless green eyes. It was perfect.

Adalynne walked in the Roth house and walked straight up to her room, not stopping until she reached her dresser. She opened the small jewelry box and rummaged through her belongings until she found the small bee charm on a silver chain. She was right about never forgetting her first kiss. It would be with her forever.

Chapter Seven

Adalynne had just fallen asleep when her cell phone rang, pulling her from her dreams. She fumbled for her phone in the dark, her senses failing her because of her drowsy state. "Ugh!" When her fingers wrapped around the smooth cover she looked at the screen, revealing her mother's number. It was 2:15 a.m. Panic bloomed within her as she accepted the call. The world snapped into focus around her as her heart raced with anticipation.

"Mom?" Adalynne listened to her mother's frantic voice stream through the phone. When she finally hung up she kicked her blankets off and scrambled out of bed, frantically wiping the hot tears that began to fall. She flicked on the bedside lamp and rubbed her hands down her face. She needed to focus so she could get her things together.

The bedroom door swung open. "Girl, you missed one hell of a party! You better have a good reason for leaving…Addie? What's wrong?" Katie stormed across the room, kicking off her heels.

"My dad had a heart attack. He's in the hospital," Adalynne said numbly. More tears washed down her face.

"Oh, Addie." Katie wrapped her arms around her and smoothed her hair.

"I have to go," Adalynne mumbled.

"I'll help you get your things." Katie grabbed Adalynne's suitcase from her closet. "Do you want me to come with you?"

"No…Mom is sending a car. I'll call you later. Okay?"

Adalynne was so grateful for Katie's help. She took over packing while Adalynne got dressed and took a moment to collect herself. When Adalynne stepped out of the bathroom, Katie was zipping up her suitcase. "I packed all your favorite clothes and your phone charger is in there too."

"Thank you, Katie." Adalynne tucked her cosmetic bag in her purse and swung it over her shoulder.

When she got outside, the car her mother organized was already waiting for her. She was glad that all the arrangements were made because she didn't feel capable of even the smallest of tasks at the moment. She couldn't think about anything other than the fear of not seeing her father again. The long ride to the hospital seemed endless until finally she watched the large building come into view on the horizon. Adalynne prayed she would be met with good news when she walked in.

"Thomas Fairweather," Adalynne blurted when she approached the front desk.

"He's in intensive care on the fourth floor…" the

small mousy woman behind the desk read from the screen after pulling up his name. Adalynne turned on her heel and headed toward the elevators before the woman finished speaking. She thought she heard her call out something but the only thing she cared about was making it to his side.

Every hallway looked the same. Everything was painted the same sterile white. When she neared the nurse's desk her mother's form caught her eye. She quickened her steps.

"Mom?" The tears flowed fresh again at the sight of her mother. It was the first time she remembered seeing her mother without her perfectly manicured appearance. Her shoulder length blonde hair hung loose from its normal sleek up do and her face only bore traces of makeup that had been long since wiped away with tears, revealing dark circles under her haunted eyes. It was strange seeing her mother without her flawless demeanor. She had never witnessed her in an emotional state before. It was refreshing to see that her mother could feel after all this time thinking she resembled a robot more than a human being.

Adalynne wrapped her arms around her mother tightly and was surprised when her mother returned the gesture in kind. It was the first time in a long time that she could remember her mother showing affection. Adalynne let a sob escape her lips as she cried with her mother. Her mother was just as fragile as she was. Adalynne cried for fear of losing her father and for the realization that her mother was capable of love after all. "He went to dinner with his associates after work. When he got home he started complaining that he wasn't feeling well." Her mother wiped her eyes with a tissue. "You know how he is with fried foods. I thought he just overdid it. I told him just to go to bed." Her mother broke off into fresh tears.

"It's not your fault, Mom. You didn't know." Adalynne rubbed her mother's back as she let her calm down. It was a strange feeling to be comforting her mother but she welcomed the distraction as they waited for word. They both held their breath when they noticed the doctor approach them in his pristine white coat and unreadable expression.

They both listened intently when the doctor explained her father had suffered a massive heart attack, resulting in a lot of tissue damage. Though they were able to get him stabilized, his condition was still serious. Adalynne walked away with the doctor's words thick in the air around her. She needed to go to his side. She pushed open the glass door to his room with her mother close behind her.

He looked so small and fragile lying on the bed, hooked up to all the monitoring devices. She searched for hints of the strong man that used to throw her into the air as a child and the man that used to eat the vegetables off her plate when her mother wasn't looking so she would be allowed to have dessert with him. She shared a special connection with her father that she drew strength from, even now that she was grown his presence was still essential to her. She needed his words of wisdom, his way of pointing out the important things when chaos clouded her mind. He understood her and knew the part of her that her mother couldn't begin to comprehend. He was the glue that bonded their family together.

Though her father had always been a busy man, with work consuming most of his time, she treasured the little time that they shared. Her father was warm and loving where her mother was cold and demanding. They always seemed a strange pair to her. When she was old enough to see the dynamics in their relationship she asked her father why he loved her mother and he said, "A heart loves who a heart loves." It was as simple as that.

Adalynne reached for his hand that lay by his side. His skin had an unnatural grey color to it that pained her. "Dad...don't leave me," she whispered, leaning in to kiss his cheek. Her mother's hand was on her back, giving her comfort. They both stared at him, praying he would open his eyes.

***

Adalynne fell asleep by her father's side, leaning against his bed with her hand covering his, haunted by restless dreams. She woke to a soft touch of someone smoothing her hair from her face. When she opened her eyes she looked up at her father. He was looking down with a weak smile. She took his hand and a large smile overwhelmed her face despite the tears that began to flow.

"My baby girl," he whispered roughly.

"Daddy." She squeezed his hand. "I was so scared you weren't going to wake up."

"I could never leave you without making sure

you were okay first." He smiled weakly. She could see how tired he was. The strength she loved in him was lost to the fragile version of him now.

"I will never be okay if you leave me," she whispered, wiping away her tears.

He touched her cheek. The simple gesture held so much meaning for them both. Adalynne held onto him, terrified to let go.

"Thomas!" Adalynne's mother gasped with relief as she walked in the room.

Adalynne stayed by her father's side as long as she could. For days she did nothing but sit in the chair beside his bed reading him articles from the paper. When he slept, which was often, the silence was heavy with emotion as she and her mother watched the steady rise and fall of his chest, nervous that any one of them could be his last. The doctor still wouldn't say he was improving. His color remained pale and his body exhausted. Not wanting to miss the rare moments he was awake, Adalynne couldn't bring herself to leave the room.

"You should go back to the house. Have a hot bath and some real food." Her mother was the first to break the silence accompanied by the steady noise of the machines that monitored her father's sleeping form.

"I can't leave." She turned to her mother, who was looking more like herself. She had left this morning to take care of some business that could not wait. She took the opportunity to tend to her needs. She looked more like her usual refined self, which Adalynne had to admit made things seem a bit more normal. It made it easier to believe that the worst was behind them.

"You should listen to your mother." They both swung around. Adalynne stood up out of her chair to reach for her father's hand. "I won't go anywhere, I promise." He attempted to brighten his frail words.

"Are you sure? There's a brand new paper waiting for you with some juicy gossip." Adalynne tried to entice him.

"I'm sure. It will make me feel better if you took care of yourself. You're looking a little thin."

Adalynne shook her head in disbelief.

"Go, Addie. I can read him the paper," her mother insisted.

"I'll be back as soon as I can," Adalynne sighed in defeat.

"Your mother will stay with me tonight. Go home…get some sleep. I'll be here in the morning. I promise," he encouraged when Adalynne didn't move.

"But…" Adalynne began.

"No buts…go, baby girl. You need to take care of yourself." Adalynne smiled at the name he called her when she was small. He hadn't used it in so long that she almost forgot about it.

After a reluctant goodbye, Adalynne left her parents and headed home. Her footsteps echoed as she walked in the foyer and turned on the lights. She had only been gone just over a month but already the house seemed strange to her. Something was different and she couldn't place exactly what it was until she studied the walls. Her mother must have had it painted after she left. The color was just slightly different than before. Adalynne always felt like her house looked more like a showpiece than a home. There were so many rooms she was not allowed in because they were her mother's formal rooms for entertaining guests. She dropped her mother's keys on the round mahogany table that stood before the grand curving staircase leading upstairs. A large vase of fresh flowers sat upon it, giving the air a sweet smell, pleasing her senses.

Adalynne walked upstairs to her room, dropping her bag on her neatly made bed. The room smelled fresh and recently cleaned, with not a thing out of place. She glanced across the room at her window and noticed it was locked. Out of habit she walked across the room and unlocked it, pulling it all the way open. She knew that Fox wouldn't come but for some reason it set her at ease.

Adalynne turned the water as hot as she could stand and stood under the shower head, letting the heat embrace her. Soon steam filled the air and she lost track of time. She felt so fragile and tired. She hadn't realized how drained she was and couldn't bring herself to leave the comfort the heat provided. When her fingers were saturated she finally turned the water off and wrapped herself in her old robe hanging on the back of the door.

Adalynne walked down to the kitchen and opened the fridge. It was stocked with fresh groceries, making her mouth water as she realized how hungry she was. Her mother must have known she was going to talk Adalynne into going home because all of her favorite things to eat stared back at her from the open fridge. She grabbed the strawberries, package of sushi, and chocolate milk. She greedily devoured them all. The last few days at the hospital she was barely able to stomach anything but now her appetite returned and the food tasted delectable.

On the way back to her room, she walked toward her father's office. It was not a place she went into often but she right now she needed to feel close to him. She was met with his familiar scent mixed with old books and wood. She turned on the light and looked at the photos that covered his walls. Her parents were big entertainers so there were many pictures of her father with many recognizable people of high society. Judges and other reputable lawyers along with the police chief and other people in various positions of law, some familiar and some not, all stared back at her. Her father's bright smile beamed back at her with his cheeks full of color.

On her way out of the room Adalynne ran her fingers over the chess table sitting in the room. Her father adored the game and she remembered when he taught her how to play, she was only a small girl. She turned back and looked around the room before turning off the light. She told herself that her father was going to recover and when he came home she would challenge him to a game of chess. It would just like old times.

Walking by the sitting room she was beckoned by her piano. She hadn't touched the keys since she had left for school. Sliding onto the smooth seat, she took in the room around her. Her mother must have had her decorator in recently to change the layout of the space. The only thing that was familiar was the large stone fireplace and the grand piano. The keys welcomed her touch as she ran her fingers over their smooth ivory. She played the first song that come to mind and the music resounded through the large quiet room. A smile played on her lips as she remembered the first time she played this song for Fox.

It was years ago when life was simple and their relationship was as innocent as they were. It was an afternoon when spring was growing mature with its warming temperatures and blooming flowers. Adalynne had told Fox how she was practicing really hard for her piano recital that was approaching. He always brightened up when she spoke of music and her lessons.

Adalynne had been trying to convince Fox to come to her house to see her play, insisting that her parents were not home. He always refused until this one afternoon, after much convincing, he finally agreed. She remembered how nervous he was walking into her house, ready to flee at a moment's notice. She grabbed his warm hand in hers as she led him toward the living room, giving him a reassuring squeeze. Adalynne could still remember her excitement finally seeing him in her world. It made him seem more real venturing outside their normal limits. When they reached the piano she hopped upon the seat, patting the spot beside her for him to join her. Adalynne watched him look around the room before he glanced at her. He practically trembled as he took in everything around them. He was reluctant to move any closer to her. She would never forget the look of awe on his face as she played. It was then that she discovered their shared love of music.

After that she started bringing her guitar with her to their place in the woods if they were unable to come to the house to play the piano. Fox was a fast learner when it came to music and she enjoyed teaching him everything she could. Soon she found she was running out of things to teach him as his remarkable ability to play any instrument surpassed her own. Eventually she began to watch him create beautiful music of his own accord. She encouraged him to show his father his talent but he always refused. He never wanted to show the world what he could do. For years she was the only person in the world who knew of his affinity for music.

Adalynne remembered the day she convinced Carmen to drive her to the music store to buy a guitar. Carmen didn't ask any questions and Adalynne was grateful for it. Adalynne knew it would be the perfect birthday gift for Fox. She wanted to find one that was the perfect fit for him. She knew when she saw it hanging up in the store it was the one. It had an intricate green design on it that was the same vibrant green as his eyes and she thought of him as soon as she saw it.

The day she gave it to him was the first time she saw Fox with tears in his eyes. She had seen him endure so much pain from the physical marks his father left on his body but he never cried. He hugged her so tight that day and she never wanted him to let her go. She didn't know he was capable of such intense feeling. She listened to him play for hours that day as he familiarized himself with his new guitar until the day threatened to end.

"I have to go home now." Adalynne stood to leave. She leaned down, wrapping her arms around him again. "You're my favorite person, Fox," she said with a smile before turning to leave.

"Bee?" She turned back when he called her name. "You're my favorite person too."

Adalynne smiled so brightly she could barely contain her happiness. When she broke through the treeline toward her house, Carmen was waiting for her on the back porch. "You started to worry me, Addie," she said, giving Adalynne a firm hug and then directing her inside the house. "Your parents will be home soon. Let's get you cleaned up for supper."

"Carmen?" Adalynne asked thoughtfully.

"Yes, child." Adalynne loved how important Carmen always made her feel by always giving her full attention when she spoke to her. No question was unimportant.

"What is it like to be in love?" Adalynne asked curiously.

Carmen's smile lit up her warm brown eyes. "It is the most beautiful thing in the whole world and it makes you feel happy from the tip of your toes to the top of your head."

That was when Adalynne realized she was in love with Fox. "I thought so."

Chapter Eight

Adalynne was startled by an unexpected knock on the door. Her first instinct was to ignore it but when it was followed by several rings of the doorbell and more persistent knocking she realized this person wasn't making that an option. Reluctantly she stood up and walked toward the door. When she pulled it open she was surprised to see Katie standing on the other side.

"Surprise!" Katie tried to sound cheerful but the gesture was quickly dropped and replaced with concern.

"Katie? What are you doing here?" Adalynne was genuinely shocked to see her friend on her doorstep. "And how did you find me?"

"Your short answer texts and not answering my phone calls made me worry. I went straight to the hospital and your mother told me where to find you…" Katie rambled off.

Adalynne just stepped forward and wrapped her arms around her, cutting off her words. "Thank you."

"When I was there, your mother said that the doctor just checked on your father and noticed some improvement." Katie patted her back affectionately. "Your mother also thought it would be a good idea that I provided a distraction for you tonight."

"A distraction would be wonderful." Adalynne smiled until she looked at Katie's face. She knew Katie had something on her mind that she was dying to tell her. She knew her well enough to know she could not hold things in and when she had something to say it practically busted through her seams. "Go on and tell me whatever you're dying to say before you explode all over the floor."

"You will not believe what happened to me!" Katie practically squeaked out the words through her excitement. "On the way into the hospital, I ran into the lead singer of the band I love, Outcome. You know the music I have been obsessing over and I make you listen to all the time? The lead singer is ridiculously hot and I. Met. Him. Can you believe it? He has to be one of the most beautiful people I have ever seen!"

"Wow." Adalynne did appreciate his talent. The guy had an amazing voice that always seemed to comfort her. His music was practically the theme song to their lives lately because it was all Katie played in their room. "Did you take a picture?"

A look of devastation came over her features. "Why didn't I think of that? It was the perfect opportunity."

Adalynne couldn't help but laugh at her. "Well, maybe you'll meet him again someday."

"That someday is tonight, my dear sweet, Addie.

Guess who is not only gorgeous, but generous as well." She reached into her purse and pulled out two black tickets and waved them in front of Adalynne's face.

"I can't." Adalynne smiled weakly.

"Listen, you aren't supposed to go back to the hospital until tomorrow, so why don't you call your mother and get an update? If your dad is doing good we'll go and if not, we'll plan to stay put. Let's let fate decide the *Outcome*. Get it?" Katie beamed at her cleverness.

"Yes, you are a slick one, Kat." Adalynne shook her head with a smile.

After Adalynne made a phone call to confirm the good news that her father was improving, she reluctantly caved to Katie's evening plans. Both her mother and Katie were insistent that she needed some time to unwind after spending days by her father's bedside. After hanging out with Katie for a while in her room, her mood drastically began to change. The sorrow was lifted as things began to feel normal again. Katie's good mood was contagious and before long she was laughing and picking out what to wear for the concert. Adalynne decided on her favorite jeans and a fitted blouse that wrapped and tied around her, accentuating her slim waist. Then she finished her look with her favorite red pumps.

"You look so hot! I wish jeans made my butt look that good," Katie gushed as Adalynne stood in front of the mirror to see the complete look.

"What are you talking about? Didn't you tell me you won nicest butt in your high school?" Adalynne picked up one of her throw pillows that had fallen off her bed and threw it at Katie, lounging across her bed.

"Yeah." Katie sighed. "That was fifteen pounds ago."

"Well, since we are on the topic of your butt, I noticed that Matthew's friend Steven couldn't take his eyes off it the other night." Adalynne watched Katie's face turn as red as her shoes. "Tell me what is going on." Katie's reaction revealed that she had news to share on the subject.

"Well, we may have been spending time together the last couple of days." She looked up bashfully at Adalynne.

"Details!" Adalynne ordered as she grabbed her hoop earrings, looking expectantly at the now silent Katie.

"Well...I really like him so I didn't sleep with him yet." Katie confessed in a rush.

"Wow. It must be love." Adalynne laughed.

"Seriously...I'm nervous. It seems too good to be true. What if the sex is horrible? I thought if I wait the sex will be better if it has more meaning. I just want it to be good with him. I really like him."

"Katie? Are you growing up? Ohhh...I am so proud of my little Katie." Katie screamed as Adalynne kicked off her heels and jumped on the bed, tackling her. "I'm glad you came," Adalynne admitted after they settled on the bed. Katie wrapped her arms around Adalynne.

"I love you, Addie. I would do anything for you."

"Love you too, Katie." Adalynne was so glad

Katie had come into her life. Without Katie's friendship she would be lost. Their connection was instant and natural, like they had always been friends. "I think it's good to wait. If anything, you will be able to determine if he wants more than sex. If he's willing to wait then you might have found yourself a keeper. And if the sex does turn out to be less than what you hope, you'll be able to work on that together."

"Yeah, you're right."

"I have my moments." Adalynne giggled. She jumped off the bed and straightened her clothes. "I'm ready to go when you are."

"Matthew is going to die when he gets a look at you tonight." Katie smiled and then instantly looked guilty.

Adalynne swung around with narrowed eyes. "What are you talking about?" Her hands found their way to her hips.

"Okay, don't get mad. Matthew has been harassing me about you since you left. He's been acting like an adorable insecure little puppy. You didn't return any of his calls either. He called me just after I had my fabulous encounter and since I made him listen to me gush for like half an hour, I offered him a ticket. He and Steven wanted to come to the concert too and for it to be a surprise that we meet them there." Katie smiled awkwardly after she finished rambling.

"Argh...I don't think I can see him right now, Katie. I think this is a bad idea," Adalynne said, deflated. "It's not a good time for me to be getting into a relationship and I can't even think about

Matthew right now."

"No pressure. I already told him that. He said he just wants to see how you are doing. No expectations." Katie promised. "Tonight is only about the people who care about you wanting to be with you."

"Oh Katie, what am I going to do with you?" Adalynne sighed.

***

When they pulled up in front of the large night club, a line stretched down the length of the street. The night was warm and balmy without a star in the sky that could be seen from the glow of the busy streets. The outside of the club was very simple with black and silver lettering spelling the bar's name, Night. Adalynne had heard of it but had never been there. It was a popular bar and hard to get into unless you had connections, but tonight if you held a ticket you were granted access. They climbed out of the taxi and started toward the end of the line.

"Addie! Katie!" The girls both turned to see Matthew and Steven in line. "Looking good, ladies." Matthew complimented as the girls walked toward them.

"Matthew! Wow, this is weird meeting you here." Adalynne lacked any real conviction as she lied.

"Katie spilled." Matthew shook his head with a smile. "I knew she couldn't keep it a secret."

"I can't keep secrets from Addie." Katie laughed,

walking gracefully into Steven's embrace. He wrapped his arm around her shoulder and kissed her on the cheek. Katie beamed and Adalynne could feel the glee radiate off her friend. Adalynne wished she could slide her arms around Matthew and lose herself in the excitement of a new relationship too. Forget about the sorrow and loneliness that seemed to surround her heart. "How are you doing? Katie told me your father's condition is improving." Matthew's sincerity was touching as he leaned closer to talk to her while Katie and Steven giggled together.

Matthew was gorgeous. His physique was well formed from his athletic lifestyle. He looked amazing in his dress shirt and well-fitted khakis. He was tall, his blond hair still bleached from the summer's sun, and his smile was infectious. She wished she could will her heart to fall for him. She wanted to crave his kiss and yearn for his touch but she was only left with an unfulfilled feeling she could not shake. A vital piece of the puzzle was missing. She smiled as earnestly as she could and humored his questions. He seemed oblivious to her internal struggle and Adalynne was grateful for it. She almost fell for her own guise of happiness while she engaged in flirtatious exchanges with Matthew.

The two of them carried on playfully. Matthew was easy to get along with, which made his company enjoyable. She could temporarily forget to think about anything else. It was a welcome feeling. The problem was she knew when she wasn't in his company, her mind started to question her attraction to him and doubt everything.

Inside, the bar had a comfortable atmosphere with dim lighting and fresh décor. A sea of round bar tables surrounded the round stage in a semi-circle. Two levels of balconies overlooked the main stage area and many faces were currently enthralled watching the opening act. It was a female singer backed with male musicians on the guitar and drums. She was slim with her sparkly tank top that exposed her stomach. Her dark brown shoulder length hair was streaked with cherry red.

"She can really sing!" Katie hollered over to Adalynne so she could hear her over the music. Katie was right. She had a velvety quality to her voice that was easy to listen to. Matthew sat down beside her after disappearing to one of the many bars in the establishment. He insisted on buying her drinks for the evening. Whenever she finished one, Matthew would replace it with another. She felt guilty, especially since he wasn't drinking, but he refused to let her buy her own. They were heading back early in the morning and Matthew had to drive.

"Did you know they were on tour? This was an unscheduled trip they booked last minute," Steven informed them, leaning in to kiss Katie's neck. She squealed in delight when it tickled.

"Worked well for us," Matthew said as he leaned back and rested his arm on the back of Adalynne's chair.

"This was meant to be, right, Addie?" Katie beamed as she snuggled into Steven's side.

"Looks that way." Addie smiled and sipped on

her drink. It tasted like pink lemonade and went down too easily. Before Adalynne knew it she found herself giddy and lightheaded and lost in the moment. Matthew focused his attention on her and took opportunities to lean in close, brushing her hair back from her face or gently running his fingers over her arm. "I'm not really sure I should drink anymore," Adalynne stated while looking at Katie, who was throwing back her drinks eagerly. "One of us has to be able to find our way home."

"Don't worry about that. I'll make sure you get home safe." Matthew was older than she was and she appreciated his maturity. He only had one year left before he officially graduated and joined the work force. Adalynne could see the excitement in his eyes when he talked about his plans for the future. Like Adalynne, his father was a lawyer, and the chase for justice was passed down to Matthew who hungrily awaited his turn to join the system.

Adalynne currently felt far from the right path for her career. She had taken a year off after she graduated high school to study art and music with the promise to her parents that she would enroll in University the following fall. The past year before she enrolled in school she poured herself into her passion of painting and composing music, this was when she felt at peace with herself but she knew it wouldn't last. It was only a temporary visit in the world she craved before she would take part in a life that was planned by her parents. She had traveled occasionally throughout the year to expose herself to the arts but mostly she stayed close to home and volunteered at a local music school to teach music.

She loved introducing the beauty of music to children. The appreciation in their eyes was all she needed to keep her going. It reminded her of Fox and his love of everything musical, how he gave himself to it completely and became a part of it. She thought of him every day, wondering if she would ever see him again. There was no closure from their last encounter and it left her mind restless with thoughts of him. That was part of the reason she didn't want to venture too far from home. The thought of never seeing him again was devastating. Unfortunately the entire year she stayed close to home she never heard so much as a mention of his name. It was as if he vanished from her life and it broke her heart.

Adalynne was grateful for the table they managed to find; it was situated beside one of the large pillars holding up the balconies above them. They had privacy but they still had an excellent view of the stage because they were so close. She wasn't sure how they pulled off getting seats so close with the amount of people packed in the bar but she was grateful.

The opening band wrapped up their act to make way for Outcome. Adalynne leaned into Matthew's arm that he had swung over the back of the chair and his fingers brushed her bare shoulders causing a smile to spread across her face. This was nice, she thought, looking over at Katie and Steven, who were cozy as well. Maybe this was a sign. Maybe she had to stop fighting it. She looked back at Matthew who smiled at her in return and gave her shoulder an affectionate squeeze.

"I'm glad you are here with me tonight." He whispered in her ear.

"Me too. Thanks for coming. I needed this." Adalynne kissed his cheek and leaned into him.

Chapter Nine

Adalynne watched the band walk onto the stage and immediately her heart began to hammer in her chest. She leaned forward in her seat, staring at the lead singer, who sauntered out onto the stage with his long, lean, beautiful body. Matthew's hand reached out to touch her lower back but she ignored the contact and the words he said. She was awestruck with the man that walked out on the stage.

"What did you say the lead singer's name was?" Adalynne called over to Katie without taking her eyes off of him.

"Brolan Pierce," Katie called back before cheering loudly with his entrance, like the rest of the room around them. The noise level of the room became deafening as everyone hollered in excitement.

Adalynne rolled the name over her tongue, it felt foreign to her. It wasn't his name and she would never use it. She didn't like the way it sounded to her ears in regards to him. He would always be Fox to her. She watched his confident movements as he walked around on the stage absorbing all the energy the crowd threw at him. A mischievous smile played on his lips as he scanned the people around him. "Good evening." His raspy masculine voice flowed through the room, radiating from the speakers that surrounded them. "I hope you're all ready for this," Fox said before pulling his guitar strap over his head. The crowd erupted into cheers.

His dark hair was long and disheveled like she remembered it but he had changed since the last time she had seen him. He was taller, his shoulders broader, and his form exuded a power that his younger self did not possess. His arms and chest were carved to male perfection, with new ink that stretched down the length of his forearms from under his black t-shirt. Adalynne couldn't help but appreciate the pure sex dripping from his presence. She wasn't the only female in the room completely entranced by him. He commanded the room and all eyes were on him expectantly. The rush of emotions that assaulted her when it came to Fox twisted her insides and made her world spin. The feelings she was waiting for when she searched Matthew's eyes, the reasons she couldn't move on, the reasons she was stuck. Fox kept them all.

Adalynne watched in awe as he strummed the guitar and his band mates followed suit and dove into song. He was in his element on the stage, entrancing the crowd that sang along to his lyrics. Adalynne could not envision a more beautiful sight then the show he displayed upon the stage. She could not believe that she did not recognize his voice until now; it was the most amazing sound she had ever heard.

"Do you want me to get you another drink or something?" Matthew leaned forward to get her attention.

Adalynne just shook her head. She knew she shouldn't ignore Matthew but the sight of Fox before her was so captivating she couldn't bring herself to sit back in her chair to engage with Matthew. The only thing going through her mind was that she never wanted to forget this moment in case it was the last time she saw Fox. She wanted to remember everything about him, his movements, his voice, and his body.

Fox flawlessly flowed into another song and the band kept up perfectly, knowing his habits and his methods. He was comfortable with the crowd, drawing them in with his words. He started into a guitar solo when he looked up and captured Adalynne's gaze, his eyes remaining on hers as he played. Heat flowed to Adalynne's cheeks and her breathing quickened as she lost herself in the moment. She knew he recognized her but she couldn't tell what he was thinking. He was never an easy person to read. His eyes continued to find her as he moved around the stage and she never wanted him to look away. Matthew must have noticed the attention Fox was giving her because he pulled his chair closer, leaned forward, and wrapped his arm around her. "Hey...you are being quiet," he whispered, gently skimming his lips along her ear.

"Just enjoying the show." She forced a smile for Matthew and shrugged her shoulders. He seemed a little put off that she wasn't submitting to his touch; instead she remained angled toward the stage. She made an effort to reinforce her interest in him but it was so hard when every cell in her entire body was pulled toward the stage. Matthew insisted on keeping his arm on her chair possessively and she didn't dissuade him. She wanted to allow herself this one performance to reconnect with all her old emotions before she had to walk away from him again.

Song after song played on and Adalynne craved his glances toward her, she wanted to know how he felt about her being in the audience as he looked down at her from the stage. Thoughts of the last time she had seen him flooded her mind. It was after Christmas break in her senior year. Fox had been keeping his distance from her since the night he had come to her room. Molly was keeping her posted on all the school gossip especially anything involving Damon Knight, as he was known to everyone else.

Adalynne would never admit her feelings toward him to Molly and Brooke, but she knew they had their suspicions. Molly was always sure to tell her when she heard something about him. Adalynne didn't put much value in the gossip that floated around the school, knowing most of it was probably fictional, but when the rumours persisted that Fox was involved with drug dealings and seen hanging around with people that had criminal records, she began to worry. Her concern only intensified when he showed up less and less to school and eventually stopped coming.

Late one night after Adalynne had gone to the movies with Molly and Brooke, they were walking down the street chatting about the show. The weather was unseasonably warm and many people were walking the downtown streets enjoying the calm night.

"Let's go get a hot chocolate!" Brooke suggested excitedly. "There's this little place around the corner that has the most amazing hot chocolate ever and they're open late," she gushed at Adalynne.

"Brooke is obsessed with the guy that works there," Molly explained. "She fails to let the fact that he's married with children get in the way of her fantasy of him sweeping her off her feet one day."

"A girl can dream, can't she?" Brooke sighed with a dreamy smile on her face.

The sound of sirens rang through the night, drawing their attention. A few figures with dark clothing ran around the corner, fleeing the pursuing officers. Adalynne and the girls didn't have time to move before the two dressed in black collided into their path. The first crashed into Molly, she yelled her displeasure at him as he kept going past her, making her almost fall from the impact. The second tried to maneuver around the girls but faltered slightly when he looked at them. Adalynne stumbled backward when he came to an abrupt stop in front of her. His hands instinctually went out to catch her from falling, his bag slid off his arm and crashed at her feet. Fox's beautiful eyes peered at her from under his dark hood. She froze in a state of shock at the realization that Fox was running from the police.

She could hear a police car come to a stop behind them. Fox immediately dropped his arms, pushing past her as if she were a stranger. The officers chasing them on foot turned the corner and almost collided with the girls as well. Fox did not attempt to flee, knowing it was useless, there was no escape. "Don't move!" the officers yelled at Fox. The other guy was already in police custody, leaning over the police car with his hands being cuffed behind his back. "Move back, girls!" the officer ordered, standing before them.

Molly and Brooke immediately shuffled back against the wall. Adalynne reached down and picked up Fox's bag and quickly made her way over to the girls. The officer didn't pay any mind to the bag, assuming it was hers and she was thankful. She didn't know what she was doing. All she could think about was protecting Fox.

"Are you out of your mind?" Molly breathed hotly in her ear when she came up beside her.

Adalynne gave her a warning glare as she noticed one of the officers approach them. "Are you girls all right?" the officer asked, studying them.

"Yes, just a little shaken up. They ran right into us," Adalynne said.

"Are any of you hurt?" the middle aged officer asked. "Did they say anything to you?"

"No sir," Adalynne answered and the girls shook their heads in confirmation.

"Okay then, ladies. You are free to go." The officer dismissed them and began walking toward *the others. Adalynne watched them search Fox, with his hands on the hood of the car. She turned to leave with the girls and didn't look back, although it took everything she had not to. She didn't want the officers to suspect anything. She didn't know what was in the bag but she assumed it had something to do with why they were running. Dread pooled in her stomach at the thought of Fox getting into trouble with the law.*

When they were a safe distance from the scene, Molly spoke up. "Throw it in the trash! Have you gone completely mad? You could have gotten in so much trouble!" The words tumbled out so quickly that Adalynne was surprised she contained them as long as she did. "Why in the world would you protect him? Have you not been listening to everything I've told you?"

"What is with you and Damon anyway? I know he is unbelievably hot but even I know not to go there. It's only a matter of time before he ends up in jail for good," Brooke said, looking over her shoulder to make sure they weren't being followed. "What's in it?" Brooke was eyeing the bag. "Are you going to look?"

Molly just shook her head. "I don't want to know." She put her hands up and walked on ahead.

"Let's just go home." Adalynne quickened her pace to catch up with Molly.

When Molly dropped Adalynne off, she went straight to her room and sat on her bed with the backpack beside her. She couldn't bring herself to open the bag for fear of finding what she suspected inside. She knew Molly was mad at her. She was constantly sending text messages to turn the backpack over to the police or get rid of it and what Adalynne had done made her an accessory to the crime. Adalynne didn't respond to any of her texts; it was just a continuation of Molly's rant from the car drive home. She knew what she had done better than anyone with her father being a lawyer but in the moment her need to protect Fox overrode her logic and she knew she would do it again if faced with the opportunity.

A tap on her window drew her attention. She released her grip on the strap of backpack. It slid off her bed and hit the floor with a thud. Fox opened the window and slid through surprisingly graceful considering his height. He looked at her briefly before his eyes narrowed onto the bag sitting beside her bed.

"That was stupid, Bee," he muttered before walking toward the bag, "and start locking your window."

"I thought they arrested you?"

"They didn't have any evidence."

"What are you doing, Fox?" Adalynne pleaded.

"I'm doing what I have to. Not all of us live a life of privilege," Fox said, waving his hand around the room.

"Who are you? This isn't the Fox I know," Adalynne asked in frustration, trying to stay the tears that threatened to fall.

"That's because you don't really know me," he said stonily as he stepped closer to her.

"Don't say that, Fox. You don't mean that." A tear slipped down her cheek as she held her ground *in front of him.*

"Do me a favour and don't help me again. I'm not worth it." He came close enough that she could smell his familiar scent. She wanted to reach out and touch him but this side of him scared her. It was as if he had never cared for her at all. He was cold and unfeeling.

"What's in the bag?" she whispered, still staring into his green eyes.

He reached up and touched a lock of her hair, twisting it in his fingers before letting go quickly. "You didn't look?" He almost sounded surprised. When Adalynne attempted to touch his hand he recoiled and stepped away from her. The gesture was heartbreaking, causing her vision to blur with tears.

"Is it what I think it is? Are the rumors about you dealing true?" Adalynne asked hesitantly, trying to keep her words steady.

"Yes." He turned and slipped out the window before she could stop him.

Adalynne stared at the window long after Fox left. She didn't know where to go from here. Fox was in trouble and she wanted to help him. She didn't even know how to begin because he put so much distance between them. They were practically strangers now. The only thing she knew for certain was she would not let him go down a path that only led to destruction. He deserved better.

The next day Adalynne knew she had to find Fox. If she didn't seek him out she feared she might not see him again. He never came to their place in the woods or to her window at night anymore and she couldn't bear the thought of something happening to him. She needed to reach him while there were still pieces of her Fox left to save.

Adalynne told her driver she needed to stay after school to prepare for a test in the library. With the approval of her mother, the driver agreed and was to return to pick her up later than usual. When the bell rang for lunch that afternoon, Adalynne discreetly left the school property, heading toward the bus stop just a few blocks away. She had never skipped school or ridden on the public bus before. She could hardly contain the knot that formed in her stomach, a mixture of excitement and nervousness.

Adalynne hadn't been to Fox's house before, although she knew the general area where she should start her search. It was a subdivision that was located not far from her house. He had managed to walk the distance day after day when he was young so she knew it couldn't be far. She had asked around school as discreetly as she could but no one seemed to know where he lived. She wasn't sure exactly how she was going to find it without a street address but she figured someone in the area would be able to direct her. She was determined and hoped that was enough to set her plan into motion. She figured she would have to knock on a few doors but she was more than willing if it meant finding Fox. The bus pulled up in front of a rundown building. The bus driver informed Adalynne this was the only stop in the area. She thanked the driver and nervously departed the bus. She stood frozen as she watched the bus pull away, leaving her in an area that, although it was a short drive from her home, seemed a world apart.

The homes were old, and in dire need of a fresh coat of paint to brighten up their dull, weathered appearances. Old rusted out cars lined one driveway, while another was overgrown with wild grass as if it had sat abandoned for some time. Across the street an old man sat upon the step smoking his pipe. Adalynne waved but he did not return the favor. He merely continued watching her as if he was trying to determine what she was up to.

Adalynne turned and approached the building, hoping someone inside might know of Fox's family and direct her to his home. As she neared she noticed it was quite old, showing years of neglect. A couple of the windows were boarded up and a few others were cracked. The remains of an old dilapidated playground added to the eerie feel of the old structure. Other than the few cars in the parking lot Adalynne would have thought it long abandoned. She stopped walking toward it, even with signs of people she had no peace of mind to enter the building. She was about to turn around and head up the street when someone pushed the old creaky door open.

A woman in her late forties exited, carrying a couple of boxes stacked on top of one another. She struggled with the door and then proceeded toward her vehicle. Adalynne quickly caught up with the woman who didn't even notice her presence until she spoke.

"Can I give you a hand?" Adalynne offered the

woman, who was balancing the boxes as she was frantically patting her pockets in search of keys.

"Oh heavens! I didn't see you there, dear. Yes, that would be lovely." She smiled up at Adalynne through glasses that had slid halfway down her nose. Her graying hair was pulled back into a knot on the back of her head with a couple of pencils weaved in the bun. The woman wore a long skirt that flowed around her legs and a loose fitting blouse that she had tucked haphazardly into her skirt. Adalynne couldn't help but smile at the tousled woman. She had a warm energy about her that shone through and an inviting smile that caused Adalynne to smile in return.

Adalynne took a few of the boxes from the top of her pile. "May I ask what this building is?"

The woman looked back at the building and sighed. "Well, I have been trying to get a building for years in this community to create an after school music program. Unfortunately, it is something a lot of children in this neighborhood don't have the opportunity to be exposed to. To keep them out of trouble, you know. I was a music teacher all my life and I watched some of the brightest children fall and lose their way. I want to give them a chance at something better. This building came up and it's the best I could afford." She looked up at the building. "I have a lot of work ahead of me to get this place safe enough to let children walk in the front door. It might be a long road before I can start to make a difference but knowing eventually it will happen is exciting. My name is Elizabeth, by the way." She extended her hand toward Adalynne after placing *the boxes into her trunk.*

"Adalynne," she responded brightly, placing her hand in Elizabeth's. "I would like to help you with your music school. I'm a fellow music enthusiast and I think it's a fantastic idea."

Adalynne watched Elizabeth's eyes brighten. "That would be wonderful. I'll take all the help I can get."

Adalynne arranged to come back another day so Elizabeth could show her what she was trying to accomplish. The more Adalynne talked to Elizabeth, the more she fell in love with her vision. Adalynne wanted to be a part of it. She wanted to help Elizabeth make a difference.

Luckily Elizabeth was familiar with the Knight family and directed her toward Fox's house, although not without warning. Apparently Fox's father had a reputation for not being a reputable citizen. Adalynne assured her she would be careful before she headed in the direction she sought.

Chapter Ten

Adalynne walked toward the house. She could see traces of the charm it once possessed but it was obvious the property lost the loving touch of its owner long ago. It was now left to fade into its surroundings, like so many of the properties in this area. She wondered why the people stopped caring about the places they called home. The garden was overgrown with weeds, with little remains of the plants once placed there. A couple of the shutters hung at odd angles and looked about ready to fall off and the paint was faded to a dull gray. The wide front porch was bare of any personal items, no chairs or potted plants. The only thing that showed the house was occupied was the truck sitting in the driveway—the same one she had seen Fox drive to school on occasion. The whole property looked like the embodiment of sadness and neglect. She didn't like knowing that this was the place that Fox called home.

Adalynne barely made it up the front step when the door swung open and Fox's form filled the door frame. He wore only sweat pants hanging low on his narrow waist. His chiseled chest was exposed and the deep grooves of his stomach showed his muscled physique. It took her breath away. His dark hair fell in dark messy waves and his beautiful green eyes stared back at her.

"Why are you here?" Fox asked softly, the anger from the night before no longer in his tone. She could sense nothing but sadness from him now.

"I need to talk to you." Adalynne stepped closer. She could feel excitement pull her toward him. When she was younger she used to think they were like magnets and now that she was older she realized how accurate she was. The closer she came to him physically the harder it was to pull away.

"Who's there?" a deep raspy voice called from within the house.

"Can I come in?" She looked up at him. His eyes stayed with her. She could tell he was struggling with something by the way he looked at her. He closed his eyes and then stepped back. Adalynne walked in quickly before he could change his mind. When she stepped into the house it was also bare of any personal items to indicate a family lived there. The living room only consisted of a sofa and chair with a television sitting on what looked like the coffee table pushed against the wall. An older man sat upon the sofa. When Adalynne looked at him she knew without a doubt he was Fox's father. She could see his once handsome features behind the gloom clouding him. His unshaven face and his unkempt hair could not hide the similarities.

"Dad, this is Adalynne," Fox said quickly as he

tried to usher her toward a different part of the house. He seemed anxious, not wanting her to be in his house. Adalynne had pictured what Fox's father looked like many times over the years and from the marks he left on Fox's body, she had always pictured him as a large evil man, like a villain you would see in a movie, but the man before her looked like a ghost. Sorrow consumed him. She could see the toll it had taken on him. His eyes were gray and shadowed heavily with dark circles. He did not pay any attention to her or Fox as he stared lifelessly at the television.

Adalynne stepped forward, carefully avoiding the beer bottles lining the floor, extending her hand to him. "Nice to meet you, Mr. Knight."

She could hear Fox sigh in frustration behind her. "What business do you want with my son? Girls like you don't pay mind to the likes of him." He didn't move to shake her hand. "You will be the end of him," he grumbled more to himself than to Adalynne, taking a long draw of his beer. He stood up abruptly, kicking the bottles at his feet. Adalynne moved out of his way as he brushed past her and shuffled into the kitchen without another word.

She turned back toward Fox. He was staring after his father with his jaw clenched tightly. He turned and walked down the hall without saying anything. Adalynne followed quickly, walking into a room she assumed was his. Once she entered Fox gave the door a shove and it slammed, startling her. "Well, I hit it off with your father. I think we're going to be good buddies," Adalynne said sarcastically, accompanied by an uncomfortable smile.

"Don't take it to heart. I'm his son and I don't think he has ever liked me." Fox smirked. Adalynne let the smile fall from her face, turning around to take in the room. Like the rest of the house it was bare, except for a bed with simple bedding and a dresser that sat on the opposite side of the room. She had tried to picture his room many times over the years. She never imagined it was quite so plain. She moved toward his bed and sat down on the edge. "Where is your guitar? Do you still play?" she asked, curious when she did not see it.

Adalynne looked up into his intense gaze from across the room. She was not sure what he was thinking. "Oh...is it okay if I sit on your bed?" Adalynne asked nervously, ready to move to stand should he object. She hadn't realized how overwhelmed she would feel sitting in his room with his shirtless body standing so close. Her heart beat wildly in her chest as she tried to remember what she wanted to say to him. Thoughts of the night when he had come to her room played in her mind after the dance, the scent of his skin and the feel of him against her was so fresh in her thoughts.

A smile played on his lips. "No, it's good. I've always wondered what you would look like in my bed," Fox said heatedly.

"You did?" Her voice cracked and her eyes widened in embarrassment.

"I have to warn you that in this moment, seeing you in my bed, I lack all will power." He moved toward her and heat flooded Adalynne's face. She swallowed exaggeratedly. He leaned in close to her

before he dropped down, reaching under the bed to pull out his guitar. "Yes, I still play." He chuckled.

"Will you play for me? I miss it," Adalynne asked. Looking at the guitar brought back so many memories. He used to play it so often when they still visited their camp. It seemed like a lifetime ago since she had heard it.

"Not now." He nodded toward the direction of his father and Adalynne dropped it immediately. She did not want to cause any trouble even though she missed the sound desperately.

"It's really hot in here," Adalynne said as she unbuttoned her cardigan. Fox sat on the floor looking up at her.

"It's getting hotter." He smiled. It had been a while since she had seen his genuine smile, way too long. She loved how it played on his handsome face. Adalynne slid off the bed, sitting down in front of him. She touched the dimple on his cheek and he submitted to her touch. "Why are you involved with that stuff?" She couldn't bring herself to say it but she knew he would understand her meaning regardless.

Fox closed his eyes and sighed. "I don't want to talk about it." His smile vanished. "Let's just stay like this, like old times when things were simple."

"We need to talk about this…how about we play a game?" Adalynne tried to bring him back from his sudden mood change. He was beginning to shut her out.

"What kind of game?" He looked up at her curiously. Those green eyes were so deep she wanted to dive into them. Her body screamed at her

to touch him, to kiss him, and relive the moment that found its way into her thoughts every day since. In this moment, she too had no will power.

"How about for each of my questions you answer truthfully I take off an article of clothing?" Adalynne moved closer, sliding her legs over his to straddle him. The feel of his body against hers was intoxicating, her clothes suddenly felt restricting and she wanted nothing more than to press her flesh against his. She had dreamed of this for too long.

"Okay I'll play your game." Fox exhaled a breath he was holding. "What's your first question?" His skin felt so warm, so wonderful. She felt intoxicated.

"Why are you doing it?" she whispered in his ear, gently caressing it with the slightest touch of her lips. Adalynne smiled against his neck when he shuddered in response. Goose bumps rushed across his skin. When he remained quiet, Adalynne pulled away. "Don't feel like playing?" Adalynne barely got the words out when he grabbed her arms and brought her back against him.

"Don't," he pleaded. The desperation in his voice touched her. "I want to, please."

She looked into his eyes. His confidence was stripped away and he was vulnerable before her, he had let down his guard. Fox slid his hands down the length of her calves and reached down and pulled off her socks. "Hey," Adalynne complained.

"Socks don't count. I owe someone money and I have no way of paying them back except to work off my debt by moving their product."

Adalynne slid her cardigan off her shoulders and

threw it on the floor. "Why did you borrow the money?"

"Because my father was and is too drunk to work. There was no way to pay the bills and when it was offered it seemed like the only option at the time, so I took the money," Fox said softly. She knew it was not easy for him to tell her this. He nodded toward her shirt after his answer. "Your turn."

Adalynne slid her shirt slowly up her stomach, watching his hungry gaze consume every inch of skin she exposed. Pulling it over her head, she watched his gaze memorize every line of her body before his eyes found hers. A smile spread across his face. "This is an awesome game."

"How much do you owe him?" Adalynne pressed on while he was still giving answers.

He was silent for a moment, contemplating whether or not he wanted to tell her. "How much, Fox?"

He closed his eyes tightly. "Ten thousand."

Adalynne stood up and unbuttoned her pants and slid them down her legs, kicking them off. Fox pulled his body up to full height in front of her, her skin flushed hot as he looked down at her. His chest rose and fell with exaggerated breath. The hunger she felt for him was reflected in his eyes and she desperately wanted him to feast upon her.

"How long will it take you to pay it off and what happens if you don't?" Her voice faltered slightly as she was losing her composure. Her mouth watered and her stomach felt as if it was reeled too tight.

"Isn't that two questions? I believe you're cheating." He smiled playfully at her.

"It is technically worded as one question." She bit her lip.

I will let you get away with it just this once. A long time, and truthfully if I didn't pay it off, he would probably kill me." His answer caused her breath to catch in her throat. "You wanted truthful answers," Fox accused lightly.

Adalynne reached up to unclasp her bra. She watched Fox clench his fists at his sides. She dropped her bra to the floor. He leaned in toward her, causing her to back up against the bed but stopped short of touching her. His breathing was laboured and he was close enough for her to feel the heat radiate from his skin. The room felt like a thousand degrees.

"Once you pay it off are you done with it?" Adalynne asked, watching him study her body.

"Yes." His intense eyes found hers.

Leaning back upon the bed, she raised her hips off the bed to remove her panties.

"Who do you owe money to?" She was surprised by the heavy voice that escaped her saturated with the desire she felt for him.

"The game is over. You have nothing left to take off." He smiled down at her. "I think I won."

"This one is to touch me," she whispered.

"No fair...what if I don't answer that question?"

"Then I put my clothes back on and walk out the door." She smiled at him and the pained expression on his face told her she had won. He was defenseless against her.

"Slim," he whispered reluctantly.

"Slim?"

"That's his name." He placed his knee against the bed, between her legs, and leaned down over her.

"What kind of a name is that?" She found it hard to concentrate and wasn't even sure the words had passed her lips until he responded.

"It's his, but ironically he is built like a tank." He looked down at her with a hooded gaze. "Can I touch you now?" Fox asked breathlessly.

"Yes," she said and he brought his mouth down upon hers. His kisses were desperate as he devoured her in his passionate embrace. Adalynne wanted this moment to last forever. When she was with him she truly felt alive. He made her whole body pulse with life, and ache with a need so great it consumed her.

"I want you so bad. It's all I think about," Fox whispered breathlessly between kisses. He unbuttoned his pants and kicked them off. His body was like a work of art, beautiful and strong. His heated gaze roamed her body. He leaned down and kissed her lips, her cheek, along her jaw and then slowly continued down her chest. Adalynne felt herself melt into the bed. Everywhere his lips touched left a path of pleasure lingering after his moved on. Adalynne gasped when he took her nipple in his mouth. She stilled as she realized what was about to happen. "What's wrong?" he asked, noticing her hesitation.

"I'm just nervous," she whispered, looking up at him through her lashes.

He pulled back so his arms were fully extended, looking down upon her naked body. His brow furrowed, he seemed to be tormented with thoughts that she could not even begin to understand. She brushed his hair from his eyes and wished with all her heart the world could go back to when nothing else mattered but each other.

"What's wrong?" she questioned when she could no longer bear his silence.

Fox growled, defeated, as he rolled off her onto the bed, rubbing his hands over his face. Adalynne sat up and looked down at him, touching his arm gently. "Did I do something wrong?" she whispered.

"No." He opened his eyes and looked up at her. "I need you to get dressed," he said, putting his hands back over his eyes.

"Why...don't you want me? I don't understand. I want this." She reached up and pulled his hand from his face. He was gorgeous with his features so perfect and his green eyes so mesmerizing. She knew with everything in her heart she wanted to be with him. She didn`t understand why he never let himself get close to her. He always pulled away when she needed him the most. She didn`t understand why he couldn't love her. "I love you," she whispered.

"You're making this so difficult." He pushed up off the bed and grabbed his pants from the floor before retrieving her clothes and tossing them to her. "We can't do this, Bee. It was a mistake. I don't want to be your first...I don't want to be your anything." Those last words stung as if he slapped

them across her face. It took everything she had not to collapse under the weight of them.

"Now what?" Anger slipped into her voice. She was embarrassed and angry he turned her down. She hastily pulled her clothes back on.

"Nothing," he replied coldly. His guard was back up and he was pushing her away like he always did and it infuriated her. "You need to go."

"Gladly." She fumed, pulling her shirt back over her head and making a show of flipping her hair out of her shirt and then stomped toward the door.

"Adalynne?" Fox called her back. Adalynne spun around and looked at him through narrowed eyes. "Don't love me."

She glared at him. "Too late, Fox. I have always loved you." She slipped through the door, making sure to slam it behind her.

"Sorry, Mr. Knight, but your son has made me incredibly angry. Have a nice day, sir." She apologized for her dramatic exit when his dark eyes watched her stomp out from his son's room. He did not respond to her as he tipped his bottle up to his lips. She continued past him and made sure to close the front door more gently as she exited the house.

Adalynne did not look back as she walked away from Fox's house. She headed back toward Elizabeth's building, hoping she would not have to wait long for the bus to return. As she walked she noticed two guys coming in her direction, on the opposite side of the street. When she neared she took in their rough appearance, with tattoos and sly smiles. They watched her the entire time and it made the hairs on the back of her neck stand up. If she hadn't have been so driven with anger she would have listened to the warnings of danger and avoided them all together but as she got closer she realized one of them looked familiar. She had seen him at school hanging around with some of the people Fox associated with. She had an idea.

"Now what is Adalynne doing hanging around these parts? If I would have known you liked to toy on this side of the tracks I would have shown more interest." Apparently he recognized her too. He was tall and lean, with oversized clothes hanging off his form. His head was shaven and a tattoo reached up from under his shirt and extended up his neck just below his ear. The other guy had longer hair that flipped out from under his twisted ball cap. He too had a lean build but slightly shorter with wide set shoulders. A devious smile spread across his narrow lips as he raked her entire body with his eyes. Adalynne wanted to cringe but she thought better of offending these two.

"You know my name?" Adalynne was genuinely surprised.

"Girls like you get noticed." He shrugged his shoulders. He was less threatening in his demeanor than the guy in the baseball cap so Adalynne focused her attention on him. "I'm Teeter, by the way, and this is Josh."

"You lookin' for a good time?" Josh's smile made her want to back away and find safety in distance.

"Ah...no." She tried to dismiss his offer casually. "Actually I just wanted to ask you guys if you knew how to get a hold of Slim." She tried to *say his name confidently.*

"Whatcha want with him?" A confused scowl formed on Teeter's face. His expression bordered on suspicion.

"I just need to talk to him." Adalynne crossed her arms, trying to provide cover from Josh's uncomfortable stares. She thought she was pulling off enough confidence as to not seem like a fish out of water.

Teeter pulled out his phone. "Are you sure?" He seemed reluctant to give her the information.

"Yep." Adalynne smiled and Teeter rambled off Slim's number. With a quick "Thank you" she left the guys behind as she made her way back to the bus stop. She didn't turn back but she could feel their eyes on her the entire time she was still in their view. Luckily she didn't have to wait long before the bus arrived and she was heading back to school with more than enough time before her driver would be there to pick her up. Her body still thrummed from her emotional experience. She took a deep calming breath before she pulled out her phone to dial Slim's number, before she lost her nerve. She had a sinking feeling she was getting in way over her head. Her relationship with Fox may have collapsed under the painful truth that Fox did not love her but it did not change how she felt about him. She wanted to save him from the trouble he had gotten himself into. She wanted to be able to sleep at night knowing she did everything she could.

Chapter Eleven

"Who the fuck is this?" a deep voice with a less than welcoming tone spat out on the other end of the line.

Adalynne was glad no one was sitting next to her on the bus because his voice traveled too well from the other end. "Hello, I'm looking for Slim. Do I have the right number?" Her voice sounded much smaller than she intended. She couldn't help but cringe at her lack of conviction.

"Yes," he answered frankly.

"Well...I am calling about the debt that Damon Knight owes you." This time she managed to get her tone somewhat more assured.

She closed her eyes and shook her head when Slim erupted into laughter. "Damon's got a girl doing his dirty work, does he? Tell him he's mine now and he's putting in his time until his debt is paid."

"Actually, he doesn't know I am calling. I want to pay off what he owes you." Adalynne was met with silence for a moment on the other end of the

105

line.

"Fifteen grand." His reply was short and to the point.

"I thought it was ten?" Adalynne countered.

"His interest just went up. If he wanted fair rates he should have borrowed from the bank. So tell me there, sweet stuff, still planning on bailing out your boyfriend?" he mocked.

"Yes. How do we do this?"

"87 George Street. Now or never," he proposed. Adalynne looked at the time. She knew where George Street was—it was on the edge of town. If it was a quick exchange, she would still make it back to the school in time before her driver became aware of her absence.

"I will be there soon. Give me an hour," she confirmed.

"Sure thing, sweetheart, looking forward to your visit." And he was gone. Fear pumped through her veins strong and potent.

The bus dropped her off at her bank. Adalynne drew a deep breath and tried to create the illusion of calm. She needed to be convincing as she causally pushed through the doors and pushed a smile upon her face. Fortunately for her, school had already been dismissed so it looked better than if she had been there when she was supposed to be in class. Adalynne was never much of a spender. Her parents always bought her whatever she needed so her account just accumulated funds that her parents had put away for her over the years.

"Hi Greta!" Adalynne walked up the teller with a wide smile. Adalynne's parents were customers at

this bank for as long as she could remember. Over the years she had come to know some of the regular tellers when she came with her parents. The plump woman behind the desk smiled. "Adalynne, look at you! Completely gorgeous, my child. Where did the time go?" She shook her head before continuing. "What can I do for you today?"

"Well, I need to make a withdrawal of $15, 000. It's for something that I'm planning for my parents' anniversary coming up. It's a surprise." Adalynne winked at her.

"Ooh, that must be quite the gift. Just a moment, dear. With such a large withdrawal, I will have to get a manager's approval." Adalynne couldn't help but feel the lump of guilt in her throat but at least her excuse seemed to appease Greta's curiosity and hopefully keep the transaction a secret from her parents. She felt like her entire body was pulsing with the crazed pace of her heart as she waited for Greta to return with a manager. It wasn't long before an unfamiliar face approached her.

"Hello Adalynne. Greta tells me you're making a large withdrawal today. May I ask what it is for?" This man was all business. His features were pinched and looked like he lacked any sense of humor. He was immediately suspicious.

"I found a local artist who has agreed to construct a sculpture for my mother's garden. He was highly recommended by a good family friend. We came to an agreement on the price based on paying with cash. I didn't think it would be a problem since I do not have a limit for withdrawals placed on my account." Adalynne did not know

where that lie came from but she was so thankful she had overheard her mother raving about an artist who had done a sculpture for someone she knew recently.

"I see." The manager contemplated her words as he studied her.

"Oh my, that sounds so lovely, Adalynne." Greta leaned in with a smile. The manager seemed reluctant but finally agreed to permit the transaction. Adalynne dodged a few more of Greta's prying questions before she was handed the envelope of cash and gained her leave. She tucked the cash securely away into her bag before exiting the bank. Once outside she took a deep breath and tried to calm her nerves. Today was definitely an emotionally exhausting day and she suspected it was about to get worse.

George Street was an approximately twenty minute walk from her location. She needed the time to build up the courage to confront this Slim guy. She convinced herself to start walking despite the fear growing strong within her. The perfectly manicured properties quickly declined as she neared her destination. She knew it was a rougher area of town but she didn't realize how on edge she would be as she made her way closer to the street. As she turned the corner onto George Street, she stopped short.

A group of people had gathered in front of the weathered house with the number 87 displayed beside the door. The three guys and one girl looked hardened and crude as they stared back at her. The girl had shaggy black dyed hair that was in desperate need of tending. Her makeup was over applied and hid any natural beauty that she might have possessed. It was hard to determine what was underneath the thick layer coating her face. Her see through lace shirt exposed her red lace bra and her jeans squeezed her excess weight over the top, giving her figure an uncomplimentary look. The three guys in her company didn't look that much better. They looked unkempt and raw, with cold stares.

"You lost, princess?" the girl snarled at her. The guys chuckled at her words.

"No." Adalynne steeled her shoulders and marched across the street, passing them without a backward glance and ignored the whistle one of the guys directed toward her.

"When you're finished in there, princess, I have some business that needs tending."

"In your dreams, Tim," the girl retorted.

Adalynne knocked on the door, trying to block out the conversation that carried on behind her because apparently she was their topic of choice. The door swung open and a large wide shouldered man appeared in the doorway. She took a step back unconsciously. Her self-preservation kicked in and told her to flee. It took everything she had to keep her feet planted. The man stared down at her with the darkest eyes she had ever seen, almost black in color. His arms looked larger than what seemed humanly possible. Adalynne barely squeaked out her intention under his intimidating stare. "Slim is expecting you," he grumbled in a voice so deep that it sounded raw and harsh.

She entered in a wide circle around him, nervous to get too close in case he suddenly decided to squeeze the life out of her. She had no doubt this guy could crush her with one hand. The interior of the house was dark and musty. The wallpaper in the hall was peeling away and the floors creaked under her feet.

"In here, sweetheart." She heard Slim's familiar voice from the phone call. He was in the closest room off the hallway. She backed away from the large man still hovering near the door. She quickly slipped into the room and away from his trailing black eyes. "My, my, you are sweet, aren't you? How has Damon kept you a secret?" He mused as he caught sight of her.

Adalynne side-stepped into the room and took in the surroundings. "Your doorman is the scariest man I have ever seen," she confessed. When she took in the room her eyes fell on two men reclined on a large leather sofa positioned in front of a large flat screen television. Controllers in hand, the sounds of explosions filled the room as a violent war game unfolded on the screen.

They both erupted in laughter at her admittance. The screen paused and both men turned to fully address her. She wasn't sure who Slim was, both men had similar builds of excessive gym goers. They both were relatively well-dressed with buttoned shirts and jeans. One had short cropped hair and his face was shadowed with a couple of days' growth. The other was cleaner shaven with wavy hair that fell longer around his face and deep brown eyes that studied her.

"We have business to attend to, don't we...?" The one with longer hair stood up to address her. He trailed off, waiting for her name.

"Adalynne," she offered quickly, knowing now who she was here to see. Adalynne reached into her bag and pulled out the envelope.

"In a hurry, I see." He smiled at her. *"Leave us."* He motioned for the other guy to leave the room and he quickly abided, leaving Adalynne alone with Slim.

"Please sit." He motioned toward the sofa.

"Um...I actually can't stay." Adalynne tried to talk through her nervousness.

"Sit," he replied flatly and waited for her to obey.

"Right...okay." Adalynne sat on the edge, ready to flee if things went wrong, though she doubted she would get past the door guy. The mere thought of the predicament she put herself in caused her heart to beat so loudly she could barely hear anything else.

Slim sat down next to her, close enough that his leg touched hers. Adalynne moved away from him, sliding down the sofa. He didn't take offense to her obvious retreat, instead an amused look spread across his face. He moved closer again and Adalynne moved to stand because she could not move any further down the sofa. He grabbed her arm and pulled her back down forcefully. *"I like you."* He breathed hotly in her ear. Adalynne tried to pull away but he was strong.

"Please don't...I have your money." She tried to hand him the envelope.

111

"I see something I want more." His dark eyes fixated on hers and fear spiked through her. A whimper escaped her lips before she could stop herself and it seemed to excite him. *"You are exquisite."* He looked hungrily down her body.

He moved to touch her and she fought off his advance, struggling against his firm grip until she tumbled to the floor. *"You're even more beautiful when you're angry."*

A large crash at the door pulled both their attentions. Then a loud grunt followed by a thud of something heavy hitting the floor. *"Adalynne!"* Fox's voice bellowed through the house.

"Fox!" she sobbed, trying to scramble to her feet. Fox suddenly filled the frame of the door. Adalynne pushed herself up and slowly backed away, toward Fox. Slim didn't move, he just leaned back against the sofa and smiled smugly. Feet shuffling behind Fox caused him to turn. She was surprised how quickly Fox moved with the oncoming threat, bringing his elbow in direct contact with the guy's face. Adalynne recognized the guy who fell to the floor as the one who accompanied Slim when she arrived. He dropped to the floor with his hands on his face.

"I've always liked your style, Knight." Slim seemed completely unaffected by the fact Fox had dropped two of his men.

"Fuck off, Slim." Fox stepped forward to grab Adalynne's arm and pull her toward him.

Slim smirked and leaned forward to pick up the envelope of cash Adalynne dropped. *"Seems your little Sugar Momma here—"* Slim slid his gaze toward Adalynne "—bought you for her shiny new toy." Adalynne looked up at Fox and watched him clench his jaw but he never took his eyes off Slim. "When she gets bored with you be sure to come back and see me. You have certain qualities that are good for business."

"Not a chance," Fox spat, pulling Adalynne towards the door. "If you ever fucking mess with any of mine I will hunt you down and kill you. You know I will." His voice was foreign and dangerous. She thought she saw fear flash across Slim's face before he collected himself.

"This will not be the last I see of you, Knight. You can't live between the lines. You will mess up eventually." Adalynne could still hear Slim's laughter as Fox shuffled her past the two bodies in the hall. The one with the bloodied face was leaning against the wall trying to stop the bleeding now soaking his shirt and the large guy at the door was face down on the floor, not moving.

When they walked outside the people who were lingering out front were long gone. Fox didn't stop pushing Adalynne forward until they reached his truck parked on the side of the street.

"Get in," he barked at her after he swung her door open. Adalynne hopped in quickly before Fox slammed the door. They drove in silence for most of the ride. She watched his eyes frequent the rearview mirror but Adalynne was too scared to ask if he thought they would be pursued. He didn't look at her, keeping his eyes on the road. She knew he was furious with her from the way he clenched his jaw, and his forced breath.

"Can you drop me off at school? My driver will be picking me up soon," Adalynne asked weakly. Fox didn't respond but when she noticed he made the necessary turns she was relieved. Fox pulled to a stop in front of the school. Everyone had long since gone for the day. She looked over at him and finally gained the courage to speak.

"I was just trying to help you," she explained.

"I didn't want your fucking help," he replied, leaning back against his seat, not turning to face her.

"How did you know where I was?" She reached up and placed her hand on the door lever but didn't pull.

"Teeter and Josh were bragging about the fact that they had talked to you. It didn't take much to make them spill about what you had asked them."

"But how did you know I would even go there?"

"I didn't. I called Slim and he said he couldn't talk because a very interesting proposition was about to walk through the door. I fucking panicked!" Fox hit the steering wheel so hard that it startled Adalynne. "Do you have any fucking idea what you walked into back there?" Fox leaned back and closed his eyes, visibly trying to calm himself down. "I should have realized you would have done something like this when you asked all those questions. Did he hurt you?"

"No," Adalynne whispered. "I didn't know you could fight like that."

He looked over at her; his eyes were blurred with emotion. "I don't want you getting involved in my business...I will get you your money back."

"I don't want it."

"I need you to leave me alone." Fox looked directly at her, his eyes pleading.

"Okay." Adalynne pulled the door open and moved to step out. "Can I—"

"I mean for good. This thing that we have…whatever it is, it isn't good for you," he interrupted her. "I want you to forget about me."

"Don't say that." Adalynne looked down at him through her wet lashes. The emotions of the day had finally caught up with her. She was exhausted and didn't want Fox to say any of this. She wanted to go back to this afternoon when he looked at her like she was the only person in the world. She wanted that always.

"It was my fault you were there today. I put you in danger." His voice showed strain.

"What? No, Fox. I'm sorry. I was trying to help you," Adalynne sobbed. "I don't want you to shut me out. I know you don't love me but can't we at least be friends?"

"Goodbye, Bee." His serious green eyes looked up at her and she knew he meant it. Their beautiful world together was over. She watched him drive away and drag her heart behind him. She stood there silently trying to figure out how something so beautiful had turned into such a complete mess. She didn't move until the driver pulled up in front of her.

"Everything all right, Miss Adalynne?" he asked, opening her door. Her driver, John, was always so kind to her. He was a very proud grandfather of six. His grey hair was thin and

cropped short. His kind eyes were creased with many years of smiles. She couldn't bring herself to answer. Instead, she just climbed in the backseat and cried quietly the entire drive home. The only reprieve she had was the fact that now she knew Fox was free of his debt.

Chapter Twelve

When the set finished the band exited the stage. Adalynne watched Fox leave and she realized how much she missed him. An unbearable ache formed in her chest. People began shuffling around the room and music blasted on the speakers surrounding them. A heavy beat thrummed through the entire club, keeping the good mood alive and thriving in the many bodies that lined the floor.

"I'm going to check my messages." Adalynne held up her phone. "I can't hear anything here." She didn't wait for anyone to respond. Leaving her seat, she headed toward the back of the bar toward the restrooms.

"I'm coming with you." Katie jumped up and followed on Adalynne's heels through the crowded floor of people. When they were away from the guys, Katie pulled up beside her. "What was going on with you and Brolan Pierce? Do you know him? Please tell me you know him. You were practically eye doing each other." Katie looked up at Adalynne's face. "*Oh my God!* You know the lead

117

singer of Outcome? Why didn't you tell me you knew him? Is he the one you're so hung up on?" Katie's eyes could not get any wider as she stared at her. Her nails were digging into Adalynne's arm.

"Katie, please be quiet." Adalynne noticed the girls waiting in the bathroom line turning to observe their conversation. "Yes, I know him and I didn't tell you because that's not his real name. I didn't know it until he walked onstage. It was a long time ago. Anyway, I'm not that hung up."

"Oh please. You barely look at all the hot guys that practically drool on you. Look at Matthew over there. He's not used to having to work to gain a girl's attention. He's used to girls handing him a free pass to their vaginas. Besides, I have never seen two people look at each other like that; I thought he was going to jump off the stage. It was beyond attraction." Katie looked like she was going to swoon as she leaned against the wall.

"Do me a favor and forget about it." Adalynne tried to dismiss their conversation. She listened to the message her mother left telling her everything was still fine.

"Why should I forget? You obviously can't." Katie folded her arms across her chest. She stomped her foot defiantly. "You cannot let this opportunity slip by. I seriously want to strangle you! You should be asking to speak with him. He owes you that much after he eye-fucked the hell out of you onstage!"

"Oh my god, Katie! It wasn't like that. He was probably just surprised to see me." Adalynne shrugged her shoulders and tried to seem casual.

"He never wanted me like that and he doesn't now."

"Are you Adalynne?" A tall man dressed completely in black came to a stop in front of her. He looked like he walked out of the gym after spending most of his life there. A black shirt stretched over his massive chest, his hair was cropped short, and his severe eyes glared at her with a very serious expression. He had the science of intimidation down perfectly and Adalynne just nodded at his question, backing up against the wall.

"Will you follow me?" he continued, taking a step back, expecting her to comply but halted when she did not move.

"Why?" she asked when he looked back at her.

"You are requested by Mr. Pierce," he stated simply, his patience wearing thin.

"I'll cover for you!" Katie pushed Adalynne toward the large security guard. Adalynne looked back over her shoulder at Katie, who continued to wave her on encouragingly. The eyes of all the other girls who witnessed the scene stared after her as well.

Adalynne tried to calm her breathing as she followed the man through a dark, narrow hallway until he came to a door and knocked. The door opened narrowly but Adalynne couldn't see in the room at her angle.

"Adalynne," he said to the person who opened the door. The door closed and a moment later it swung open wide and Adalynne watched the band members leave the room. They nodded approvingly at her. The one she recognized from the drums spoke to her as he passed. "Hello there, beautiful."

Adalynne tried to manage a smile in return but she was overwhelmed with nerves. He smiled widely at her before continuing down the hall with the others.

Adalynne didn't move. Her feet felt planted in place until the security guard gave her a gentle nudge of encouragement. She walked in slowly and he closed the door behind her, narrowly missing her. Adalynne took in the room. The sofas were covered in discarded clothing. The walls were covered with posters and framed photographs.

Fox walked out of a connecting room with a beer in his hand. His hair was messy like he had just run his fingers through it. He leaned against the door frame and stared at her from across the room. The emotions that overcame her were crippling. She had been living so long without her heart and now it was right in front of her and yet so far. She couldn't think of anything more striking than his muscled lean frame. The way his jeans hung so low and how his shirt hugged his body that held a promise of so much pleasure. He was a drug to her and she was addicted to him in every sense of the word.

"You are so beautiful." His voice was raw from singing. He walked over to the sofa and sat down, not taking his eyes off her. "I can't get you out of my fucking head." Fox ran his hand down over his face.

Adalynne walked toward him until her leg touched his. He ran his fingertips across her stomach gently. The touch was so soft she could barely feel it. "Are you really here?" he said softly like he wasn't even really talking to her.

"Yes." Adalynne leaned down, climbing onto his

120

lap, straddling him on the sofa. She couldn't control herself. She was driven with need and she had far too many drinks to think clearly. Adalynne took the beer from his hand and leaned back to place it on the table. He stared up at her through a hooded gaze. He was so perfect and she wanted to kiss his beautiful full lips. The alcohol that coursed through her system numbed anything but the desire for him that pulsed wildly through her body. She moved her hips against him and a low moan escaped him. He didn't move, his hands remained by his sides, gripping the fabric of the sofa. Adalynne took his hands and placed them on her. He immediately began caressing her body.

"Who was that guy with you?" A hint of jealousy tainted his words and Adalynne couldn't help but feel the thrill of this fact.

"A friend," Adalynne responded quickly, not wanting to think about Matthew while she was in Fox's arms.

"He didn't look like just a friend," he countered flatly. Fox brushed her hair back from her face, cupping her face.

"My father is in the hospital." She had always felt the need to tell him the things that mattered to her.

"I know. That's why I came back here. To make sure you were okay." He looked up at her with his focus suddenly sharp. She knew he was under the influence of something, she could tell by the look in his eyes but she didn't let it stop her. She leaned forward and claimed his lips with hers in a beautiful kiss. They fought to get closer to each other as they pressed their bodies together. His hands slid under her shirt and he caressed her skin until her need became desperate. He pulled her shirt over her head and smiled as he bit his lower lip. Adalynne in turn pulled his shirt off and ran her fingers over the lines of his hard body. She could feel his need for her, his body craved her as much as she did him. He responded to her every touch. All of the heartache she had suffered was worth this moment with him. Fox unbuttoned her pants. She stood up so he could slowly pull them off her hips, gently kissing her legs as he ran his hands down the length of them. His touch lingered on her skin, making her dizzy for more.

"I want you to be the first to have me. I don't want anyone but you," Adalynne breathed in his ear as she leaned into his chest. His hands immediately stilled on her back and she realized she ruined the moment. It was so easy to forget he didn't feel the same about her when he looked at her like he had only moments ago. "Forget I said that," she said frantically, trying to kiss him, but he turned away from her. He dropped his hands to his sides. "No, please don't do this. I want this more than anything. I don't care if it doesn't mean anything to you. Please, Fox." A tear slipped down her cheek as she pleaded with him.

"No, you don't. You don't know what you're talking about. I never wanted you to save yourself for me, Bee. I told you that a long fucking time ago." His voice was desolate. "I just wanted to fuck you and get you out of my head."

"Don't say that," Adalynne sobbed.

"I never asked for you to love me. I don't want you to." He ran his hands through his hair and shut his eyes tight. Adalynne was so close to him but she never felt so far.

"It's the only thing I am sure of in my life," she whispered softly. "Why do you always shut me out when things start to feel real?"

Fox pulled himself out from under her and stood up. "Fuck!" he yelled, hitting the bottles off the table and they shattered on the floor. A sob escaped Adalynne's lips as she stood up and pulled her shirt back on.

"What do you want from me? Do you want me to tell you that I don't care about you? Do you want me to tell you that all I want is for you to screw me and then we can part ways and never think about each other again? To tell you that I have been with lots of people and sex has no meaning for me? Would that make you happy? You are the most confusing person in the world. You want me one moment and hate me the next." Adalynne tried to keep her voice down but she was angry.

"I want you to hate me," he said, defeated, as he looked down at her. "It would make this so much easier. I want you to slap me in the face and storm out of here and never fucking think of me again."

"Why did you send for me then? Was it just to rub it in my face that you don't have any feelings for me and leave me humiliated?" She was yelling now but she didn't care. She was furious with him.

Fox leaned back, his shirt still discarded on the floor displaying his impossibly hard body. He just looked at her with his jaw set. Turmoil brewing in the sea of green as they remained set on her.

"Screw you, Fox!" She stormed over toward the door. Swinging the door open, she came face to face with the security guard. He didn't say anything as he looked down at her seething form. "What are you looking at?" she yelled at him before she pushed past.

"Adalynne!" Fox called to her from the doorway. Adalynne disappointed herself by stopping in her tracks, turning around to face him. He held an envelope in his hand, extending it out toward her.

"What?" she sobbed.

"Your money." He indicated toward his hand. "I told you I would pay you back."

"Is that what this was about?" Adalynne dropped her shoulders. "I'm such an idiot." She sighed. She closed her eyes tight through her embarrassment. She had thought he had called her back there because he wanted to see her, when he merely wanted to pay her back from bailing him out of Slim's influence. She felt like a complete fool throwing herself at him. No wonder why he recoiled from her when she proclaimed her feelings. "Take your money and shove it!" she yelled at him, trying to salvage her damaged pride.

Adalynne stalked across the floor packed with bodies lost in the music. When she came in view of the table, Katie jumped up and met her. "Are you okay?" she said in Adalynne's ear.

"I want to go home." She wasn't even able to pretend she was okay for the sake of their company. Matthew was on his feet quickly, coming to her side.

"Is it your father?" Matthew asked with grave concern.

"No, she just needs to go home. The last few days have been hard on her," Katie said for her as Matthew looked at her expectantly.

"I'll drive you," Matthew insisted.

When Matthew and Steven dropped the girls off, he promised to call her tomorrow before they left to head back to school. Adalynne tried to tell him it wasn't necessary but once again he insisted. Adalynne felt guilty he was here for her and all she could think about was Fox and the lingering sensation of his touch on her skin. Matthew kissed her hand gently before turning to leave her and Katie on the doorstep. Adalynne wished she wanted to be with Matthew; he was safe. What if being with him would save her from the heartache that Fox caused her every time he didn't return her love? She couldn't get hurt by someone who didn't control her heart.

***

The next morning came quickly and when Adalynne woke up she still felt exhausted. Her body ached and her stomach felt uneasy. She was determined to be at the hospital early to check on her father; she forced herself to get motivated. She left Katie to sleep. Leaving a note on her pillow explaining she left early for the hospital, she closed the door and headed downstairs.

Adalynne walked toward the kitchen when she heard a commotion. Unsure of who would be rummaging around so early in the morning, she knew it wasn't her mother because she had taken her car last night when she left the hospital. "Addie girl, you're up early." Carmen's warm familiar voice floated down the hall. A smile blossomed on Adalynne's face. "Carmen!" Her feet quickened their pace and rounded the corner to the kitchen. Carmen was standing at the island and the familiar sight almost brought tears of joy to her eyes. "I missed you!"

Carmen's strong embrace was comforting and Adalynne melted into her. "Look at you. It never ceases to amaze me the woman you have become, so beautiful darling." Carmen sighed, stepping back to look at her, smoothing Adalynne's hair back from her face. "It's not the same here without you. I miss all the trouble you used to get into." She winked. Adalynne had always felt closer to Carmen than her own mother. Seeing Carmen made it really feel like she was home. "How are you holding up?"

"I'm okay. I'll be better once Dad gets to come home." Adalynne stepped back. Carmen gave her a sad smile. "Are you making pancakes?" Adalynne's eyes widened.

"Yes dear, your mother called me yesterday and said you would be staying at the house so I knew my Addie would want her favorite breakfast when she woke up." Carmen smiled.

"You are too good to me. Can I help?" Adalynne looked around for something to do.

"Sit." Carmen motioned to a stool at the island. "And tell me about life outside of these walls." She smiled expectantly. "How is the world treating my

126

Addie?"

Adalynne could never lie to Carmen so she didn't try to glaze anything over and the words tumbled out from deep within her. She told Carmen how everything felt wrong. She felt stuck in someone else's life, going through the motions but not really living. She tried to focus on her classes but her heart wasn't in it and she found herself directing all her energy on managing to get through the days. She didn't want to let her family down so she was intent on getting through it. Especially now that her father was sick she wouldn't do anything to cause any more stress.

Adalynne even found herself telling Carmen about Matthew and how she couldn't find it in her to return his affections. She found it so frustrating her heart would not cooperate with what her mind was trying to convince her was the best choice. He was handsome, passionate about his career, and on the path to success, and most important, seemed to genuinely care about her. He wanted to spend time with her.

Adalynne spent her whole life loving a boy that would never love her back. She wondered if she would spend the rest trying to fall out of love with him. Fox had inspired a love so encompassing that she feared she would be left with only fractions of feelings that would always pale in comparison. She wished her love would have been enough for him. It didn't matter how big and bright her feelings shone for him—it was never enough. His heart did not feel the same and she was left chasing a dream.

"You are still hung up on that boy, aren't you?"

Carmen asked but it didn't really sound like a question as much as speaking a truth she already knew.

"What boy?" Adalynne tried to play dumb. Over the years Fox warmed up to the fact that Carmen welcomed his presence. When he knew Adalynne's parents were in no risk of coming home, he would submit to entering her house. They spent many hours in front of the piano, or sitting at the kitchen table sampling Carmen's cooking. Adalynne never openly talked about her feelings toward Fox. Though, she knew Carmen could tell Adalynne's heart swelled when that green eyed little boy was near. Even at their young age Fox had become the center of Adalynne's world.

"Don't play dumb with me, child, you are so transparent." Carmen tried to be stern but ended with her signature smile.

"What? *Fox*. No. That was so long ago."

"You don't fool me. I'd seen the way you looked at that boy even when you were just a small child. There was no mistaking that look, my dear." Carmen shook her head slowly as if shuffling though old memories, her eyes not really focused on anything in particular in the room. A smile played on her lips.

"Fine. I'm such a pathetic mess." Adalynne dropped her head in her hands.

"Life is not meant to be easy. It is hard, complicated, and sometimes seems impossible. All we can hope is getting it somewhat right." Carmen smiled encouragingly. "Despite what your mother thinks you cannot put a neat little bow on everything and pretend it's perfect. We need to make a mess before we can make something of it."

"Do you think there are different kinds of love? Do you think that if you cannot be with the person you love, you can learn to love someone else?" Adalynne asked hopefully.

"In my life I have seen many different types of love. Some make us happier than others. Some start with good intentions and fall apart over the years. Though, there is one type of love that is very rare and special. I have witnessed this only a few times in my lifetime…"

"Morning." Katie shuffled into the kitchen, still in her pajamas. Adalynne wanted to continue the conversation with Carmen but the moment was lost. "Ooh, pancakes." Katie clapped.

"I didn't think you would be up before I left." Adalynne was surprised to see Katie up so early. She was never one for mornings.

"Yeah, well, as much as I love sleep, my stomach had other plans."

Chapter Thirteen

After stuffing her face with Carmen's ridiculously good pancakes Adalynne said her goodbyes to Carmen and a very reluctant Katie. Adalynne was anxious to get back to her father's bedside. Katie was heading back to school and made Adalynne promise she would keep her updated on her father's condition.

When they had arrived home last night Katie insisted Adalynne explain in detail how she knew Brolan Pierce before she would let her go to sleep. Despite Adalynne's exhaustion and sullen mood from her encounter with Fox she humored Katie's request. She started with the fact that Brolan Pierce was actually Damon Knight and Fox to Adalynne. Katie thought it was the most romantic story she had ever heard but Adalynne tried to convince her it was more of a tragedy than anything else. Katie was so easy to talk to and her story with Fox just flowed from her memories to words as Katie listened intently. It was strange talking so openly about Fox. He had always been such a private part of her life.

Catching Fox

***

When Adalynne walked into her father's hospital room she was overjoyed to see him awake. He was perched up with pillows and sipped on some broth her mother was feeding him. The sight warmed her heart. Her parents had both led such demanding careers, the time they allowed themselves to show affection for one another was scarce. Adalynne could hardly recall moments when they expressed love for each other throughout her childhood. Sometimes she wondered if there was any love left between them after all these years but the affectionate touch her mother bestowed upon his shoulder now, spoke of much love.

"Addie girl, you are looking so much better this morning," her father said. He still did not have the strength back in his voice but the smile upon his face reached his eyes and it lifted the weight from her shoulders.

"Good morning. You look as handsome as ever." Adalynne wrapped her arms around her father's neck, being careful not to hurt him. His shoulders relaxed under her touch and she could tell the smile was still on his face by the warm energy he emitted.

"Your friend Katie is lovely," her mother stated when Adalynne finally let go of her father and seated herself on the chair beside his bed.

"The greatest," Adalynne confirmed. She felt so relieved to see her father looking so well, all the tension from last night seeped from her body.

"Can we have a moment, dear?" her father asked her mother after their conversation had long since died away and they just continued in comfortable silence.

"Sure, I was actually going to find the nurse and ask for another blanket." She forced a smile and gave her husband a quick kiss on the cheek before leaving. Adalynne wondered why her mother seemed uncertain about leaving them to their private conversation. The look in her eye told Adalynne she knew what was to be discussed and did not approve.

He patted the side of his bed for Adalynne to come closer and she complied, settling as gently as she could next to him. "Your mother doesn't necessarily agree with me on what I am about to say to you but she doesn't want to argue because it's not good for my heart. Doctor's orders, you see." He smiled, placing his hand gently against his chest.

"It's actually quite wonderful how she's always biting her tongue despite the fact she's desperate to say something. I'm going to have to start taking advantage of her agreeable state, get her to let me play more golf or perhaps get out of the operas she's always dragging me to. I can't stand that shit. Excuse my language." Adalynne couldn't help but laugh.

"After this little scare I have put a lot of thought into things, especially the fact I know it is not your preference to follow in our footsteps. As much as your mother and I have always wanted it for you, it is not our decision to make. I know that you're miserable. Your friend Katie confirmed it. That girl can talk but I'm sure you already know this. You might not want to tell her your secrets." He winked at her.

Taking her hand in his, he continued talking. "I want you to do what makes you happy, and if that means pulling out of school and teaching music lessons at the place you spent most of your time last year, so be it. I want to see that smile on your face again. I miss when your eyes used to light up when you talked about what was happening in your life. You're not like your mother and I. You never have been. You have always wanted to follow that sweet little heart of yours toward the sound of music. It is one of the things that make you so special. It was foolish of us to try to force anything on you. I want you to embrace what your heart wants, otherwise your life will be full of regrets and we don't have time for that. Life is too short."

"But Mom…" Adalynne began.

"Is a very difficult woman, I know that more than anyone, but she made her choices and now I want you to know that you are free to make your own. You don't owe us anything." He patted her hand reassuringly as her mother walked back in the room with a tight smile on her face. Adalynne could practically feel the tension coming off her mother. "Think about what I said."

"I will." Adalynne kissed him on the head. "We will have plenty of time to talk later about life plans when you come home and I challenge you to a serious game of chess. This time I will beat you because you'll still be recovering. You are weak and I am going to take advantage." Adalynne smiled and her father accepted the challenge happily.

"Even at my weakest you don't stand a chance against this reigning champ." He laughed playfully but ended up sending himself into a coughing fit. Adalynne slid off the bed to give him space and her mother came over with a glass of water.

"You need to rest now." Her mother adjusted his pillows so he could lay back.

"I'm all right," he said softly, looking up at Adalynne reassuringly.

"Excuse me. Am I interrupting?" Adalynne turned to see Matthew standing in the doorway. He looked every bit the gentleman with his pressed shirt and fitted pants.

"Matthew?" Adalynne stood up with a surprised expression on her face. "I wasn't expecting you."

"I wanted to see you before I left." He smiled brilliantly. He looked handsome standing before her with flowers in his hands.

"Mother, Father, this is Matthew Murphy from school," Adalynne introduced quickly when she remembered her manners.

"It's very nice to meet you, Matthew." Adalynne's mother said approvingly.

"These are for you, Mrs. Fairweather." Matthew passed her a beautiful arrangement of flowers displayed in a glass vase. Adalynne's mother showed her appreciation with an honest smile. It was quite a feat because her mother was usually more reserved toward people she didn't know.

"Please call me Adalynne," Her mother offered.

"I see Addie not only got your name but your beauty as well." Adalynne watched Matthew's signature smile spread across his face and just like

134

that, he won over her mother's favor. Her mother was almost giddy as she situated the flowers on the table.

"Yes, our family has passed down the tradition of naming all our firstborn daughters Adalynne." She laughed light heartedly. "Tradition is a funny thing."

"And for you, Mr. Fairweather." Matthew lifted up a box in his hand, pulling the cover off to reveal a bottle of Scotch. "It's for after you recover, of course." Matthew winked at her father. "Father said it was your preference."

"I knew there was something familiar about you; you're Max Murphy's son." Adalynne's father smiled at the connection he made when Matthew smiled to confirm. "Good man, your father. Tell me, are you studying law?"

"Yes, sir," Matthew stated proudly. As Matthew and her father launched into a conversation regarding their field of interest, Adalynne watched her mother's face light up at the prospect of Matthew being in her daughter's life. She could almost see the wheels turning, planning her and Matthew's life together and picturing what her grandchildren would look like.

"Addie?" Matthew's voice reached her through her clouded mind. She had tuned out the conversation taking place in front of her as she thought about what her father had told her, wondering if her mother would actually permit her to follow her own career path. At least one of them was on her side now with her father's change of heart. It was better than none.

"What? Yes? Sorry, late night," Adalynne apologized for her attention wavering.

Matthew smiled knowingly. "I just asked your parents if it would be okay if I took you for a quick lunch before I left. Would you like to join me?" He looked at her expectantly.

"What about Steven? Isn't he waiting for you?"

"He decided to go home with Katie, so I'm all yours if you'll have me." He leaned in and touched her shoulder gently. She couldn't help but appreciate his ability to always be completely at ease and know how to conduct himself around people. Even her normally hard to please parents were completely enamored with him. She had to give him credit. He knew how to win over a room. It was one of the qualities that would make him a great lawyer one day.

"Of course." Adalynne smiled.

"Wonderful, I won't keep her long," Matthew assured her parents.

Adalynne really enjoyed herself in Matthew's company over lunch. He took her to an Italian bistro with a patio overlooking a busy city street. She had heard of the place and always wanted to try it. They sat in the warm midday sun and the conversation flowed seamlessly between them as they asked each other questions to get better acquainted. Matthew genuinely seemed interested about getting to know her and she found herself laughing at the many questions he insisted on asking.

"What is your favorite time of day?" He smiled at her over his iced tea.

"Umm...I would have to say dusk. When

everything gets quiet and the stars come out in the sky. I like to just look up at the stars and think about all the things that are possible." She smiled. "Yours?"

"I was going to say mornings but you have convinced me to change my mind. You have a way of making me see things differently." His gray-blue eyes looked across from her and Adalynne couldn't help the blush that crept into her cheeks. "I think you are the most beautiful girl I have ever seen, Addie."

The waitress came over and Adalynne was grateful for a moment to collect herself. The waitress leaned in toward Matthew and laughed at his charming demeanor when he made a comment about the food. Adalynne wondered if she should feel jealous as the waitress openly flirted with him. Instead she found herself understanding of the behavior because he was handsome and poised. The power he exuded was compelling and not common for someone his age. He had a way of drawing people in Adalynne appreciated. He had so many characteristics telling of the success he would obtain. She could see why her parents were so taken with him. She thought how perfect he seemed, everything a girl would want in a guy but for some reason she could not picture being by his side when he claimed his success.

Matthew reached across the table and placed his hand over hers gently. "What is your favorite type of music?" He raised his eyebrow expectantly.

A smile spread across her lips. "Everything. I love to listen to everything and play everything."

"You play? What instrument?"

"I have tried everything I could get my hands on. Piano, guitar, violin...I love being able to grab any instrument and just play. I challenged myself when I was younger that I would learn to play everything." Adalynne smiled at remembering her parents trying to convince her to settle for a few of her favorite instruments but she was hungry for everything so her parents eventually caved and provided her with instructors who exposed her to what she wanted.

"Have you then? Tried everything?" He mused.

"Not yet." She smiled. "But I hope to."

"I suppose it's hard to do when you are tackling such a demanding career path. We have to make sacrifices." He squeezed her hand gently.

She knew that he didn't understand her passion, the way he dismissed it so easily like it was only a hobby. It reminded her of the way her parents had always viewed her music, nothing more than something to pass the time. When she played she was happy, truly happy, and that was where she wanted to be. She didn't bring up the fact she might be changing her career path after her conversation with her father but she knew that given the chance she would take it. As much as she enjoyed Matthew's company she did not want to confide in him. The first person who came to mind who she wanted to share her exciting news with was Fox, even after what had happened. He was the only person who truly understood her passion. He would be the only one who would truly know how important this was to her, being able to follow her own path.

"Favorite present you ever got?" he asked, pulling her attention back.

"Hmm…" Adalynne thought about everything she had gotten in her lifetime. Her parents were always giving her gifts since she was an only child and their careers were so demanding. They made up for their lack of attendance in her life by buying her things but none of those things stood out in her mind as special. She thought about the necklace Fox had given her, it was her favorite piece of jewelry but there was something else that came to mind, bringing a smile to her face.

It was a summer when they were younger. Fox spent almost every night with her that particular summer, crawling in her window at dusk when the stars became visible in the darkening sky. He was always so impossibly quiet. She never knew he was there until he slipped through the window. Adalynne knew things were bad with his father even though he never talked about it. She never forced the issue but she was glad he came to her when he needed her. He would always crawl into her bed and Adalynne would wrap her arms around him. Sometimes she would sing softly when he was quiet. Others times they talked until they could no longer keep their eyes open. Adalynne didn't want to fall asleep because she always knew that he would be gone when she woke in the morning.

Fox would always complain her feet were cold, saying he was going to stop coming over because of it and they would always end up in giggles. One night when he crawled in next to her he placed something soft in her hand.

"What's this?" she asked excitedly. She flicked on the light. In her hand was a fluffy pair of socks with little bees all over them.

"For your feet." He smiled at her. She touched the dimple on his cheek that she loved so much.

"I love them." She pulled them over her feet. They were the softest socks she ever felt. Pulling them up to her knees, she laid back down, turning off the light. "Better?" She cuddled in close to him and nuzzled into his neck. She felt him tense at her touch but she didn't pull back. She wanted to be as close as she could.

"Perfect," he replied quietly after a moment. And then she let herself fall asleep.

"I can't really think of anything off hand," she lied, unwilling to share the memory she held so close to her heart.

"I will have to change that then." Matthew smiled and she found herself doing the same.

When Matthew dropped her back off at the hospital, he insisted on opening her door for her. She thanked him for the wonderful lunch before he leaned in and kissed her unexpectedly. "Was that okay?" he said breathlessly after pulling back. Adalynne reached up unconsciously and touched her lips.

"Yes, it was nice." Adalynne said softly, looking up at him. It was the truth. His lips were soft and gentle against hers. She had responded to his kiss with the same gentle touch that he applied but it was missing the hunger she felt when her lips touched Fox's last night. The desire to remain connected after they pulled apart was lacking. It was the feeling that overwhelmed her when she was with Fox because of her insatiable hunger for him. Heat flooded her face at the memory of her kiss from the night before and Matthew was elated by the reaction he received from what he believed was his kiss. She smiled at him. Maybe nice was what a kiss was supposed to feel like, gentle and beautiful. Maybe she had it wrong this whole time.

As she watched Matthew drive away her phone rang in her pocket. Pulling it out, she looked at the caller. "Mother? Is everything okay?" Adalynne listened to her mother's frantic words on the other side of the line before she took off running through the doors. She ran past the elevator and the surrounding sounds around her faded away as her senses numbed. She couldn't bring herself to comprehend anything other than forcing herself up the stairs as fast as her legs could move until she pushed through the door on her father's floor. She didn't slow her pace as she rounded the corner and her father's room came into view. Her mother was outside the room and she turned to meet Adalynne. She quickly closed the distance between them. Her mother wrapped her arms around Adalynne's shoulders, squeezing fiercely. "He was doing fine…" her mother sobbed. "Then…" Adalynne tried to support her mother, who leaned into her, tears staining her face as she tried to speak.

Adalynne looked into his room as the doctors and nurses frantically worked to resuscitate him. All the machines monitoring him were all making frenzied beeping noises. She felt disoriented as she watched helplessly as the scene unfolded in front of her eyes. The truth of the severity of the situation played on all of their faces as they shuffled around the bed, hastily working. Adalynne's insides felt like lead as she waited.

Adalynne wasn't sure how much time had passed until finally the door swung open in front of her. She searched the eyes of the doctor and knew before he spoke that her father did not survive. The machines were turned off and only the echo of them lingered in her thoughts. Her mother pushed her in the room after the doctor left; she wasn't sure who was supporting who as they entered the room. Her mother immediately went to her father's bedside. Adalynne stood at the bottom of his bed looking at his still form. He looked like he was sleeping and any moment he would wake up and this nightmare would be over. Her mother placed her hands on his chest and wept as she looked down upon her husband's face. Adalynne's eyes fell to his feet under the blanket. She reached out and touched his toes. She could still feel the heat lingering in his body, making her mind refuse to process the reality of his passing. She watched her mother grieve like she was a stranger in the room. She could not let herself accept the truth in front of her because she knew the pain would be unbearable. Time seemed distorted as she stared at her father lying in the bed. Her mother's cries blended with everything else and washed into the background.

When a nurse walked into the room, hesitantly

calling her mother's attention, panic consumed Adalynne at the realization they were going to take him away.

"Dad?" Adalynne moved quickly to his side across from her mother, who looked up at her with confused, swollen eyes. "Dad! Don't leave me!" Adalynne shook his shoulder. Her vision blurred as tears claimed her, spilling from her eyes. "We need you. You can't leave us." She became more frantic as she took his lifeless hand in hers. He did not respond to her and he never would again. "Please…" Her voice trailed off weakly. She knew he was gone but she didn't want to accept it. "You said you wouldn't leave me as long as I needed you…I still need you."

Her mother's hands tightened on Adalynne's shoulders and pulled her toward her. "Say good bye, honey." Her mother's voice was heavy with sorrow.

Adalynne looked back at her father and then the nurse, who stared at them with a pained expression on her face. Taking a deep breath, Adalynne leaned in and kissed her father's cheek for the last time. "I love you, Daddy."

Chapter Fourteen

When Adalynne's mother pulled into their driveway she could see her aunt's car already there waiting for them. It had been a couple of months since she had seen her aunt but she had no desire to see anyone right now. Her Aunt Shiralee was a younger, friendlier, brunette version of her mother. Adalynne adored her and used to secretly wish she had been her mother when she was young. Aunt Shiralee always made her feel so special when her own mother had little time for her. When she visited Adalynne they would do wonderful things together. In fact, she introduced Adalynne to music when she was only two years old. She would play the piano for her when she visited and Adalynne was instantly in love with it.

Adalynne's mother pulled into the garage and turned off the car. "Come on." She reached over and touched Adalynne's leg and smiled weakly. They were the first words spoken between them since they left the hospital.

"I just need a moment," Adalynne replied,

making no effort to move from her seat.

Her mother looked at her before she replied. "All right, but don't be long," she said before she opened her door and entered the house. Adalynne unclipped her seatbelt and opened her door. She needed to be away; she couldn't bear going into the house and facing anyone right now. She walked toward the exterior door in the garage and opened it, walking outside into the late afternoon air. She walked away from the house slowly at first. Her feet seemed to walk on their own accord until she realized where she was heading. She quickened her pace and ran through the trees, not stopping until the view of the camp came before her.

She unclipped the lock and pushed open the door they had fastened out of plywood, pushing it closed behind her. She looked around the small interior. It had been awhile since she had stepped foot in this place. She and Fox used to spend hours in this place, but now it seemed like a different life. She rubbed her hand along the wall where she had painted a mural of a fox and a bee in the forest. She remembered when she had painted it.

"Stop staring at me. You're making me nervous," Adalynne ordered playfully. "I want this to be perfect."

"It's already perfect," Fox said as he leaned back against the wall watching her put the finishing touches on the mural. "This is now officially my favorite place in the whole world." He said, smiling.

"How do you know that? You haven't been

anywhere else in the world," Adalynne said just for the sake of being argumentative.

"I know because it's where you are." His eyes lit up with his words, making Adalynne blush.

"Fine. Okay then. But only because I'm stupid enough to believe you." Adalynne turned back to her painting and she heard Fox retrieve his guitar. He began strumming a tune, before long he was singing along with his music.

"Bee is painting a mural on the wall...she doesn't like to be watched at all...but I can't take my eyes off of her especially when I can see her pink lacy panties..." he sang playfully.

"Hey!" Adalynne reached back behind her. Sure enough, her underwear was sticking up past her pants. She pulled her shirt down quickly.

"I wonder if she has a matching bra...'cause I like what I saw..." Fox sang with a mischievous look in his eye.

"You wish you could find out," Adalynne teased. Fox dropped his guitar and reached out to tickle Adalynne. He was always merciless in his tickling attacks, causing Adalynne to scream out as she laughed. "I'm...trying...to finish..." She tried to say between her laughing. He leaned in close to her face so his cheek touched hers as she struggled against him. She could hear him take a deep breath. "Did you just smell me?"

"Yes, when is the last time you took a bath?" he teased. "You stink."

"Stop...you love how I smell." He looked into her eyes and Adalynne became lost in them. He got up suddenly, stepping away from her. "I gotta go.

146

I'll see you tomorrow."

"Sure," she said, disappointed. She always hated it when he left her like that. She was left wondering what she did to make him want to leave. "I'm gonna stay and finish this," she called after him but he had already slipped out the door.

***

Adalynne leaned against the wall and slid down to a seated position and let the tears of grief overcome her as the realization she would never see her father again assaulted her. She let herself cry as the day grew old and the light faded into darkness around her. She was surrounded by stillness, the soothing quiet of the evening settled upon the land, and she wanted to fade away with the day.

She didn't bring her phone or anything with her when she left her mother's car. She had no way to know how much time had passed. Adalynne couldn't bring herself to stand, she wasn't ready to go home and face her family. Even when she was completely surrounded by the darkness of night, she refused to move.

Adalynne closed her eyes tightly when she heard her name called. Fox was looking for her. It felt almost like a dream. It was so long ago that he had come to see her at their camp, Adalynne thought she was imagining it. It wasn't until the door swung open and his tall form entered she knew that he was really with her. "Bee, there you are," Fox said, relieved. He leaned down next to her in the darkness. His hand barely brushed her knee. The concern in his voice made the tears well in her eyes again.

"How did you know I was here?" Her words felt strange in her mouth as she spoke.

"When I heard about your father, I tried to call your cell. Your mother answered and was upset you left without telling anyone where you were going. She's worried about you." Fox sat down next to her and leaned against the wall beside her.

"I wasn't there...when it happened. I had left for a lunch date. How pathetic is that? I wasn't with my father when he died because I was on a stupid date." Adalynne wiped her eyes. "What is wrong with me? I am a horrible daughter. He deserved better than that."

"Your father knew you loved him, Bee. Don't ever doubt that. Grief does horrible things to people." Fox spoke from experience. He had dealt with the loss of his mother at a young age and she knew it had taken a toll on him.

"Does it ever stop hurting?" Adalynne asked, turning toward him to look at the outline of his dark figure beside her. The only light was the dim moonlight and it did little to penetrate the darkness that swallowed the inside of the camp.

"No...but I promise you it will get easier." Fox stood up and rummaged around. It was too dark for Adalynne to know what he was doing.

"You still have my cell phone number?" Her voice was shaky. His words finally registered about trying to call her.

"Of course." He lit a match, shedding light in the darkness. She watched the light dance off the contours of his face. He was so handsome it was almost painful to watch him. He lit a candle sitting on the floor...it was gingerbread scented. Adalynne remembered bringing it to the camp because she knew how much he loved gingerbread. It seemed like so long ago now but as the smell enveloped the small space it was soothing, and she couldn't help but relax her tense shoulders.

Fox sat down facing her but didn't say a word. She watched him sitting as still as she was, staring back at her. His features were shadowed in darkness as the candlelight danced along his back. Everything about him drew her in, the way he moved his tall muscular body, the way his high cheekbones and masculine jaw gave the perfect canvas for his handsome features and endless green eyes. The way he smelled, the way he smiled. She loved everything about him except the fact he didn't love her. She couldn't help but think how cruel fate was, her father was taken away from her and Fox didn't want her...she wasn't allowed to have the two men she loved most in the entire world.

"I wish you could have known my father. He was a great man." She couldn't manage much more than a whisper with her unsteady voice. For a moment it looked as if he wanted to say something but he remained quiet. Fox got up, opened a box, and grabbed a sleeping bag from inside, laying it out on the ground, and retrieved a folded blanket, spreading that out as well.

"Come here." He reached his hand out for Adalynne but when she didn't move, he leaned down and scooped her up effortlessly, pressing her against his chest. The feel of being held against his body was the most comforting feeling she had ever felt. His heat was wrapped around her; she wanted to stay like that forever because she felt protected. It was like she finally released the breath she was holding since the news of her father shocked her. She ran her hands up his chest and wrapped her arms around his neck as he sat down on the blankets.

"Tell me what I can do," Fox whispered in her ear. Her body heated with his lips so close. Being so close to him made her forget the pain that made it hard for her to breathe. She wanted to hold on to the contentment of being in Fox's arms and forget about what awaited her.

Adalynne leaned up, placing her hands on either side of his face. She could feel him hold his breath in anticipation of what she was doing. Adalynne leaned close to his lips. She closed her eyes, breathing in his addictive scent fueling the fire erupting inside of her. Leaning in to his neck, she grazed her lips along his skin. She could feel him tremble beneath her touch.

"Give me tonight," she whispered in his ear as she pressed her body into his. She could feel his grip tighten on her shirt with her words and his body tensed under hers. "I don't want to think. I'm tired of thinking."

"I can't say no," he breathed painfully.

"Good." Adalynne smiled as she brought her lips to his. His response was gentle at first as she encouraged him, holding back for a reason Adalynne didn't let herself think about. She wanted to be lost in him and every touch and caress he gave her halted her thoughts and roused her body. She refused to let any words pass her lips in fear that he would leave her if she expressed her love for him, like he had done so many times before. Adalynne just let her body speak for her as she ran her fingers through his wavy hair. He smelled tantalizing. She kissed his neck as she felt the goose bumps rise on his skin under her lips. Adalynne pulled off his shirt, exposing his hard flesh that enticed her fingers. She felt every line of his muscles that etched his skin. Fox was her favorite place to be, wrapped in his strong arms and teased by his soft lips.

Adalynne could feel his hunger growing for her as he moved with her in a beautiful rhythm as they explored each other's bodies. Adalynne leaned back and pulled her shirt off as his hands slid up her back to unclasp her bra. She had played this moment through her mind so many times as she desired to be with him but none of her imaginings came close to the intensity of this moment as they devoured each other with their ravenous hands. Adalynne kissed a moan that escaped his lips as she pressed her naked flesh against his.

Fox positioned Adalynne on the blankets and leaned over her. He looked down at her exposed curves as the candlelight illuminated her body for him to see. Adalynne reached down and unbuttoned her pants and he aided her in sliding them down the length of her legs before discarding them on the floor. He was on his knees, looking down at her naked body.

"You are so beautiful, Bee," he whispered before leaning down to claim her mouth. Adalynne unbuckled his belt. His hand firmly clamped around hers. "Are you sure?" he whispered hesitantly. Adalynne nodded in response. "Bee?" He urged, looking into her eyes. "I don't want you to regret this."

"I never would," she whispered back breathlessly. With her words of reassurance, Fox shed his pants and leaned down against her body. Adalynne couldn't help the moan of pleasure that escaped her lips at the feel of his strong naked body against hers.

"That was the most beautiful sound I ever heard," he said against her neck. His mouth explored her, trailing kisses over her entire body. Her breasts became heavy with desire, and her hips moved to the rhythm of their song as he teased and drew her pleasures from deep within. He treated her body like a treasure and soon she was swimming in a sea of pleasure.

Adalynne gasped as he slid inside her but the tension soon melted away with his gentle touch, leaving her awash with overwhelming bliss at the beauty of what she was sharing with Fox. Fox allowed her to escape the torment that was tearing her soul and gave her a light within the darkness.

Adalynne let herself fall asleep in Fox's arms, spent from the intense emotions of the day. Though it did not take long to turn into a restless sleep, she found herself wrestling with painful thoughts that insisted on pulling at her consciousness. They tried to lure her awake to face the demons awaiting her.

When she stirred, Fox would tighten his hold on her, wrapping his arms around her to make her feel safe. She wasn't ready to face the world, she wanted to stay here forever and sleep with the rhythm of Fox's heart beating against hers.

When the first light of morning crawled across the floor, Adalynne opened her eyes. Fox was asleep beside her, his arm around her waist as his breathing caused his chest to rise and fall, slow and steady. His thick dark lashes fanned out over his tanned cheeks. She wanted to kiss his full soft lips to say goodbye but she didn't want to risk waking him. Thoughts of the beautiful night lingered in her mind, allowing a smile to cross her lips but she knew what they shared would not change anything.

She would always be in love with Fox. She had been in one way or another for her entire life since he wandered into her backyard that fateful day. Her need for him was sewn into her very being and she could never escape it, just like she could not escape the fact that her father was now gone. A tear slipped down her cheek and Adalynne quickly wiped it away. She wished she could hide out in their camp forever and never have to face the truth that waited for her in the real world.

Adalynne knew it was unhealthy for her to devote her life to someone who did not share her feelings. She knew in her heart she needed to distance herself from Fox and move on with her life. She couldn't keep throwing herself into his arms only to be turned away time after time. A heart was only so strong and right now hers was far from the best. It felt torn and bloodied, struggling to

Aimee McNeil

continue beating when she felt so much loss.

She hoped in time the pain of losing both the important men in her life would fade to the point where she could carry it without feeling like it would break her. She remembered what her father had said the last time she was with him—life was short and she needed to start living hers.

Adalynne would always hold the memory of last night close, it was beautiful and perfect and it would always be in her heart, just like every memory of Fox. It was a moment of pure escape she needed to survive the very devastating day. She was so grateful he was there to help her through it.

Adalynne picked up the notepad and pen that sat upon the small table in the corner. Scribbling quietly on the paper, she placed it on the floor next to Fox's sleeping form.

I will never forget.
Goodbye, Fox.

She knew he would know what it meant. Although she left the camp with sadness in her heart, it was without regret. She was walking back into her life to deal with the loss of her father. There was only so much pain she could handle and now the thought of being close to Fox and never being able to have him was worse than staying away from him. Her decision was made.

This was the beginning of a new chapter in her life. She needed to accept the fact that she would no longer be able to throw herself into the arms of her father, for him to kiss her upon the head and tell her

154

that everything would be all right.

She also needed to accept the fact that Fox was not hers to love and she had to let him go to live the life he was meant to, a life without her. Adalynne would wade through the pain of loss and find herself on the other side, no matter how long it took.

Chapter Fifteen

Adalynne walked quietly into her house so as not to alert her aunt or her mother of her return. She climbed into her bed and fell to sleep as soon as her head met the pillow. Her body was exhausted and Adalynne felt like she would never be able to quench it even if she spent the remainder of her life in bed. The sensation weighed every part of her body down. Even the world around her seemed darker and colder despite the heat the rising sun promised. She was consumed with sorrow. Her moment of escape last night was over and the real world closed in around her as dark as night.

Adalynne was not sure how long she slept, but when she awoke to stirring in the house, she saw something on her pillow. She wrapped her hand around the envelope Fox had tried to give her the other night, with the money he wanted to return to her. She ran her finger over Fox's handwriting.

Goodbye Bee.

Tears started anew. She sat up and looked toward her window. It was closed tight and no sign of Fox. Adalynne lay back down and pulled the covers over her head and sank back into a restless sleep once the tears stopped flowing and she had nothing left.

She awoke when her bedroom door opened and someone sat on the edge of her bed, shifting her mattress. She knew it was her mother but she didn't acknowledge her entry. Her mother lay her hand gently on Adalynne's back for a moment before getting up to leave and closing the door behind her. Adalynne drifted in and out of consciousness, unaware of the passage of time before her door opened again and her mother once again came to her side.

"Adalynne?" Adalynne lowered the blankets but did not turn toward her mother. "We were so worried when you took off. The only reason we got any sleep last night was because your friend Damon sent me a message telling me you were fine and would be home soon." Adalynne did not respond to her mother. "He's a nice boy," her mother said in a tight voice.

"Don't worry, Mother, it was over before it started," she said without pleasantries. She could feel her mother's relief without even turning to see her face. Her mother was so predictable. Adalynne knew when she mentioned Fox had called her she was trying to see how he would interfere with her plans for Adalynne and Matthew. Adalynne had never felt like her mother truly wanted what was best for her. It was more like what was best for the family and more specifically her image.

157

"Come down soon and eat," her mother said before she left the room. When her mother closed the door, Adalynne slid from her bed and locked her bedroom door. She didn't want to do anything but be left alone and stay in bed. A few times through the day there were knocks at the door that pulled her from sleep but eventually they stopped and she drifted away again. Not even sure when she was awake or asleep anymore, reality blurred.

"Abbie girl?" It was Carmen's voice outside her door. "You need to eat, sweetheart." Adalynne wasn't sure how long Carmen stayed at the door but eventually, like her mother, the footsteps retreated when her efforts proved futile. Her body felt tired and her muscles rigid. She felt like she was slowly disappearing into the gray fog settling around her.

"Katie keeps calling. You should really let her know how you're doing," her mother's voice carried through the door.

Soon darkness and quiet enveloped her as night fell over the house. The persistent knocks at her door ceased and she was left to her own misery of restless sleep in the still of the late hours. She knew she couldn't hide in her bed forever but the thought of getting up and facing what awaited her seemed too hard to bear. The next morning made its appearance before she was ready for it and the knocking started again.

"Addie? It's Katie. I'm worried about you. Open up...I'm not going anywhere until you open this door." Katie knocked again. "Addie? Fine, I can wait as long as I need to," Katie said defiantly after many unsuccessful attempts to get Adalynne to open the door. She slid down the door and seated herself out in the hall before she started belting out every song she could think of.

When Adalynne could bear it no longer, she slid out of bed and unlocked the door. Katie immediately stopped singing when she heard the lock give. The door opened and Adalynne crawled back in bed. Katie didn't say anything as she walked into the room. She climbed in bed next to Adalynne, wrapping her arms tightly around her.

"You're supposed to be at school," Adalynne said flatly with her face in her pillow.

"It will be waiting for me when I get back but right now I'm needed elsewhere and that's right here in bed with my un-showered best friend who I love very much." Katie smiled warmly. Adalynne couldn't bring herself to smile in return. Her face felt too tight.

"I hope you don't mind but I ordered some of Carmen's yummy food to be sent up because I'm starving. Your mom called me first thing this morning so I drove straight here without eating anything. That's how much I love you."

"I love you too."

"I'm not going to pretend I even know what you're going through but I will promise I'll be here for as long as you need me." Katie tucked Adalynne's hair behind her ear as she lay beside her.

"But school?" Adalynne whispered.

"Don't even think about it."

Adalynne grabbed Katie's hand and held it close. She was glad Katie was here. She didn't realize how much she needed her until now. They stayed in bed until Carmen walked in with a tray of all Adalynne's favorite treats. "Addie girl." Her face was filled with concern when she looked at Adalynne's exhausted form in bed curled up beside Katie.

The smell of all the delicious things that Carmen made reminded Adalynne that her body required food to survive. She knew she couldn't hide out forever. She wouldn't let her father down. She was going to find a way to be happy again.

Katie spent the next couple of days with Adalynne as she adjusted to resuming normal daily activities. Adalynne showed Katie family photos to shed light on the type of man her father was. It was painful and comforting at the same time. Things seemed so much more bearable with Katie by her side for support. There were even a few times that Adalynne forgot to be sad. Katie even insisted on doing Adalynne's makeup to cheer her up, claiming that pampering always made her feel better.

"Seriously, Katie?" Adalynne questioned her friend's cosmetic abilities. "I look like I'm ready to do some pole dancing, with sparkly tassels hanging off my nipples."

"Okay, I guess it is a bit much," Katie confessed before they broke into a fit of laughter. "But you would make a lot of money as a stripper, that's for sure." Adalynne ended up painting Katie's face up as well before they headed down to meet her mother for supper. The look on her mother's face was priceless when the girls walked into the kitchen.

Adalynne's mother, who rarely showed emotion

under normal circumstances, seemed to be faring very well, diving back into her work instead of dealing with her loss. She knew it was only a matter of time before reality caught up with her mother and she hoped that she would be stronger then to help her through it. Even though Adalynne was not as close to her mother as she would have liked, Adalynne did love her.

She didn't know how she would ever repay Katie for the light that she gave her during those first few days. Katie was everything she needed, a shoulder to cry on, a friend to laugh with and confide in. Katie listened as she spoke of her father, even when all she did was cry. She also told her about what happened with Fox and the decision to move on and see if she could find a way to get her heart to love another in time.

"If you think that it's the best decision, then I won't say otherwise." Adalynne could tell Katie wanted to say more on the subject but Adalynne was grateful she left it alone. She needed to believe it was the best thing right now because it seemed the safest course of action to avoid any more pain to her already fragile heart.

The morning of the funeral was a step of regression for Adalynne as she prepared to face the world with the loss of her father. Until now she was able to avoid everyone. She was sheltered and safe to deal with things on her own terms. Adalynne hadn't even checked her phone for the last few days. It was nice to deal with her pain in private but now she had to face everyone. She knew she wouldn't be able to hold herself together long with all the familiar faces that would be there to share their condolences.

When they were dressed for the funeral, she and Katie made their way downstairs to see the commotion made by the caterers preparing for the gathering after the service. Everyone who wished to do so was invited to come back to the house afterwards. Flowers were being carried in the front door and everyone who laid eyes on Adalynne gave her a tight smile which she could barely return.

The house looked beautiful, as if it were to be presented on the cover of a home magazine. It did not match the sullen gray of her mood, making everything feel strange and unreal. She still felt so disconnected with the world.

***

Adalynne looked at the rectangular hole in the ground which would be the final resting place of her father. The service had been difficult and draining. She stood in the cemetery feeling exhausted, a feeling fast becoming her new normal. Her father's casket was carried and placed over the opening with much care. Many solemn faces surrounded the grave in their funereal best to honor her father. Many of them were familiar to her. Her father had many associates she had come to know over the years and others she recognized from the photographs in her father's office. She found it hard to distinguish between who she actually knew and who she merely recognized from the pictures.

The words spoken of her father's life

accomplishments and his character hung heavy in the air; she missed him dreadfully. The sound of sniffles and soft whispers surrounded Adalynne as she closed her eyes to embrace a gentle breeze. She took a deep collective breath to relax her tight chest.

Katie touched her shoulder and Adalynne opened her eyes to see her mother had stepped forward to place her flower upon his casket. Adalynne stepped forward and leaned down, placing her hand on the smooth wood before she gently laid her flower upon the other. "You will always be in my heart, Daddy."

Stepping back, she watched them lower her father into the ground. Adalynne stood frozen in place as everyone around her gave their sympathies before leaving, until the only people left were his closest loved ones. Katie hooked her arm through Adalynne's, giving her not only emotional support but physical as well. Adalynne's mother turned to her, continuously dabbing her red eyes with a tissue as to not disturb her makeup. Adalynne had no energy to consider her appearance for her tears could not be controlled. "We should head back to the house. I don't want to keep our guests waiting," she said, touching Adalynne's shoulder. Adalynne looked at her mother—even though she remained composed she could not hide the pain in her eyes. Her mother still looked so poised and graceful amid her grief, while Adalynne felt like she was falling apart. Adalynne merely nodded in response. Taking one last look at her father's grave, she followed her mother to the waiting car.

Adalynne's attention was drawn to a figure standing off in the distance. She knew who it was the moment her gaze beheld him. The sight of him took her breath away. Fox made no attempt to approach her. When he noticed her attention, he gave a quick nod. She had never seen him in a suit before and she had to prevent herself from running to him. It would be so easy to lose herself in his strong embrace, to seek the comfort only he could give. She realized how difficult it was going to be to stop needing him. Katie's eyes looked up at her with concern when she noticed who Adalynne was watching.

"How are you holding up, dear?" Adalynne turned to see Carmen standing beside her. Carmen looked lovely in a black wrap dress and blazer that looked very slimming on her round figure. Adalynne smiled when she looked into Carmen's warm brown eyes; it felt heavy and foreign on her face. She knew it did not convince Carmen, who could see through the façade. She wondered if it would ever feel right to smile again. Adalynne was glad Carmen was with her today. She had grown so close to their family after working for them for over twenty years. She was always the constant in Adalynne's life and she felt more like family than her blood relatives. She needed her close.

"Not good," Adalynne replied honestly. There was no point lying to Carmen, she always knew the truth without Adalynne even having to put it into words.

"I know, dear, and unfortunately it will take some time. Eventually it will hurt less, I promise. We will all miss him dearly. He was one of the greatest men I knew." Carmen looked over at Fox and then reached down and took Adalynne's hand in hers. "Remember when I told you how rare true love is." Adalynne nodded at Carmen's question. It was the conversation that they never did finish the morning before her father's death. "Well..." Carmen continued. "I saw it in your eyes when you looked at that young man." Carmen tilted her head toward Fox. "You were so young at the time and it was the most beautiful thing I have ever seen, Adalynne. I watched it flourish in you over the years. It radiated from you in everything you did. Then I saw it again when he looked back at you. That boy is more in love with you than any boy has ever loved a girl, I can be sure."

Adalynne wrapped her arms around Carmen's shoulders. "I wish it was true, Carmen, but things are not always what they seem," Adalynne whispered softly before turning to get into the car.

"No, they're not," Carmen said with a soft knowing smile. "In time." Carmen patted Adalynne's hand. "Some things just need time."

"Are you coming back to the house?" Adalynne asked Carmen hopefully.

Carmen looked over quickly at Adalynne's mother, a reflex that she could not break. She tried to be discreet about the action but was unsuccessful. She almost looked guilty when she looked back at Adalynne. "No, dear. The day has taken its toll on this old body. I'll see you tomorrow, bright and early." She gave Adalynne's hand a final squeeze of affection before she left. If Adalynne was of usual mind she would have confronted her mother about why Carmen did not feel welcome coming back to

165

the house as a guest, she had more of a right than any of the others to be there. Her mother always frowned upon the relationship that Adalynne had with Carmen, but over the years turned a blind eye because it made her absence easier. In public she never allowed Carmen to be viewed as anything other than the housekeeper that she was, but to Adalynne she was much more than that. She was family.

When they arrived at the house there were so many faces she had not even noticed at the service. The house was full when they arrived, guests mingled throughout the main floor. The decorators had prepared the house beautifully. It reminded Adalynne more of a wedding reception with the exception of the somber mood.

"Adalynne." Molly walked toward her with a warm smile. Adalynne had not seen Molly in months. They had conversed through email on a regular basis since they graduated high school and it was nice to see her familiar face. "I know everyone has probably asked you this a million times, but how are you?"

"I will be okay, just not yet. Molly, this is Katie." Both of their faces lit up at the familiar names. Adalynne had told them about each other and now they finally had a face to go with the names.

"Brooke is here too. I think she was hanging out at the dessert table." Molly looked around for her but could not see her through the sea of people floating through the rooms. When Adalynne looked up she could see all the faces waiting to speak with her and she was overwhelmed.

"Save me," Adalynne whispered. Her friends immediately came to her aid, shuffling her toward the kitchen past the crowds trying to gain Adalynne's attention.

"Geesh. They're like sharks. It's not hard to tell that most of them are lawyers." Molly sighed as they walked into the kitchen. Luckily with the exception of the caterers, the kitchen was free of people.

"I have some news that might cheer you up." Adalynne looked up at Molly's bright face and knew she had some juicy gossip. "Are you familiar with the band Outcome?" Adalynne and Katie both looked at each other. "What? You already know it's Damon Knight? How amazing is that? Who would have thought?"

Brooke walked into the kitchen catching the end of the reaction from Molly's news. "Oh, the Damon thing? I wanted to be there when Molly told you." Brooke sighed before wrapping her arms around Adalynne.

"She already knew anyway," Molly pouted.

Once the introductions were done for Brooke and Katie, Brooke filled them in on her latest career path idea. Since they had graduated high school over a year ago, Brooke had changed her mind more times than Adalynne could count. To date, she still had not committed to anything but it was still nice to see the excitement she exuded over the latest possibilities. The girls hid out as long as they could before Adalynne's mother tracked her down to make her rounds to see the guests. The small reunion of her friends had significantly improved her mood and Adalynne was able to face her duty.

Brooke's excitement about her new career endeavor reminded Adalynne about the conversation her father had with her. She was going to do what made her happy. Unlike the indecisive Brooke, Adalynne already knew what it was she wanted to do. She would follow her dream of music. She was going to start living her life the way she wanted. With that thought in mind, she could feel the dark cloud give just a little. She had hope.

Adalynne was surprised to see Matthew among the guests. He sought her out through the crowd when he noticed her walk in from the kitchen. "Adalynne, how are you?" His hair was tamed from its usual carefree style, giving him the appearance of the professional he would soon be. He was handsome and drew eyes from all over the room. "I've been looking for you but no one seemed to know where you were."

"I'm not feeling particularly social today," Adalynne apologized. "I didn't know you were here or I would have found you. We were hiding in the kitchen."

"That's definitely understandable. I came with my parents. I was worried about you. You haven't been returning any of my calls. I needed to see you." Adalynne appreciated his concern but she was in no place to entertain him at this point in her life. She couldn't give him what he wanted. She couldn't be in a relationship right now.

"Matthew, I can't do this right now." Adalynne indicated between them. "I need—"

"Don't say anything. I told you before I would wait for you. I understand you need time after what happened." He tipped her chin up to meet his eyes. "As long as it takes. Besides, my parents got a look at you and I don't think they'll let me do otherwise. They are quite taken with you." Matthew smiled.

"I know the feeling. I think my mother is already planning our wedding." As soon as the words escaped her lips, Adalynne regretted it. His eyes lit up with expectation. "Matthew, I don't want you to wait for me. I can't ask you to put your life on hold for me, especially when I have no idea when I will be ready for a relationship."

"Don't worry about that. You do what you need to do." He smiled. Wrapping his arm around her shoulder he gave her a comforting squeeze.

Chapter Sixteen

Over the next few months Adalynne made major changes in her life, much to the dismay of her mother. She knew she needed to take control of her future. Her fragile heart needed to find a source of strength after her fall to the painful dark of loss. She set out to follow a path leading to happiness and hers lay in the instruments her hands yearned to play. The day after her father's funeral she sat in front of her piano and let her music find her. The last conversation she had with her father was never far from her thoughts. Following through with her mother's plan to pursue a career in law was no longer an option. She was standing her ground and breaking the Fairweather tradition of rearing a new lawyer every new generation. Her dreams could not correlate to a future in books and working within the lines.

Adalynne wanted to color outside the lines, play music that had never been written. She wanted to feel free to be the person that was hiding within her, waiting to stretch her arms and let the world know who she was. She was Adalynne Fairweather and she would carve her own path in a world both giving and harsh. She didn't know where she would end up, just that she would follow her heart on the way. That was enough for her.

When Adalynne withdrew from the school her mother had insisted she attend since she was a little girl, it caused a rift between them. Her father's death affected them in different ways. While Adalynne was inspired to not let her life slip away from her, her mother focused on maintaining their old life. She resisted all change. Adalynne had become a wild card that no longer fit into her perfect plan. They had never been so distant.

Adalynne found herself back at Elizabeth's music school the first opportunity she had. When she walked through the door she was awash with the feeling of coming home. She missed the old decrepit building desperately and the wonderful souls within.

Adalynne felt bad for losing touch with Elizabeth the last few months. Their relationship grew strong over the year she helped Elizabeth establish the school in the community after that fateful day she stumbled upon it when looking for Fox. She spent every day at Elizabeth's side, building it from the ground up as they tried to establish themselves in a community that did not welcome them with open arms. It took time and persistence but eventually the local businesses found value in their efforts and gave their support. A local music store donated second hand instruments, starting their collection that began to accumulate over the course of the year.

The amount of children who came to their door grew and soon the two of them could not handle it all themselves. Luckily there were others who shared their passion and a few retired music teachers who knew Elizabeth offered to help out. Other musicians soon began using their amenities to teach lessons. Part of their earnings helped offset the cost of the free lessons they provided to the children who could not afford it otherwise. The whole operation was a growing success and Adalynne was so proud of what Elizabeth had accomplished.

When Elizabeth threw her arms around Adalynne when she walked back in the door, it brought tears to her eyes. She had missed her music family. They were the ones that shared her passion.

With Elizabeth's connections in the music industry, Adalynne was able to swing a late enrollment in a renowned school of arts in town to study music. All of the time Adalynne had devoted the year working with Elizabeth's beautiful dream to teach music lessons and to organize programs for children who could not afford the luxury inspired her. She knew she wanted to have the capacity to bring music into people's lives.

It wasn't long before Adalynne began her search for an apartment closer to town. The animosity between her mother and her made it impossible to remain at home. Her mother's wrath was a powerful thing and it suffocated Adalynne. Despite the fact that her mother disagreed with her career choice, she also gave her a hard time in regards to Matthew.

At first Matthew had given her the space he said he would, but slowly his calls became more frequent, until she began avoiding them all together. Her mother quickly picked up on the fact that Adalynne was pushing him away. The guilt of knowing he was waiting for her became too much. She knew what it felt like to wait for someone to return your affection and Matthew deserved better. She wasn't in a position emotionally to start a relationship but Matthew wasn't an easy man to deter.

Molly had come with Adalynne when she finalized the lease for her new apartment. When the landlord handed Adalynne the keys, she took Molly up to take a look at her new place. She swung the door open and flicked on the light. "What do you think?" Adalynne waited expectantly for Molly's answer.

"Wow! I love it." Molly spun in a circle in the large loft.

"It definitely has potential." Adalynne took in everything around her. The decision to rent the space was hastier than she would have liked but she felt good about it. She looked at the interior that was now hers. It looked so large without furniture. She loved its rustic charm. The glazed cabinets gave them a worn and loved appearance and the exposed brick walls added to its unique character.

"I guess you need to buy some furniture now." Molly gestured to the vast empty space. Her voice echoed through the room.

"Yeah, I guess so."

It wasn't long until Adalynne became settled in her new life. Her new studies came easily to her and she found herself excelling through her classes, which only supported the fact she made the right decision. She began to find her smile again without forcing it for the benefit of those around her. Her schedule also allowed her to resume her work with Elizabeth, who was delighted when Adalynne requested to step into her old role.

The school was slowly taking shape and becoming a very welcome addition to the community. When Adalynne arrived there was a new wooden sign out front with Music House carved beautifully into its surface, musical notes bordering the letters. It replaced the old makeshift sign Elizabeth had temporarily put up outside. There were a few new minor adjustments to the interior, making the space more conducive to their needs. A few more rooms were set up for lessons, fully utilizing the entire building. Adalynne was impressed how things were coming along so wonderfully.

When Adalynne walked into the building she could hear the music coming from behind many of the closed doors stretching down the hallway. The occasional squeaks and complaints of pained instruments brought a smile to her face.

The mural Adalynne had painted in the entrance still covered the walls, bringing vibrancy to the space. She still remembered the hours she put into it trying to make the entrance inspirational to the people who walked through the doors. A small stage still existed from when the building had been used as an elementary school, and was put to full use. Elizabeth used it for concerts and for the children to play for each other. Adalynne remembered organizing the concerts last year and all the people who had shown up to see the children's progress. It was such a rewarding experience to see everyone enjoying the hard work taking place within these walls.

"The sign looks great!" Adalynne complimented.

Elizabeth looked up from her stack of papers with a vibrant smile. Her eclectic style and her wayward hair tied in a knot on the top of her head embodied creativity, and were among her many endearing traits that Adalynne adored. "I wasn't expecting you 'til later. Are you all settled in your new place?" Elizabeth grabbed hold of her and pulled her into a tight hug.

"I got tired of unpacking. I needed a break." Adalynne sat down next to the mess of papers surrounding Elizabeth. When she was unpacking she came across the envelope that Fox had left on her pillow. She knew the moment she picked it up where it belonged. "I have something for you." Adalynne placed the envelope on the desk in front of Elizabeth. "I know you're in need of a new piano."

Elizabeth opened the envelope and gasped. "Addie, I can't take that from you."

"Yes, you can. I need this money to go somewhere it will make a difference. It's important to me, Elizabeth. *Please*," Adalynne pleaded. "We both know how important it is to have a proper piano here." She indicated the walls around them and smiled when she knew she won the argument.

Elizabeth looked into Adalynne's eyes and her

features softened. "How will I ever repay you for everything you have done for me and this place?" Elizabeth shook her head. "You are the reason I have made it this far. You have more heart than anyone I know, Adalynne." Elizabeth smiled brightly, crinkling the skin around her eyes.

"Don't give me that much credit," Adalynne said. "You brought this place to life."

Between her work with Elizabeth and her studies, Adalynne found her days filled. She hadn't seen Katie as much as she would have liked because of school and Katie's new relationship with Steven. Katie had given her so much of her time when her father died that she was trying to allow her to catch up on the other parts of her life. They spoke frequently on the phone and Adalynne loved to hear what Katie was up to.

Katie was always quick to fill her in on all the drama she was missing and the fact that Matthew always showered Katie with questions and sulked because Adalynne refused to return his calls. True to her word, Katie never brought up Fox even though Adalynne knew she wanted to. Thankfully, Adalynne's busy schedule allowed little time for her to dwell on the matter.

Late at night was a different story, when her mind refused to slip away into a restful sleep. Thoughts of Fox filled her mind. It had been months since that night she had given herself to him. The days grew colder as winter settled in but the clarity of the memory refused to fade. She could still remember his smell as if he were still with her, her skin remembered his body pressed against hers. The feel of his strong body still lingered upon her fingers as she remembered exploring his flesh. She wondered how she would ever escape the torment her heart inflicted upon her.

***

"I finally finished my apartment. It now officially looks like someone lives here." Adalynne told Katie when her number lit up her screen. "You would be so proud of me." Adalynne paused her playlist on the computer so Katie couldn't hear the music in the background. A list of all of Outcome's songs filled her screen. She couldn't resist teasing herself by listening to Fox's music.

"That's wonderful news. How about you let me in and show me around?" Katie practically screamed with excitement.

"What? You're here?"

"Let us in! It's cold out here," Katie complained in the phone.

"Us?" Adalynne said as she buzzed them in the front door.

"Don't be mad," Katie blurted into the phone before hanging up.

A moment later, Katie walked in her apartment door, followed by Matthew. "I wanted to surprise you and he insisted on coming." Katie smiled awkwardly, in hopes that she would be forgiven.

"Hey, Matthew." Adalynne smiled over Katie's shoulder as she hugged her friend. "Come on in." She was actually glad that Matthew had come. She didn't realize she missed him until she laid eyes on

177

him. The possibility of a relationship didn't seem so far from her thoughts anymore now that life had calmed down. She wrapped her arms around Matthew in a warm embrace.

He immediately returned the gesture and pulled her close. "I missed you," he whispered, leaning in close to her ear. The way he looked down at her, his infectious smile brightening his handsome features, she couldn't help but think that maybe there was still a chance for them.

She spent the day with Katie and Matthew and it was a nice reprieve from her usual activities. Katie even insisted Adalynne take them to Elizabeth's music school because she was always talking about it. Adalynne proudly toured them through the facility and introduced them to Elizabeth. Katie loved the school and was instantly impressed with Adalynne's involvement.

During their visit, Elizabeth insisted Adalynne break in the new piano that had arrived that morning. Katie encouraged it because she had never heard Adalynne play before. She played some classic tunes she knew Katie would love. It wasn't long before Katie was singing along to the music, drawing the children to the excitement. Katie's energetic personality was a perfect fit with the children and she encouraged them all to dance along. Everyone was having a great time except Matthew, who stood off to the side, looking slightly bored. He kept his attention on his phone. Adalynne knew he was not musically inclined but was discouraged to find out that he didn't appreciate the art, either. Adalynne tried to push any of these tentative thoughts aside. Sharing the love of music was not a necessity for a relationship. She and Fox loved music and that relationship was a failure from the beginning.

Matthew and Katie stayed with her that night. They indulged in wine and take-out Chinese as they covered every topic of importance. Adalynne could not escape the hint of jealousy as Matthew and Katie carried on about the latest dramatic developments on campus. She felt so removed from their lives first hand and couldn't help but feel like an outsider. She missed Katie and secretly loved the fact Katie told her that her new roommate was a bore.

"You know what those law students are like," Katie teased Matthew, giving him a little playful punch on the shoulder.

"Hey now. I'd like to argue that comment," Matthew disputed.

"I bet you would." Adalynne giggled.

"You look really good, Addie!" Katie gushed. "I was so worried about you. It's so wonderful to know that you're doing what makes you happy. I wish I could visit more." She ended with a pout.

"Yes *but* that would mean leaving Steven's bed more often," Matthew tormented Katie.

"Hey!" Katie's face turned bright red. "I'm not there *that* much." Katie defended her honor to Adalynne. "But he does this thing with his—"

"Don't!" Matthew covered his ears. "I don't want to know the freaky shit you guys do in there because it is right next to my room."

Adalynne laughed at this lighthearted side of

Matthew. She was used to his carefully strategized demeanor as he procured his position among his friends. Adalynne remembered how the other guys at the Alpha house looked up to him but here in her home he was relaxed. She felt this was the first time she'd really glimpsed the man he was and she liked what she saw. They laughed and argued playfully for hours and the girls soon learned it was almost useless to try to build a case against him. His skills as a lawyer were definitely sharp, even with the vast amount of wine that he had ingested. The girls found it fun to wind him up and he took everything in stride. Adalynne couldn't remember when she had laughed this much and she didn't care her cheeks were sore. It was a welcome pain, from what she had experienced as of late.

Matthew was the perfect gentleman when it came to his behavior around her. His eyes always followed her and he would lean into her when she was close. Adalynne found the attention appealing and by the end of the night was extending some of the same gestures toward him. It wasn't long before Katie caught on and excused herself to make a phone call.

Matthew took the opportunity to pull Adalynne aside. "I can't think of anything but you, Addie." The wine had made him even more forward than usual. "I need to know eventually you will want more." He seemed to be struggling to keep his distance from her, his hands searching for a response from her as he touched her leg and caressed her shoulder.

"What if I say that time is now?" Adalynne

looked up from under her dark lashes to see the smile spread across his handsome face.

"I'd say that it would make me very happy." He claimed her lips, guiding her body back so she lay against the sofa as he deepened their kiss. "I've wanted to do that for so long," he breathed against her lips before he kissed her again. The kiss did not stir uncontrollable desire but it felt good.

She placed a hand against his chest to catch her breath. "But...can we approach this a little more slowly?" Adalynne chuckled at his enthusiasm.

"Of course." His smile tried to hide the disappointment she saw flash in his eyes. "I couldn't help myself."

Katie opened the door and walked out slowly, unsure of what she would walk into. Adalynne stood up to meet her, encouraging her to rejoin them. Although Matthew did not trigger the same intense response from her Fox did, she refused to get discouraged. Getting involved with Matthew was a good choice. He was handsome, successful, and most important, he wanted her. She wanted to feel loved.

The next morning Matthew left with his promise lingering in the air. This was the beginning of a wonderful thing between the two of them. She wanted to believe his words. She wanted her heart to accept what they were creating was the potential for love. She had to accept she would never have what her heart truly wanted.

Adalynne placed her hand against her chest, feeling the beat of her heart. She needed to let go of Fox so there was room for her to love someone else.

She hoped more than anything Matthew was her reset button.

Chapter Seventeen

"*So* this Matthew guy?" Elizabeth asked with raised eyebrows.

Adalynne had come over to the Music House early to help Elizabeth with some things she was working on. Adalynne always enjoyed time with Elizabeth. Their relationship was always easy and natural.

"Yeah." Adalynne shrugged her shoulders. "We're seeing each other now." It felt so strange to admit it. It felt like she was talking about someone other than herself.

"He is very handsome," Elizabeth stated, studying Adalynne's response. "I was starting to think you spent all your free time here. It's nice to know that you're taking time to date. A beautiful girl like you needs to feel the excitement of young love." Elizabeth smiled, looking like she was calling to mind an old memory.

"Yeah." Adalynne bit her lip.

Elizabeth looked at her for a moment before changing the subject. "Did you hear there was a fire at the Knight house last night?" Elizabeth watched for her reaction. "No one was hurt, thank goodness," she added quickly. "John apparently decided to burn his shed down after he had a few too many. Rumor has it that it was filled with his late wife's old belongings." Elizabeth watched Adalynne perk up with the news. "Why do you never ask me about the Knight family? So many times I have watched the questions form on the tip of your tongue and then you dismiss them when someone mentions something about the family." Elizabeth peered at Adalynne closely.

"Your heart is tied to them and I have a feeling I know why. I've seen that beautiful boy. Not much gets past me, Adalynne. I may be getting old and crazy but I can still figure things out. Especially when a beautiful girl hides out with me all the time and always looks toward the Knight's house when she walks out this door, like you're drawn to it."

Adalynne collapsed in a chair. She didn't realize how transparent she was. "What happened to his family? How did his mother die?" It was the question she wanted to know the answer to for long as she could remember. She wanted to know why he was the saddest boy she had ever met.

Elizabeth leaned back in her chair and sipped her tea. "I went to school with John Knight. He was a few years older, but I knew who he was. He was so handsome, just like his son." Elizabeth smiled as she visited her memories. "He was a bit of a troublemaker back then, but it was his mischievous youth to blame, nothing serious. He just made a lot of parents nervous." Elizabeth winked. "Shortly after he graduated high school I heard he met a girl named Karen and he never looked back. They were married after they dated for a couple of years. John had developed a name for himself as a talented carpenter. He used to make the most gorgeous furniture. It wasn't long after they got married that she became pregnant with their first child but unfortunately after Damon was born news of her depression spread. The family struggled with it and it took its toll on all of them, even that poor baby never knew his mother's love because the depression robbed her of everything. Eventually she took her own life." Elizabeth shook her head sadly. "John and Damon found her when they came home from the store. She had taken a whole bottle of pills. Young Damon was only three at the time."

Adalynne couldn't help the gasp that escaped her as she listened to the heartbreaking story.

"That child acted out in every imaginable way. No one could get through to that beautiful boy until one day when he was about six years old, his hatred and rebellion dissipated and he gained focus and respect for others. He was still haunted, though. No one knew what happened to him to make the change, but it gave everyone hope for his wellbeing. He wouldn't let anyone close to him; his father either. They closed themselves in and lived in torment. His father turned to the bottle to ease his sadness and it wasn't long before everyone suspected that John took his frustrations out on Damon. Many times over the years Damon came to school covered in bruises but he denied everything. Always coming up with an excuse and since no one could prove it they were left to watch the family fall into the darkness of despair. Many people believe he blames his son for his wife's death."

Adalynne's phone rang, pulling her from Elizabeth's shocking story. "Go ahead and answer your phone," Elizabeth insisted when Adalynne choose to ignore it.

"Hi, Carmen."

"Adalynne, I'm glad I caught you." Carmen's voice sounded full of worry. "Your mother didn't get up this morning so I went to check on her. She never sleeps in, so I thought maybe she was sick or something. When I went to check on her I knew...your mother is finally grieving, Addie. She needs you. She won't get out of bed and refuses to eat." Carmen's tone was worried. Carmen's loyalty was unwavering even when it came to Adalynne's mother, who Adalynne felt didn't always deserve it.

"I'm on my way," Adalynne said quickly before hanging up.

"Is everything okay?" Elizabeth noticed Adalynne's tone.

"My mother needs me," Adalynne informed her while she gathered her things and headed out the door. She took a quick glance up the street and realized the habit she had formed that she wasn't even aware of before Elizabeth brought it up—she was drawn to Fox's house. Even though she knew he no longer lived there, it was still a place she associated with him and therefore she felt drawn to it just like she did to him.

When Adalynne arrived at her mother's house, Carmen was waiting for her at the door, wringing

186

her apron in her hands. "I didn't know what to do, Addie. She won't let me help her."

"Thanks for calling, Carmen. Is she still in bed?" Adalynne asked, taking off her jacket and shoes.

"Yes, dear." Carmen nodded.

When Adalynne arrived at her mother's bedroom door, she knocked quietly and then opened it, not waiting for an answer. She approached the bed and noticed her mother's form buried under the covers. She looked so small in the large bed. Adalynne's mother opened her eyes and looked at her but didn't say anything. Her eyes were swollen and her hair in a disarray from a restless sleep. It was strange to see her so vulnerable. She had always seen her mother so composed and now she looked broken curled up in front of her. She now knew why everyone was so concerned for her when she was suffering the same torment.

Adalynne slid in the bed beside her and reached up and brushed the hair from her mother's face. She knew all too well the sorrow her mother was feeling. The memory of the pain was still fresh in her mind.

"I'm here." She smiled softly at her mother. Her mother's tears started anew and Adalynne held her until her mother's breathing became slow and steady as sleep overcame her. Her mother had stayed in a state of denial so long that Adalynne had wondered if she would ever let herself face the loss. Even though Adalynne knew her mother was suffering right now, she knew it was important to finally start the healing process, like it had been for her. It was something they would both struggle with for the rest of their lives.

When her mother finally opened her eyes, Adalynne was sitting on the edge of the bed looking at a framed picture of her parents sitting on the night stand. "I remember when Dad and I went to the jewelry store to buy those earrings for you." Adalynne chuckled when she pointed to the large, hideous earrings her mother wore in the photo. "He asked the saleswoman for the ugliest jewelry she had. I remember Dad and I laughed about what ones we were going to get you. It was surprising how many choices they had. I thought it was the greatest thing. It's one of my favorite memories of him." Adalynne touched her father's image. "I asked him why he wanted something he knew you wouldn't like and he said..."Adalynne wiped a tear that escaped down her cheek. "He said he knew you would hate them but if you still wore them then he would know you still loved him."

"I think those are now my favorite earrings," her mother whispered softly. Adalynne crawled back in bed with her mother and wrapped her arms around her, hugging her tightly.

"I miss him too, Mom, every day." Adalynne held her mother while her body trembled. They stayed in bed and flipped through photo albums, struggling through tears and even sharing laughs as they voiced their memories. Adalynne had never felt this close to her mother. As much as she disliked seeing her mother in so much pain, it felt like they finally connected on a level that they had never achieved before now.

Adalynne shared the news that Matthew and she

were officially dating. She knew it would make her mother feel better and Adalynne noticed the significant improvement in her mood immediately. "That's wonderful news. He has so much potential, someone you could make a life with." Her mother smiled weakly. "Your father liked him." She sighed.

"Yeah, he did, didn't he?" Adalynne remembered how her father spoke with Matthew in the hospital. They got along so well with their similar passion of law.

"I thought I lost you too." Her mother leaned on Adalynne's shoulder. "It seemed like when your father died, I lost you too."

"I just needed to make some changes, deal with some things. I did feel a little lost but I never left you," Adalynne apologized.

"I know the feeling." Her mother smiled back. "Thank you for today. I needed this."

"I love you, Mom." Adalynne squeezed her hand.

"I love you too. Don't stay away again, okay?"

"I won't," Adalynne promised.

***

The next afternoon on Adalynne's way to the Music House she decided to make a stop. She drove up the street until Fox's house came into view. She had spent the day with her mother yesterday and even did some baking with Carmen, making her favorite banana muffins. She wasn't sure if what she had planned was a good idea but she wanted to check on Fox's father. She knew Fox wasn't around and she felt like she needed to stop by in case John needed something. She learned everyone deals with grief in their own way but sometimes they need the support of others to pull through. When she parked out front she noticed the detached garage had fire damage. The left side of its exterior was scorched.

With a basket of muffins in her hand, she walked up the front step and knocked on the door. She waited and knocked again when no one responded. The door swung open in front of her, causing her to jump in response.

"Damon's not here," he barked at her before closing the door again. Adalynne took a deep breath and tried to not let his behavior discourage her. She remembered the story Elizabeth had told her and the pain he suffered when he lost his wife. Adalynne knocked again.

After a moment the door swung open again. "What!"

"I wanted to stop by and say hello." Adalynne tried to smile but was worried it seemed forced.

"Hi," he replied bluntly. His scruffy appearance and shadowed eyes did not hide the handsome qualities he shared with his son. He was a product of his emotional state. He was consumed with sorrow and it shone through his cold gaze.

"I brought you some muffins." Adalynne offered the basket, but he stepped back without receiving the gift.

"I don't know where he is. He left, said he's not coming back." He stormed off, leaving Adalynne in the doorway. She stepped through, walked into the kitchen, and set the muffins on the counter. He showed no interest in entertaining her company, so she didn't want to push him. She left without another word, closing the door behind her.

The next day, she once again knocked on John's door. This time when he noticed her through the window he didn't even bother to come to the door. Adalynne took a breath and opened the door without his consent. "I'm coming in," she stated as she opened the door.

"You certainly are," he fumed sarcastically. "I didn't open the door 'cause I don't want you here." He sat on the sofa drinking his beer. She walked to the kitchen where the basket of muffins still sat untouched.

"I see you don't like banana muffins. Good thing I brought something different today. Chocolate chip cookies, everyone likes those." She grabbed the basket from the counter and left the container of cookies. "See you tomorrow, Mr. Knight." She gently closed the door behind her and left.

For the rest of the week she maintained the same pattern of dropping food off to Fox's father's house only to return the next day to replace it with something else because he didn't touch it. She figured eventually her persistence would pay off and eventually it did. Two weeks later she knocked on his door and was surprised when he opened it for her. She was used to letting herself in after he ignored her knocking. He then returned to his usual place on the sofa without a word but Adalynne was thrilled because even though it was small, it was still progress.

"I thought I would try a new approach because

you refuse to tell me what food you like and I ran out of sweets to try. I made lasagna." She held it up triumphantly. It was the first time she made it and she was proud of herself. She had been spending time at her mother's now that their relationship had taken a new turn and Carmen had been giving them both cooking lessons. She looked forward to their get-togethers. Her mother even started making suggestions as to what they should make. She was not a natural in the kitchen and Carmen and Adalynne found it quite entertaining to watch her attempts.

The next day when Adalynne returned her dish was sitting on the counter, washed clean. She grabbed her dish and replaced it with her newest attempt. "I knew eventually I would find something you liked." She smiled on her way toward the door.

"Those banana muffins you made smelled really good," he mumbled as she passed.

"Then I will bring some tomorrow. Take care of yourself, Mr. Knight."

"Why?" He looked at her like it was the strangest question he ever heard.

"Because Damon needs his father."

With Adalynne's busy schedule and Matthew finishing out his year of classes, their time together was very minimal, but Matthew had promised when he finished up for the year he would pay her back for his absence. Adalynne never complained. She knew how important his career was to him. The weekends he did manage to visit, he insisted on taking her out on proper dates. They tried different restaurants around town, never visiting the same

192

place twice. She was enjoying her time with him and wondered what it would be like to spend every day with him and not just stolen days in between their busy lives. Although she did like Matthew's company and the excitement of getting to know him, she enjoyed her time by herself. When he wasn't with her she didn't miss him like she thought she should. The distance between them was comfortable to her and thoughts of Fox were still what her mind lingered on when she went to bed at night, even when it was Matthew lying next to her.

Matthew agreed to take their relationship slow, no pressure in the beginning, and they focused solely on getting to know one another. She knew she was pushing her luck but he even agreed to her stipulation of waiting to have sex. She still needed time to get her head around the thought of giving herself to someone other than Fox. That night was one of the most amazing experiences of her life and she didn't want to take away from it. She found herself desperate to hold onto that memory as long as she could.

When Matthew showed his affection it did not inspire need for him. She found herself consciously making an effort to enjoy their intimate moments together, always stopping things when he tried to push too far. Sometimes it angered him but he would quickly compose himself when she reminded him of what he agreed to. She always made sure to please him in other ways. They spent hours exploring their bodies, getting to know each other without taking that last step of intercourse. She enjoyed his fascination with her body but his touch did not ignite passionate heat. Her body did not succumb to the intoxicating bliss she remembered so vividly. It did not tremble with anticipation and make her want him inside her with a need so desperate that it made the entire world fade to nothing.

Eventually she agreed to give herself to him. It was nothing like her experience with Fox. Afterward she locked herself in the washroom and cried quietly. She did not find pleasure in Matthew's arms. She did not love him.

Chapter Eighteen

Adalynne continued to make progress with Fox's father. She continued her visits with him every day and his behavior toward her softened to the point where things were pleasant. He would talk to Adalynne about the game he was watching, something on the news, or even the weather. They always stuck to the safe subjects and Adalynne didn't want to be the first to deviate from those comfortable exchanges. She never brought up Fox because she knew it was a sensitive subject considering he hadn't seen his son in a long time. Adalynne saw letters on the kitchen counter that had Fox's handwriting on them. She once snuck a peak to discover they were filled with cash, no letter or personal effect. They all were sitting on the counter untouched.

It was an early Sunday morning and spring was in full swing. The earth was thawing with the new warmth that radiated from the sun. Flowers were inspired to wake from their winter slumber and brighten the world. Adalynne had told Elizabeth she would be later coming into the Music House that day because she had something planned before.

Adalynne pulled up in front of Fox's father's house and opened her trunk. She wanted to restore the overgrown garden in front of the house. She couldn't stand looking at the sad sight every time she visited. She grabbed her gardening supplies and gloves and made her way to the garden to begin pulling out the weeds that had long since taken over. The yard needed some attention. It had not been touched since the early spring growth and now was painfully neglected.

Adalynne was hard at work for about an hour and had managed to wrangle most of the larger weeds from the bed. She looked up when the door opened and Fox's father stood on the step looking down at her.

"Good morning," Adalynne offered sheepishly. She hadn't told him of her plan to try to salvage the garden and wasn't exactly sure how he would respond. She continued to work as he stood there for a moment watching her efforts. She wasn't sure what he was thinking, his expression was hard to read. Unfortunately it was a trait that ran in the family.

"Do you think people can change?" he asked thoughtfully.

"That's why I'm here." Adalynne looked up at him. It was the first time she had seen his smile and she found herself smiling back. It was the biggest step toward progress she had made to date.

He walked down the front steps, taking a few steps toward the driveway before turning back toward Adalynne. "He loves you, you know." Adalynne knew he referred to Fox as soon as he said the words.

"I wish it were true," Adalynne said sadly, turning back to her gardening. He had no idea how much so. She had wanted to broach the topic of Fox but not about that. It would never be the love that she wanted from him.

"He does, believe me, but he just doesn't think he's good enough for you."

"Why would he ever think that?" Adalynne sighed. She wiped her forehead with the back of her gloved hand and leaned back on her heels.

"Because I told him every day of his life he wasn't." He looked down and turned to walk away, leaving Adalynne alone with the garden. She didn't know what to think of his words, though they placed a seed of doubt in her plan to move on without Fox in her life.

Adalynne broke into a chuckle when she heard the lawn mower roar to life. It felt like a huge victory. They worked simultaneously for what felt like hours until Adalynne stepped back from the garden, pleased with what she had accomplished. She sat on the front step brushing the dirt from her clothes as she watched Fox's father finish up. He had even trimmed up the edges of the grass. The property now looked well-manicured, a huge improvement from when she had arrived this morning.

"Thirsty?" he asked Adalynne as he walked toward the front steps.

"Very," she panted.

He returned a moment later with a cold bottle of water. She couldn't help but frown when she noticed that he opted for a beer for himself but she didn't comment. It wasn't her place but her gesture did not go unnoticed.

"You need a couple of chairs or something on your front step. It's such a nice place to sit and feel the sun on your face," she commented, tilting her face up to meet the sun, leaning back on the step. "I'll be back tomorrow. I want to put some flowers in the bed because most of them didn't survive the invasion of the weeds." Adalynne laughed. "Thank you for the drink." She stood to leave.

"Thank you," he said with deep meaning in his eyes. She knew he referred to more than the gardening. Like Fox, he was more expressive with his eyes when he wanted to be than he was with his words. She wished they were always so easy to read but those glimpses were few and far between.

"See you tomorrow, Mr. Knight."

"Call me John."

"Tomorrow then, John." Adalynne waved.

The next morning when Adalynne returned with a trunk load of flowers she noticed two wooden chairs sitting on the front step. She climbed the stairs to view the chairs. They were beautiful, so smooth to touch. She sat down in one and leaned back and closed her eyes. The sun was warm this morning and it felt nice on her skin.

The door opened and she heard footsteps on the porch. "You like the chairs?"

"Yes, they're beautiful." Adalynne looked up at John, shielding her eyes from the sun with her hand.

She couldn't help but notice he had shaved his scruffy beard. "Much better." She grinned, rubbing her own chin.

"Oh, yeah. About time, I guess." John touched his face.

"Where did you get these? They are so comfortable," Adalynne observed, taking in the detail of the chairs.

"I made them," he stated softly.

"Well, they are fabulous." Adalynne remembered Elizabeth mentioning that he used to make furniture. She had forgotten about that until now.

"You should sell these. Do you make anything else?" Adalynne was very curious about his skill.

"Yeah, I used to make anything that could be made with wood. It was nice to use my tools again. It's been such a long time since I was inspired to make anything." He said warily. "I missed it." John sat down next to her in the other chair. "You're right. This is a great place to sit."

"It is." Adalynne agreed.

"I went to an AA meeting last night." John looked off thoughtfully into the distance.

"I'm proud of you. That takes courage." Adalynne said. She was so touched that he was sharing this with her.

"Well, right now I feel like shit. Excuse my language." John rubbed his hands on his face. "I would do anything for a drink right now."

"Damon would be proud of you too," Adalynne added sincerely.

"Someone wise told me I have to take care of

myself because my son needs me. It's about time I tried to get my shit together for him."

Adalynne reached over and placed her hand on his arm. "If you need me for anything just let me know. I will do whatever I can."

"You have already done so much. You have been kind to me when no one else cared, not even me."

"I could tell you were a good man when I met you, just lost." Adalynne leaned back in her chair. "We all get lost sometimes."

"I was lost for a long time, Adalynne." He pointed toward the shed, still damaged from the fire. "I got so tired of being angry. I tried to burn all the memories I couldn't escape."

"I don't think we can ever escape memories. We just have to learn how to move on despite the ones that haunt us." Adalynne took a deep breath against the emotions tightening her chest.

John looked at Adalynne considerately. "He changed after he met you." John leaned back and ran his hands through his hair. "Always sneaking into those woods. I followed him one day to see what he was up to. I saw the two of you. It didn't take me long to figure out who you were. After that I told him to stay away from you or I would give him a whipping. He still went to meet you every day and I would be waiting for him when he walked out of the woods. I beat the shit out of my boy so many times…" John teared up with his words. "The day after he would still go to meet you even though he knew what was waiting for him. I have done so many terrible things, Adalynne. So many unforgivable things."

"I'm sorry. I didn't know." Adalynne's vision blurred with her own tears. "I wouldn't have let him come if I knew."

"Don't be sorry. It was good someone loved him because I didn't know how."

Adalynne got up from her chair and hugged John. He was unmoving under her embrace at first and then slowly patted her back as he relaxed.

"I loved him with all my heart and I always will," she confessed. Adalynne had finally met the man behind the wall he had built around him. The transition from what he was, until now, sitting beside her and speaking from the heart was remarkable.

***

Classes had ended for the year, freeing up Adalynne's schedule. Besides Adalynne's daily visits with John, she also committed herself to the Music House full time. The community was showing its support of the work they were doing and it encouraged Elizabeth and Adalynne to reach out even more, creating new and innovative ways to bring music into people's lives. It was a rewarding experience to have someone walk into the door and say someone recommended them to the school. It meant they were accomplishing what Elizabeth had set out to do when she bought the place. The Music House was becoming the pride of the small community.

Although Matthew always listened to her as she spoke of what was taking place at the Music House, she knew he didn't share in her excitement. Even the news of their success didn't rouse his interest. His mind was always on other things. His summer was dedicated to a temporary internship his father had arranged at a law firm. The connections he was already making in the industry were remarkable. She was proud of what he was accomplishing. There was no question he would become the lawyer he had set out to become. His dedication to the cause was similar to the amount of herself she applied to music.

The summer did not bring them closer, as Matthew had promised. Their career-driven lives kept them occupied and Adalynne began to wonder what kind of future they would have if they couldn't find the time to develop their relationship. The work had him consumed, occupying the majority of his time. Adalynne did admire his drive for success. It was an excellent quality in a man and her mother always reminded her of that when they broached the subject of Adalynne and Matthew's relationship.

Adalynne's mother had settled back into her demanding career and although Adalynne did not have that same raw connection with her mother they had experienced those few days, she would always remember it. She was glad her mother had allowed herself to grieve and now she was moving on without so much weight upon her shoulders. They did, however, make an attempt to remain close. Adalynne joined her mother once a week for dinner. Adalynne's mother mostly liked to talk about Matthew but she listened when Adalynne filled her in on what was happening at the Music House.

Adalynne liked sharing her successes with her mother even though she knew her mother didn't appreciate it like she did. It was more for her own benefit than her mother's. Like Matthew, her mother didn't share her love of music and therefore did not completely respect her career choice. Adalynne wondered if her mother's interest in her relationship was because her mother feared for her future should it be left to her own accord. She knew the career she chose was not as profitable as what her mother wanted for her but it was what made her the happiest. It was a sacrifice she was willing to make.

Matthew always accepted her mother's invites to supper. He had a charm about him that completely won over her mother. Those nights Adalynne usually let her mother and Matthew discuss their topics of interest and she would nod and smile on cue. Neither one would even notice her lack of input in the conversation. Adalynne would find herself tuning out while she played with her phone, always navigating to Outcome's web page to find the latest information or tour stops. She didn't allow herself to feel guilty because it was not specifically Fox she sought out. She convinced herself it was an innocent endeavor. She had promised no more Fox when she committed herself to the relationship with Matthew. So far she wasn't making the progress she hoped. Although she admired and respected Matthew, even enjoyed his company, she still didn't love him.

When the summer bled into fall and the season changed, Adalynne found herself back into the throes of school. Her studies became more specific to becoming a professor of music, meaning she was that much closer to attaining her goal. Elizabeth was always supportive of her, always there to cheer her on every step of the way.

Over the next few months she also watched John's painful struggle to curb his dependence on the bottle, a process proving to be a battle each step of the way. Adalynne made sure her daily visits persisted to show her support. Some days John couldn't get out of bed and needed the encouragement he was doing the best thing even though it didn't necessarily feel like it at the time. She made sure he ate and took care of himself. Most days she would leave in tears but not until she was in the privacy of her car. He refused to leave the house most days for fear he would drive straight to the liquor store. He committed his time to his garage, focusing his energy on creating his beautiful furniture. Adalynne made sure his cupboards were always stocked with healthy food so he wouldn't have an excuse to go to the store when he felt so weak against the call to drink.

His AA sponsor, Meredith, was someone who became a constant in his life as well. She was a woman who had gone through the same struggle five years ago and knew the pain John was experiencing first hand. Meredith had spiraled out of control when drinking consumed her life. She had finally found herself in a place where she could reach out and help others who were struggling to find their way back. Meredith became a steady presence in his life and soon the three of them became familiar company. Adalynne felt better leaving John knowing Meredith would not be far should he need her.

Adalynne could see the attraction develop between John and Meredith as they spent time together. She knew Meredith would not condone anything beyond their platonic friendship until his need for her help ceased. Meredith took her role as a sponsor seriously. She had a maturity about her that stemmed from the tragedy of her life. Meredith would not risk his progress to indulge in the excitement of a possible relationship between the two until she knew he could handle it. Adalynne came to respect her strength immensely. She was a woman Adalynne was truly honored to know.

Chapter Nineteen

Thanksgiving arrived and Adalynne decided to host dinner for the holiday. Matthew and his parents were coming, making Adalynne extremely anxious. She had only met Matthew's parents briefly on a few occasions and nothing as personal as dinner in her home. The feeling that she needed to impress was overwhelming. Matthew always said his parents spoke highly of her and she didn't want to disappoint them. It was the first time Adalynne had cooked a turkey dinner on her own but she felt prepared with Carmen's pointers. Although she had invited Carmen to her dinner, she had to decline. Carmen came from a large family and she had other obligations. She did come over earlier in the day to check on Adalynne's prep work and to see if she needed help before she headed home to her arriving family. Adalynne was grateful. Carmen's visit had calmed her nerves. Her presence was always soothing.

She had also invited John, Meredith, and Elizabeth. She wasn't sure how all these important people in her life would come together in one space but she loved them all and wanted to have them close for the holiday. She was also nervous how John would react to her relationship with Matthew. He knew she was dating Matthew but he had never witnessed it in person. A feeling of guilt bloomed within her because she knew John was aware of her true feelings. She feared John would judge her for the path she'd chosen when they both knew her heart did not follow.

All of these feelings aside, she still felt like she made the right decision. She warned John, Meredith, and Elizabeth that her mother sometimes came off as unfriendly. It seemed like the nicest way to refer to her mother but she knew another word might come to their minds once they'd met her. She could only hope her mother would make an effort to converse pleasantly with the important people in her life.

Elizabeth was the first to arrive. She came early to help Adalynne with preparations for dinner. "I absolutely love this place. It is beautiful and elegant but at the same time very welcoming." Elizabeth toured around her apartment. "I feel guilty I haven't been here until now," she said.

"Well, it's not the easiest task getting you out of the Music House." Adalynne laughed.

"I could say the same about you. If it wasn't for school I bet you would be there just as much as me." Elizabeth shot back with a smile. "Did I ever tell you how happy I was that you showed up in my life when you did, Addie?"

"Yes, all the time. And you always give me way

too much credit. My interest in the Music House is completely selfish and for my own personal gain." They both laughed as they worked around the kitchen. The aroma of the cooking meal soon filled her apartment with the promise of delicious food.

"I might have to steal some of these recipes. That pie smells delicious," Elizabeth gushed as she set the pie up on the cooling rack.

"It's Carmen's creation. She is the most amazing cook," Adalynne said proudly.

John and Meredith arrived together and after unnecessary introductions between Elizabeth and John, because they recognized each other instantly, an easy flow of conversation followed between all of them. Adalynne was glad she had decided to bring everyone together. Meredith and Elizabeth found common ground and before long it felt like the most natural thing to have them together.

"I brought sweet potato casserole." Meredith set it on the counter before diving into the kitchen to help Adalynne and Elizabeth. "It has been years since I've had a meal like this." Meredith smiled and a hint of sadness crossed her expression.

"Then I better not let you down," Adalynne said.

Next Adalynne's mother arrived in her pristine form. Even though her smile was not as sincere as Adalynne had hoped it would be, she appreciated her mother's attempt. When Adalynne noticed the bottle of wine in her hand, her stomach dropped.

"Mother, I told you no wine," Adalynne tried to whisper but couldn't help the scolding tone that escaped her lips.

"I thought you were joking, dear. I mean

Thanksgiving without wine?" Her mother shrugged off her objection.

"It's okay, Addie," John said reassuringly. "You don't…"

"This meal will be so good we won't need wine." Adalynne took the wine from her mother's hand and dropped it in the garbage can. Taking a deep breath, she tried to recover her composure. She could feel the heat of anger on her face.

Before Adalynne could make proper introductions, Matthew and his parents arrived and the whole atmosphere changed. Adalynne hoped she was being oversensitive and she was the only one that picked up on the tension that began to develop. She was furious with her mother for bringing wine when she specifically told her not to because there would be two recovering alcoholics attending. Adalynne figured she should have anticipated her mother's actions when she had become angry she had been hanging out with 'a strange alcoholic man'—the very words her mother used when she had spoken to her on the phone.

"What are you doing with your life?" her mother asked in outrage when Adalynne told her who was coming to dinner. She hadn't mentioned John before then. She wasn't exactly sure how to explain the connection because her mother had never known about Fox. Her mother had been so upset Adalynne didn't get the chance to explain how she knew him.

Matthew made easy conversation with Elizabeth, John, and Meredith. She could tell it was his game face but he was making more of an effort than her mother and she appreciated it. She only hoped he seemed sincere to her friends. Mr. and Mrs. Murphy engaged in pleasantries with Adalynne's mother and she couldn't complain. Things were going as smoothly as could be expected. John, Elizabeth, and Meredith were nothing but warm and wonderful guests as they took everything in stride. Adalynne served the meal with the help of Elizabeth. Once everyone had their food, Adalynne sat down to enjoy her hard work.

"So if you're not involved in music, how is it that you know Adalynne?" Mrs. Murphy asked John when conversation had drifted toward Adalynne's music endeavors.

"I know John's son. We went to Memorial High together," Adalynne offered quickly, looking at John's expression. She knew he realized her family was not aware of how well she knew his son.

"I live down the street from the Music House. She has been a big help since my son left." John smiled at her, trying to ease her obvious nerves.

"Yes, she is a wonderful girl. You must be so proud," Meredith added with a smile for Adalynne's mother.

"Of course," her mother replied tightly.

Adalynne didn't realize how unprepared she had left everyone in regards to her relationship with John and Meredith, how vague she had been about her connection as to not reveal her past with Fox. She knew she couldn't tell Matthew because it would be too easy for him to realize she was still in love with someone else. Her mother was unaware because Fox had always refused to let her tell her parents about their relationship. She hoped John wouldn't take their lack of knowledge about him personally.

"We knew how special she was when we first met her," Mrs. Murphy said.

Adalynne had always wondered what Matthew told his parents about her to make them fond of her. It seemed like they had never gotten past the awkward first encounters.

Adalynne's face heated. She wasn't comfortable with the conversation turning on her. Adalynne looked at Matthew when he stood up suddenly, pushing his chair back.

"Since Adalynne has invited everyone she cares about tonight, with a few exceptions, of course, being her best friend Katie could not join us, there is something that I want to ask Adalynne. Now seems like the perfect time."

Adalynne tried not to look scared as she watched Matthew make a suspicious speech in front of her family, his words almost blurred together in her mind as she watched the scene unfold. Suddenly he was kneeling beside her, looking up into her eyes. Adalynne stared down at a huge diamond ring that looked too large for her slender finger.

She looked at Matthew, too shocked to speak. She didn't expect this tonight. She couldn't even form words. All she could think about was Fox and if she said yes it would mean that the little hope she still carried in her heart would be gone.

"Congratulations, son!" Mr. Murphy's voiced bellowed around her. She still hadn't answered but neither Matthew's parents, nor her mother, seemed to notice as they congratulated them.

She could feel her mother grab her shoulders and bring her in for a hug. "This is the most wonderful news."

Adalynne met John's eyes, across the table. He looked back at her with a small, polite smile. She desperately wanted to know what he was thinking. Adalynne's attention turned back toward the commotion beside her as Matthew hugged his parents, who smiled proudly at their son. Adalynne wondered why they were so happy their son was marrying her. She wanted to know why Matthew had proposed to her when she had never told him that she loved him. She wanted to know why everyone assumed she would say yes when she didn't answer his question.

The excitement of the proposal carried on for the rest of the evening. Adalynne tried to not draw attention to her obvious distress by putting her best smile on. Her mother, Matthew, and his parents didn't seem to notice but she was not as convincing to Elizabeth, John, and Meredith, who gave her wary glances the rest of the evening.

When John and Meredith announced their departure, Adalynne followed them out into the hallway as discreetly as possible. "John? I hope you didn't take my mother's and Matthew's lack of knowledge of you the wrong way. Damon never wanted me to tell my parents about him and it was hard to explain our connection without that piece of the puzzle. So I guess it was easier not to say anything about it. I'm glad you came. You're both important to me and it meant the world you came even though it was a bit painful," Adalynne apologized.

"Not at all, it was the best meal I've had in a long time, Addie." Meredith tried to ease Adalynne's mind.

"You are too nice," Adalynne replied.

"You didn't say yes," John commented on the proposal, searching Adalynne's expression.

"You noticed, huh? Well, I think you're the only one." Adalynne couldn't even manage a smile.

***

As soon as everyone left, Adalynne called Katie and told her what had happened. Katie was still at Steven's parents' house for the weekend. She felt guilty for burdening her while she was trying to enjoy her weekend getting to know Steven's extended family. They all wanted to meet the girl who had won Steven's heart.

"Oh my god! I wish I could have been there. Addie, what are you going to do? Are you going to tell him no?" Katie rambled so fast it was hard to process her questions. Adalynne could hear the commotion from Steven's young cousins in the background.

"Maybe you should call me when you get home," Adalynne offered.

"What? No way, hold on." There was shuffling on the other end of the line. "Okay, continue," Katie encouraged. "There is no way that this can wait."

"I don't know what I'm going to do. I know that I would have said no if I had answered, but now that things are just moving on, I'm thinking maybe this is the best thing. My plan was to get over Fox and this is definitely moving on. I don't want to be alone the rest of my life. Matthew makes me happy. He's a good guy. He makes me laugh. I'm just…"

"Not in love with him." Katie finished her sentence. "Do you really want to marry someone you don't love? What if Carmen was right when she told you Fox really does love you? What if you called him?" Katie answered after a moment's silence. "Just talked…"

"No way! Whatever that *was* is over. It's too hard, knowing I can't be with him. I would just be submitting myself to more punishment, the same heartache I've put myself through my entire life. He never loved me back, Katie. Not the way I wanted him to, at least." Adalynne sighed, defeated.

"I'm coming over next weekend. I want to talk about this in person and I have some news for you that I don't want to tell you over the phone," Katie said quickly.

"What news? You are seriously going to tell me that and then make me wait?" Adalynne whined.

"Yes."

Adalynne's computer alerted her of an email and she opened up on the screen in front of her. It was the details of her engagement party the following weekend. "Well. I guess you'll be here for my engagement party," Adalynne fumed. "My mother just sent me an email with all the details she has already arranged. *Kill me.*"

"Well, then it's good planning because I definitely think you will need me for that," Katie responded sympathetically.

"You have no idea."

"What am I going to do with you, Adalynne? Five days and I will be there and we'll talk about all of this."

Chapter Twenty

True to her word, Katie arrived on her doorstep the following Saturday. Adalynne had tried to get her mother to cancel the engagement party but the invitations had already been sent. Her mother refused to entertain the idea. Since Adalynne was unable to bring herself to derail the engagement, things were going ahead as planned.

"Thank god you're here." Adalynne wrapped her arms around Katie, who bounded in her door. "I need you to get through today."

"How are you going to get through the rest of your life if you go through with this? I think Matthew is a great guy, but I honestly don't think this is the right move for you. You're going to end up miserable."

"It's just the engagement party that has me on edge. Things with Matthew and I are great. Matthew is working toward a great career, we get along great, he's handsome and attentive, and we're great together," Adalynne defended half-heartedly.

"Good to know things are so *great*," Katie said

sarcastically. "By the look in your eyes, everything is not *great*, by the way. You look terrified. Do you know why I had to be your friend when we first met?" Katie didn't wait for an answer. "When you look at people you do not judge them. You see all the good they can be. It is beautiful how you see the world. There is so much that is special about you, Adalynne. You have done so much to make everyone else happy but now it is time to think about yourself. You have to take back your heart. Nothing has changed. You cannot deny your feelings forever."

"It's too late."

"It's never too late, Adalynne." Katie grabbed her by the shoulders to accentuate her point.

"What is your news that you wanted to tell me?" Adalynne changed the subject. Katie rolled her eyes at Adalynne's refusal to finish their conversation.

"Okay, but only because I can't hold it in much longer. I have been dying to tell you since I found out last weekend. Don't freak out, I have already done that enough for both of us. I'm pregnant," Katie finished, biting her lip. "But no one knows yet, so you have to keep the secret for now."

Adalynne stared back at Katie without a word. It was the last thing she was expecting to come out of her mouth. "Does Steven know?" Adalynne asked the first question that came to mind when her words thawed from the shock.

"Yes, he basically had a panic attack. It was definitely not in our plan, but we had a little time for it to register and we're planning to keep the baby. It's not going to be easy, I haven't figured out what I'm going to do about school or anything, but we love each other."

"You're going to be a great mom." Adalynne smiled. "Congratulations. Am I the first to say that?"

"Yes. I told Steven that I needed to tell you first. We're not sure when we're going to tell our parents. I think Steven would wait until the baby was born to tell them but we'll figure it out." Katie shrugged. She didn't let things bother her unnecessarily. She took things as they came and always assumed things would work out for the best. It was an ability Adalynne admired.

"I have no doubt." Adalynne wrapped her arms around her and squeezed tight.

***

When Adalynne walked into her mother's house she felt Katie's hold clamp tightly onto her arm like she was preventing Adalynne from fleeing. She must have sensed her hesitation.

"I'm not going to run," Adalynne whispered under her breath so the many faces that turned to acknowledge her arrival wouldn't notice.

"Just making sure," Katie said, meeting all the faces directed toward them. "Let the games begin." She smiled outrageously and fluttered her eyelashes up at Adalynne.

"There you are, darling." Her mother parted from the crowd and drew close to them. "I was beginning to worry." She gave Adalynne a suspicious glare. "Matthew arrived some time ago with his parents.

Come this way."

Her mother directed her through the crowd of people that congratulated her as she passed. She would not let Katie stray too far as her mother weaved her through the gathering. Adalynne noticed so many faces she hadn't seen since her father's funeral. Memories of the funeral pulled heavily at her emotions.

The interior of the house looked as if it had a fresh makeover since the last time she was here a few weeks ago, giving it more of a modern feel with flowers arranged throughout the room accenting the new color scheme. Her mother must be trying to keep herself busy with the constant redecorating. New furniture was staged in the room that looked like pages of a magazine rather than a home that was loved and lived in. She noticed Tracy Gibbons, a fellow classmate from high school, among the crowd. It surprised Adalynne to see her amongst the people here to wish her well.

Tracy was Fox's old girlfriend and had despised Adalynne since the day she met her when she started Memorial High her twelfth year. Adalynne had not even spoken to her directly the entire year they went to the same school. The sight of her made thoughts of Fox surface and a dull ache lined her stomach.

Adalynne's eyes fell on Molly and Brooke across the room. They both waved and then discreetly nodded toward Tracy as if to say 'why is she here?' Adalynne shrugged unknowingly. She hadn't bothered to ask her mother who she invited but apparently it was everyone she ever knew regardless whether they liked her or not.

Matthew was dressed to impress as always. His suit was perfectly tailored to show off his masculine lines. His parents as well were perfect as they flanked their son in discussion with some other guests but everyone turned to Adalynne when she approached.

"There is the beautiful Adalynne now." Mrs. Murphy smiled radiantly.

Adalynne knew John and Meredith weren't there because her mother conveniently forgot to send them an invite. She hadn't visited John as much lately—she blamed it on the work load from school, but she was actually embarrassed to be around John because he knew she was marrying someone else when she loved his son. She could see the truth every time she looked into his eyes. She didn't know why she felt so guilty. She wasn't cheating on Fox. He had never given her the option of being with him.

Adalynne had questioned Matthew's reasoning for proposing to her when they were only officially a couple for less than a year. She knew he was in a different place. He was older than her by five years and just starting his career but she didn't share in his urgency to take this next step. He had told her he wanted to establish a strong foundation of family as he built his career. She struggled with the idea of marrying him. It felt too soon but their families were insistent they were a good match. In the world of old money, social rules, and family politics, things did not always line up with the real world. Matthew promised her that they would have a long engagement. This was only a promise they would eventually get married once they were established and ready to take that step.

Adalynne cared for Matthew. She favored him as much as she could with what remained of her heart. She figured it might be the closest she would have to happiness with someone. Her only hope was that eventually in time she would grow to love him. Right now it didn't seem to be an issue for Matthew to take their relationship to the next level regardless if she had professed her love of him or not.

Adalynne put her best game face on despite the constant stream of questions from the house full of guests, the constant fussing of her mother to make the event perfect, and Tracy hanging off Matthew's every word like he was the most fascinating thing in the world. Adalynne wondered if Tracy was attempting to make her jealous. She didn't even know if Tracy knew about the history she shared with Fox. The only thing she knew for certain was that Tracy hated her. She didn't feel jealous at all, even when Tracy leaned in and touched his arm, letting her fingers linger. She only wished Tracy would disappear off into the crowd somewhere so Adalynne didn't have to endure her annoying laugh.

Matthew's parents spoke about how proud they were of their son, only recently completing law school and already making a name for himself. They had informed Adalynne that Matthew was entertaining the possibility of a job opportunity that would take him abroad for the beginning of his career. Adalynne smiled and nodded as his parents explained how they thought it would be a good opportunity for him to travel now before they had children and how easy it would be to entertain her music hobbies anywhere Matthew led them in his career. Adalynne felt her chest tighten as she took in the conversation. She tried to keep the smile upon her face, the last thing she wanted to do was cause a scene. She wanted to object, to confront Matthew and ask him why he had never brought this up to her. He should know by now that she would not be willing to leave the Music House. She had worked so hard with Elizabeth, she couldn't just walk away to follow Matthew wherever he may lead.

Katie was never far from her side. Her mouth dropped open as she listened to Matthew's parents. She looked like she was scared Adalynne would have a break down. "Adalynne, could you join me for a moment?" Katie interrupted. "Sorry, Mr. and Mrs. Murphy, but it's an important matter and it cannot wait."

"Of course, dear." Mrs. Murphy excused herself to converse with other guests.

"I felt suffocated and I wasn't even in the conversation," Katie whispered as she pulled Adalynne off to the side for some privacy. "Who is the bitch that insists on feeling up Matthew?" Katie asked with wide eyes.

"Tracy Gibbons. She absolutely hated me in high school." Adalynne searched her out in the crowd.

"What did you do, steal her boyfriend?" Katie looked at Adalynne's reaction and got her answer.

"She was Fox's girlfriend in high school. I don't think she even knows how I felt about Fox but she went out of her way to let me know she didn't like me. She probably suspected something." Adalynne sighed and leaned against the wall. "I'm kidding myself if I think that I can actually go through with this engagement to Matthew."

"Finally you're speaking some sense." Katie squeezed her shoulders. "I thought I was going to have to arrange an intervention."

Molly approached them. "Hiding, are you?"

"Hey, Molly," they said in unison.

"I thought I would never get you away from those vultures to talk. First, congratulations on your engagement." Molly's smile fell from her lips as she noticed that Adalynne seemed upset.

"Are you okay? Is it Tracy? She is obviously trying to get to you." Molly was concerned.

"No, I couldn't care less what Tracy was up to. I'm just..." Adalynne trailed off.

"Having second thoughts?" Molly continued when Adalynne didn't finish. "I remember what you're like when you are completely head over heels about someone. I never really saw that when it came to Matthew. I just didn't want to say anything. I figured maybe you weren't over you know who." Molly changed the subject when she realized she might have said too much. "I should have the new website up and running in a couple of days. I think you're going to love it." Molly said. Adalynne had contacted Molly to set up a much needed website for the Music House. Elizabeth was not one for technology and always found an excuse to put it off so Adalynne had to take matters into her own hands. Since it was Molly's specialty, she knew the best person to call for the job.

"Thanks, Molly," Adalynne said gratefully.

"Did you hear that Damon is back in town? I heard he has a new swanky condo. You know, the new ones that just went up on the waterfront." Molly's eyes always lit up when she dished on gossip. Luckily when it came to her friends' secrets, she was very tight-lipped. Katie and Adalynne exchanged glances at the information.

"How do you find out this stuff?" Adalynne asked. Molly always had the inside scoop on all things.

"Well, in this instance my cousin Marshall works for a delivery company. He delivered furniture to his place and he recognized him." Molly winked. "I always pay special attention to things that may be important to my friends. Suite 402, I think. Yeah, that's what he said."

"I'll cover for you if you want to run off for a quick drive. You know how these things last for hours. Besides, I think you have some demons from your past you should truly settle before you can move on." Katie winked encouragingly. Adalynne only nodded, excitement pooled heavily in her stomach. She needed to get away from here and right now the only place she wanted to run was where she promised herself she wouldn't. She wanted to talk to Fox.

"I knew it," Molly proudly stated. "I knew it since the first time you I saw you staring at him."

"Thanks, Molly. Tell Brooke I said I'm sorry I missed her." Adalynne gave her a quick hug.

"I will but it's not easy to miss her lately. Her newest endeavor as a makeup artist has gone horribly wrong. She looks like a hooker. I keep telling her but she doesn't believe me. She says she has never gotten so much male attention and she loves it." Molly sighed. "She'll believe me when they start propositioning her."

Adalynne snuck out of the house without detection. Molly and Katie were going to hold off any notice of her absence as long as they could. She knew she would have to answer for her actions eventually, but not now.

***

The building was an architect's dream with its sleek design and impressive stature. It stood before prime beachfront overlooking endless blue waters.

Adalynne did not allow herself to think through her actions because she knew she would talk herself out of this ridiculous plan. Her mother was literally going to fly into a fit of rage when she discovered that Adalynne snuck out on her own engagement party.

When Adalynne parked her car she noticed a couple of guys were hanging out in the stairwell having a smoke. She thought she would take advantage of the opportunity and try to sneak into the building.

"Hi boys." She managed her best smile. "Can you let me in? I forgot my keys." They were both fairly young, dressed in painting overalls. They were taking a break from whatever project they were working on. They both smiled at her as she came to a stop in front of them, giving her an obvious once over. Normally, she wouldn't like that kind of attention but she was in need of their help.

"Sure thing." One of them winked at her and swung the door open for her to pass. She gave them an appreciative smile before starting to climb the stairs.

When Adalynne reached the fourth floor she pushed the door open to face a long hallway. The interior was brightly lit with wall sconces that lined the walls. Everything was new and impressive and smelled of fresh paint as she walked down the hallway. She tried to keep her mind from playing out the possibilities that might unfold when she came face to face with him. Her heart raced as she brought herself up to the door labeled 402 in bold black letters.

Adalynne stared at the numbers for a few minutes before she could bring herself to knock. Taking a deep breath, she waited to see if there was any noise on the other side of the door. She knocked again slightly louder when there was no answer. Adalynne was about to knock again when the door swung open and Fox was standing in front of her. Her heart felt like it was going to leap from her chest. All she could do was stare at him.

"Bee?" Her name slipped from his lips so softly she didn't know if he actually said it.

Fox wore nothing but low riding jeans that revealed his enticing lines. His hair was tousled and longer than it was last time she had seen him. His face was unshaven with a few days' growth and still incredibly handsome. She remembered how it felt to run her fingers through his hair when he kissed her.

226

Heat flared to life deep within her as her heart raced at the sight of him again. It only took a moment for all of those feelings to resurface. His expression of shock quickly melted into his unreadable, casual composure. "What are you doing here?"

"Who is it, Brolan?" a female voice called from inside the apartment. Adalynne tried to hide her surprise when a woman appeared behind Fox. Her robe was untied, exposing her naked body. When she noticed Adalynne, a malicious smirk crossed her face. She was the brunette who had opened for his concert, with the red streaks in her hair.

"I'm sorry." Adalynne stepped back from the doorway. Fox pulled the door closed behind him, stepping out in the hallway with Adalynne.

"What are you doing here, Adalynne?" There was something in his tone that Adalynne could only read as anger.

"You never call me Adalynne." She was overwhelmed with the reality of what she walked in on. It was nothing like she imagined. Truthfully, she had no idea what she had expected to happen, dropping in unexpectedly. She realized now how foolish her decision was. What they shared was too far buried in the past.

"Things change," he said bluntly.

"I came because I wanted to talk to you. I got engaged." Adalynne couldn't meet his eyes. She looked down at the ring that suddenly felt too heavy on her finger.

"Why the *fuck* would you come here to tell me that?" Fox took a step toward her and Adalynne backed against the wall. The door swung open and the girl appeared, impatiently waiting for Fox to return.

"Give me a minute," he spat out angrily. He pulled the door closed again, despite her cold glare.

"I don't know…I guess I wanted you to give me a reason not to be with him." Adalynne could barely stop the tears that threatened to fall. She was embarrassed standing on his doorstep, begging him to give her something to hold onto when he obviously was involved with someone else. She wondered when she'd become so pathetic.

"What do you want from me?"

Adalynne couldn't stop herself. She figured she had already made a fool of herself. "If things would have been different, could you have ever loved me?" she asked quietly, tears slipping down her face.

He didn't say anything for a moment as he looked at her, considering her words. She desperately wanted to know what he was thinking. Her eyes were drawn to a tattoo on his chest she hadn't noticed before. Over his heart were three letters that made the tears fall from her eyes. Her name, Bee, was written over his heart. She ran her fingers over the ink on his warm skin. He was taken back by her brazen move, stepping back from her touch. He covered the tattoo with his hand.

"Go back to your stuck up fiancé and live happily ever after." He swung his door open and slammed it closed behind him. Adalynne leaned against the wall for support. She could barely bring herself to walk. There was a large crash behind Fox's door as something shattered on the floor.

"Get the fuck out!" Fox screamed. "Get your shit and get the fuck out!"

Adalynne quickly made her way to an alcove in the hallway to get out of sight.

"You're fucking crazy!" the girl screamed. She swung the door open and it slammed loudly against the inside wall. Adalynne ducked out of sight. She watched the girl storm down the hallway, pulling on a sweater. Adalynne breathed a sigh of relief when the girl barreled past without noticing her.

The noise continued in Fox's apartment. His door was still open as she walked hesitantly toward it. The noise inside suddenly stopped. She didn't want to leave without making sure everything was all right. When she reached the threshold of his apartment, she took a deep breath and stepped inside. She noticed Fox sitting on his sofa with his face in his hands. He was bleeding quite heavily. The blood ran from his hand down the length of his forearm, dripping onto the floor.

She approached cautiously. The Fox she knew would never hurt her but he was not the same person she remembered. "Fox?" she whispered softly as she neared him.

His endless green eyes looked up and locked with hers. "We have to stop the bleeding. Where are your towels?" He stood up and swayed on his feet. Adalynne immediately encouraged him to sit back down. "Stay here, I'll get a towel. You're dripping blood everywhere." He looked down at his arm like he just noticed the red lines running down the length of it.

"Shit," he said, sitting back down on the sofa.

Adalynne quickly found a clean hand towel and brought it over to wrap around his arm. "Let me see. Please, Fox." He reluctantly surrendered his arm to her and she saw the gash that ran down the length of his hand. His breathing was heavy as he watched her examine his wound. She refused to look up into his intense eyes. "It needs a bandage. Do you have a first aid kit?"

"Yeah."

She could smell the liquor on his breath with him so close. "Are you drunk?"

"Yeah, but not enough for this." He leaned into her, his uninjured hand found her waist but she pulled away from his touch. The whole situation made her feel like she had a weight upon her chest.

"Stay here, I'll get a bandage," Adalynne ordered.

Adalynne walked into the stark white bathroom. White marble tiles covered the walls and led into a shower that was as large as the entire bathroom in her loft.

Adalynne opened the medicine cabinet to reveal rows and rows of prescription drugs. She picked one up and examined the bottle. She didn't recognize the name of the drug but she had a sickening feeling they were not legit. Finding the first aid kid under the sink, she made her way back to the living room where Fox sat on the sofa.

Adalynne took care to make sure the wound was cleaned and dressed properly. She wanted to ask about all the pills but she thought better of it. She didn't want to add anymore tension between them.

Fox was quiet. The only sound was the quiet

rhythm of his breathing. She could feel his eyes on her, the heat of his gaze as he studied her. She found it hard to be so close to him. To be touching him. It was impossible for her to ignore the feelings that stirred. Her heart and her head were at war with each other. She couldn't help but feel coming here was a horrible idea.

Chapter Twenty-One

Adalynne made the mistake of looking into his captivating gaze. "Do you think about the night at the camp?" he asked. He reached out and grazed the back of her hand with his. The sensation lingered.

"Don't ask me that." Adalynne stepped back from him.

"Why? You were the one that came here looking to dig up the past." Fox pushed himself off the sofa and walked into his large kitchen. Grabbing a prescription bottle off the counter, he flipped the cover off and tipped the pills up to his mouth. He proceeded to chase the pills with a large swig of whiskey that sat opened on his counter. The kitchen was beautiful except for the countless bottles of liquor and take out containers that littered the counters.

"Are you sure you should be drinking and taking pills at the same time?" Adalynne was uneasy with his behavior.

"My hand hurts." He tipped the whiskey up to his mouth and took a long draw. He set the bottle

232

down and walked closer to her. "What if I told you that I have been thinking of fucking you since you showed up at my door, especially after your buttons came undone?" He reached up and flicked her shirt to reveal that the top few buttons of her blouse had come undone, showing a little more skin than was appropriate.

"Oh my god!" Adalynne quickly re-buttoned her shirt. There was no way to escape the heat flooding through her veins. Adalynne was overwhelmed with the mixed signals Fox was giving her. "Sorry to break it to you, but I'm not one of your groupies you can use whenever you like."

Fox walked back into the kitchen and grabbed the bottle of pills.

"I think you took enough pills, Fox." Adalynne stormed into the kitchen and tried to take the bottle from him but he held them up over her head. "Stop it! Give me the pills before you kill yourself."

Fox grinned as she made an attempt to reach for the container he shook high over her head. He was so much taller than her. He laughed as he tormented her until it died on his lips and his eyes darkened. His nearness suddenly made her world spin.

Adalynne stepped away from him, pulling a much needed breath into her lungs to clear her head. "Stop it, Fox. This is not a game! Why are you taking so many pills?"

"I want to feel numb." He set the bottle down on the counter and picked up the whiskey.

"How many did you take?" Adalynne grabbed the bottle and counted the remaining pills, though it did little good because she didn't know how many were originally there.

"You worry too much." He waved his hand dismissively.

"And you don't worry enough. Look here…" She held the bottle up for him to see. "Do not ingest alcohol while taking this medication."

"I can't see that, it's all blurry."

"That's because you're drunk." Adalynne shook her head with a sigh. "Why do you even have pain medication anyway?"

"Because everything fucking hurts all the fucking time." Fox moved to tip the whiskey to his mouth again but Adalynne grabbed the bottle.

"You've had enough. Let's get you to bed so you can sleep this off."

Fox staggered as he walked. "Those pills are the shit." He laughed. Adalynne followed behind him to make sure he made it to his room. When he neared the doorway, he leaned against the wall.

"Fox? Are you okay?" She walked up beside him to check on him. He reached over and slid his hand around her waist, then pulled her tight against his body. It was hard to think when she was surrounded by his scent. Her body reacted to his touch. Her heart raced loud enough she feared he could hear it.

"I miss you, Bee," he breathed against her ear. He moved her so she was back against the wall and he placed his leg between hers, pinning her in place. His lips came down to claim hers. It took her a moment to regain her senses. This is exactly what she had thought about every night since they were together.

"We can't do this." Adalynne pushed away from

him.

"Why? Is Matthew the only one allowed inside you now?" He words were pained, almost angry when he spoke.

Adalynne narrowed her eyes. "I have to go." Adalynne backed away.

"Does he touch you like I did? I need to know. No, I don't want to. *Fuck*!" He screamed out, frustrated. He leaned his head against the wall, a pained expression on his face. She couldn't tell if he was mad at her or at himself.

"I should go. It was a mistake to come here." Things used to be so simple when they were young. She was happy just loving him, nothing else mattered.

"I thought you came here for a reason to not marry that shit head. I'm giving you one! Come to bed with me and I'll make you forget him." Fox backed up toward his bed.

"You have a girlfriend, Fox." Adalynne set her jaw.

"You have a fiancé but that didn't stop you from coming here."

The emotion poured into her words. "I didn't come here crawl into your bed, Fox!" She found herself yelling at him before she realized what she was doing. "I came because..."

"What?" he slurred. "If you're looking for more than just a good fuck, then you're in the wrong fucking place. I have nothing else to give you. I have nothing!" There was a storm brewing fierce behind his haunted eyes. "I never had anything to offer you."

235

"I never asked for anything. I just wanted you."

"Don't you see that there was never a chance for me and you? You are the only one that can't see that." His words cut so deep, she felt like she was bleeding out upon the floor. All the feelings she held so close, so deep, seeped from her with the realization that he could never love her the way she needed him to. Her Fox was never hers to love.

"Goodbye, Fox." Adalynne took a deep, shaky breath. This version of him terrified her beyond words. She didn't know what she expected to find when she dropped in on him. She didn't understand this side of him. He was cold and broken.

"Do me a favor and stay away next time!" Adalynne watched him collapse on his bed, throwing his arms over his face. She backed out of his room, walking straight into the kitchen to dump the whiskey and pills down the garbage disposal. Most of the other bottles were empty, so she left them alone before walking out the door.

***

When Adalynne climbed into her car and shut the door, she let the tears fall freely until she had none left to shed. Her insides twisted painfully as she concentrated on taking deep, even breaths. When she finally collected herself, she grabbed her purse to powder her nose and reapply some gloss. She couldn't walk back into reality looking like an emotional disaster. She looked at the clock and realized that she had been gone for a few hours. There was no way her absence didn't go unnoticed.

Grabbing her phone, she noticed multiple missed calls and texts.

Katie left a text informing her that she had gone back to her apartment because things got a little intense when her mother discovered Adalynne ran out on her engagement party. There was a string of irate messages from her mother, which Adalynne erased without listening to. Matthew's message made her feel the most guilt. He was upset that she ran off without telling him and rightfully so.

Instead of calling Matthew back, she drove toward his place. He had recently gotten an apartment about half an hour away from hers. It was a close daily commute to his new position in the heart of the city. She felt numb since her encounter with Fox. An eerie quiet settled over her once she shed all her tears. The only thing she could think of was fixing what was within her control. He deserved an apology and it was something she wanted to do face to face.

***

Adalynne ran her hands over her hair, sorting out the blonde tendrils and straightening her clothes before she knocked on Matthew's door. She waited for a moment, wondering if it was a mistake to assume he went home after the party. She knocked again before pulling out her phone. She had begun texting a message when the door swung open in front of her.

Adalynne looked up to see Matthew's wide-eyed expression at her arrival. "Where did you go?" It was the first time that his temper was ever truly directed toward her.

"I'm sorry. It was a little overwhelming there. I just needed to get some air."

"Get some *air*? You missed the entire fucking thing. How do you think that made me look, having my fiancée run out on our engagement party?"

"I'm sorry, Matthew. I don't know what got into me, but I am here to apologize and make it up to you." She bit her lip and put on the most innocent face she could manage.

"I think you should go." He remained unamused by her attempt to win him over. She stepped closer to him. He tried to move to prevent her from entering his apartment but she slipped by. "Adalynne, this isn't funny."

Adalynne began to unbutton her shirt slowly as she looked up at him. He grew quiet as a conflicted expression took over his handsome face.

"I told you I wanted to make it up to you," she teased as she let her blouse fall down her arms and puddle to the floor.

"Adalynne, you should go. This isn't a good time." He looked nervous standing before her, his eyes shamelessly watched as she continued to remove her clothes. Her skirt was quick to follow as she slowly pushed it off her hips and down the length of her legs. "Adalynne, please…"

"Shhh…" Adalynne cut off his words. Adalynne slid her hand over her flat stomach and dipped her fingers under the waist of her lace panties. "Do you want this?"

"Adalynne, listen to me." He stepped closer to

her but she evaded him and ran off toward his room. "*Adalynne!*" His words were full of anger again, giving chase to her.

Adalynne spun around and watched him grab for her as she approached his bedroom door. "What's the matter, Matt? Don't you want me?" Her playful mood suddenly died away when she saw actual fear in his eyes.

"The *matter* is that it's now a little too crowded in here." Adalynne turned to see Tracy in Matthew's bed, dressed only in red lace underwear. Tracy was reclined against his headboard, seemingly satisfied with the recent development as a sly smile crawled over her face.

"Still a heartless bitch, I see, Tracy," Adalynne spat angrily.

Tracy only chuckled evilly as she raked her eyes over Adalynne's naked body. In Adalynne's shock she forgot that she was naked. She wrapped her arms around her, trying to cover what she could.

"*Shit!*" Matthew raked his hands down his face. "Adalynne, when you disappeared, I was fucking mad at you. I wasn't thinking, Addie. I mean, fuck, you love that fucking Music House more than me. What do you expect?" Matthew pulled his hair in frustration.

"That is your *defense*? For a promising lawyer, you're an idiot." Adalynne said sharply.

"Addie please…it didn't mean anything. I'm sorry," Matthew begged.

"I need to leave." Adalynne pushed past him, he grabbed for her hand but she retracted it quickly, not wanting to touch him. Grabbing for her discarded clothes, she began hastily pulling them back on. "Oh, this is yours." She pulled her ring off and held it out to him.

"I'm not taking it back. Don't do this, Addie." His tone became desperate. "It didn't mean anything with her."

"I don't love you, Matt." She stepped forward and pressed it into his hand.

"You don't mean that." He grabbed her hand. His eyes looked completely gray as they pleaded with her.

"Yes, I do." Adalynne pulled her hand from his grasp and walked out the door. She drove back to her apartment in a daze, unable to process the entire disaster of a day that poured relentlessly down upon her. She made a note to never drop in on someone again. She felt like two very important chapters of her life were suddenly ripped away and she was left with a hole she didn't know how to fill.

When Adalynne walked into her apartment, Katie was waiting for her, completely beside herself with worry. Adalynne closed the door behind her and slid down to the floor.

"What the hell happened? By the look on your face, it's something huge!" Katie collapsed on her knees in front of Adalynne, wrapping her arms tightly around her. Adalynne told her what happened with Matthew. The words just flowed out of her as if it were someone else talking. When her words died away, they both sat in silence.

"Holy shit!" Katie breathed as she lay sprawled out on the floor in front of Adalynne. They were both letting everything sink in.

"What am I doing?" Adalynne sat up suddenly. "We need to celebrate."

"Celebrate?" Katie was confused by the sudden change in Adalynne's mood. "What happened with Damon?"

"Nothing happened. I don't know why I expected anything else. I don't want to talk about that right now." Adalynne pulled herself up off the floor, bringing Katie with her. "We need to celebrate two very important things. First, my best friend is having a baby! Second, I might have avoided a disaster of a marriage that I wasn't ready for. Are those not good reasons to celebrate?"

Katie turned some music up as loud as they could get away with and the two of them decided to bake a cake. Adalynne was so grateful Katie was with her. They laughed and danced as they worked together in the kitchen to create their masterpiece, a vanilla cake with chocolate fudge icing. On the top Adalynne wrote "To Baby and Freedom!" in white icing.

"Somehow those two things don't seem to go together." Katie looked at the cake. "We might be the first to celebrate these two things simultaneously." she laughed.

"Very true!" Adalynne passed Katie a fork and they indulged in their creation, eating until they felt sick to their stomachs.

"You were right. Celebrating is *so* much better than being sad," Katie mumbled between bites. The girls stayed up late laughing and talking. It was just like when they lived together, when distance did not separate them. Whenever they got together it was as if all the time that they had been apart did not affect them.

***

The next day her mother requested Adalynne meet her for lunch. Katie had offered to join her, if it would make it more bearable. As much as Adalynne would have liked to have her company, she knew Katie was anxious to head back to school to work on some papers that were due the next day. A feeling of dread closed in around her with the thought of confronting her. Adalynne only wished she had more time before she had to deal with her mother's wrath.

Her mother chose the golf and country club for the location of their meeting. It had been her father's favorite place for Sunday brunch. They came here together on occasion but that felt like a lifetime ago. Memories of her father washed over her as she walked into the familiar building. The interior was exactly the same, white tablecloths, perfectly set tables with dainty tea cups sitting upon each table.

Adalynne spotted her mother across the room, sipping her tea with her attention on the pages of a magazine. Adalynne thought of turning around and walking out—unfortunately her mother looked up, as if reading her thoughts. She sat back in her chair, the magazine forgotten as she watched Adalynne approach.

Adalynne took a deep breath that smelled of the fresh flowers from the beautifully displayed vases upon the tables. The country club always provided a beautiful atmosphere but today Adalynne could not appreciate any of the finer details because the conversation that awaited her only filled her with dread.

"Hello, Mother." Adalynne managed her best smile as she came to stand before her mother. Her mother stood and gave her a hug that was too stiff for the mood she was trying to exude to the people around them.

"Adalynne," she said. "Please, have a seat." Her mother waved the waiter over to pour Adalynne her tea before she engaged in conversation. "I was not impressed with your rude and untimely exit from your engagement party. Then this morning, I receive an urgent call from Mrs. Murphy stating that her son was devastated that you called off the marriage. Care to shed some light on your behavior as of late?" To anyone around them it would appear her mother was talking about something lovely, the way she maintained her poised demeanor as she spoke. No one would suspect the anger that lurked beneath.

"I can't marry him, Mother," Adalynne confessed, leaning back against her chair.

"Do you know how embarrassing it was to explain to your guests that you ran out on your own engagement party?" her mother continued. "Do you know how much damage control I've had to deal with?"

"It was *your* party and they were *your* guests. *I* tried to tell you not to have the party, remember?" Adalynne was not as gifted as her mother at containing her emotions. It was a trait she was glad she did not possess. She could feel her anger boiling under the surface of her skin and she liked to release the steam.

"It's just cold feet, darling." Her mother waved her hand dismissively.

"Matthew slept with Tracy Gibbons. It's not cold feet, Mother. It's over." Adalynne tried to keep her tone low.

"Listen, Adalynne, I didn't love your father when we first got married. In fact, your father had a brief affair at the beginning of our marriage. I forgave him and before we knew it you were in our lives and we never looked back. Love is never instant. It takes time and work to love someone."

Adalynne could not help the shock that overcame her from her mother's admission. "What?"

"Just take some time…" her mother started.

"Dad never had an affair," Adalynne denied.

Her mother shrugged her shoulders. "He might as well have. The first few years of our marriage were hardly joyous. It wasn't until I became pregnant with you that things changed. It was like he saw me for the first time." It was the first hint of an actual smile on her mother's lips since she arrived. "Matthew will take care of you. This is how your life is supposed to be. Your father would want this," her mother continued.

"No, he wouldn't have. Dad told me himself that he wants me to be happy. Why can't you just let me decide what is best for me? I cannot live my life for you," Adalynne argued.

"Take some time. Think about what you're doing

before you do something rash," her mother almost pleaded with Adalynne. She reached across the table to touch her hand but Adalynne pulled away from the contact.

"I am not going to marry someone with the hope that one day they decide to love me or I them. I am not *you*, Mother!" Adalynne spoke in a harsh whisper before she stood up from her seat, disturbing the table slightly and spilling the tea from their cups.

"No, you are not," she replied weakly, staring at her tea that had spilled over the side and pooled in the saucer. Adalynne turned on her heel, giving her mother a quick goodbye as she left her sitting alone in a room full of people watching them. Her mother's plan to avoid a scene backfired.

Adalynne knew she didn't want to spend her life waiting to fall in love with someone anymore. She couldn't marry Matthew and hope that one day her feelings would change and become something more. The kind of love she wanted was the kind full of passion, the instant connection that made her unable to deny its lure. The kind of attraction that made every part of her body crave his touch, his love, and his nearness. She knew exactly what she wanted because she had experienced it. Fox was her true love, the only love her heart wanted.

Adalynne was prepared to spend the rest of her days alone because she didn't want to settle for something less than what she had the joy of knowing, even if it was just for a brief moment in time. The love she experienced was beautiful while it lasted. The only problem was that it burned too bright and faded too quickly. She thought maybe she secretly loved misery and that was why she subjected herself to a love she couldn't hold onto.

Chapter Twenty-Two

"Vegas?" Adalynne asked, surprised.

"Yes, can you believe it?" Katie screamed excitedly in the phone. Adalynne had to hold the phone away from her ear. "Steven wants to make it official. It will be too hard to plan a traditional wedding with Steven finishing his last year, and he wants to be married before the baby comes. What's more romantic than running off to Vegas to get married?"

"Did you tell your parents about the baby yet?" Adalynne asked curiously.

"No. We figured why not get married first and then break the news all at once. It will be like ripping off a Band-Aid. Steven is convinced his mother will insist on having a say in everything once we break the news. He wants us to do it our way first and then if his mom demands a traditional wedding with all the fluff we can appease her later. You know I couldn't care less about the whole ritual of it all. We just want to be together..." Katie's voice trailed off dreamily.

Adalynne smiled. It had been two months since she found out about the baby. "You know that if you don't tell them soon they will figure it out for themselves when you start to show, right?"

"That's why we're going to Vegas this weekend," Katie confessed.

"Oh wow...this weekend? Okay..." Adalynne tried to sort through her memory about what her schedule held for this coming weekend.

"I know it's not much notice, but I need you, Addie," Katie whined on the phone. "Pretty please?"

"I can make it work," Adalynne promised.

"Yay! Thank you! I can't have a wedding without my best girl with me. There is one more thing though," Katie said guiltily. "I feel really bad about this but Steven wants his best man to be there for him...I'm sorry, Adalynne, but Steven and Matthew have been friends forever and..."

"Don't worry about it. It's your day and I'm not even concerned about it. Besides, we're good now," Adalynne lied. She hadn't spoken to Matthew since a few difficult phone calls after she had called off their engagement.

"*Riiight*. You're such a liar, but thanks for understanding."

"For you, I would do anything," Adalynne assured her.

Since Adalynne had decided not to marry Matthew, things seemed a lot more comfortable between her and John, which Adalynne knew was due to the fact she no longer felt guilty around him. John never really talked about it and she was grateful. She hadn't seen her mother much since their lunch together. They had spoken briefly on the phone on a few occasions but Adalynne always had an excuse not to visit her mother. She knew what to expect if she did and she didn't want to entertain anything her mother had to say.

Elizabeth thought it was exciting Adalynne was going to Vegas even when she told her that Matthew was going to be there. She thought Adalynne worked too hard for someone her age and she was always after Adalynne to enjoy her youth. Elizabeth insisted they would survive the weekend at the Music House without her.

As much as Adalynne was excited for Katie and Steven, she dreaded spending time with Matthew. She knew it was going to be awkward if they had to spend time in each other's company after how their relationship unraveled. Adalynne tried not to dwell on those worries because nothing would keep her from Katie's side as she got married. She was prepared to deal with whatever came her way.

***

Adalynne drove the two hour drive that Friday morning to meet Katie, Steven, and Matthew at the airport. She didn't want to miss a moment of the trip with Katie. The discomfort she expected being in Matthew's company was not what she anticipated. Matthew was on his best behavior and did not discuss anything personal between the two of them. Adalynne suspected Katie had warned him not to cross that bridge on this occasion and he was being respectful of her wishes. It allowed Adalynne to completely relax and immerse herself in the wonderful occasion that brought them all together.

Adalynne even found herself wholly enjoying Matthew's company. They had a wonderful conversation that had them both laughing and carrying on with Katie and Steven. Adalynne was grateful they could fall back into easy graces with one another. There were moments when it felt like nothing difficult had happened between the two of them. Adalynne didn't hold a grudge against Matthew. She never really gave herself to him like she should have when they entered a relationship together, so she figured they were even. Although she was cautious not to get too comfortable around him as to not give him the wrong impression, it didn't matter how much they got along, it didn't mean she regretted her decision.

Katie and Steven's excitement was contagious and Adalynne was looking forward to spending the weekend with them. The first night Adalynne and Katie were spending alone, shopping for dresses for the ceremony that would take place the next night. Matthew and Steven had their own plans for the night. They did not divulge any details to the ladies, insisting it was top secret. It would only technically be one night she would be in Matthew's company anyway, and seeing how easy their flight had been, it seemed silly that she worried so much about it.

"How about this one?" Katie spun around in front of a full length mirror. Katie had yet to start showing in her pregnancy, making the dress selecting mission much easier. They did not have to limit the options to maternity styles. The girls wanted to go to every dress store they could find and were having a wonderful time trying on all the options that caught Katie's eye. Katie's only stipulation for her dress was that she wanted it to be the traditional white.

Katie tried everything on from long sleeve, full length gowns to dresses that were barely enough material to be considered a dress. Katie found herself leaning to the more elegant, simple styles.

Adalynne looked at the latest dress Katie put on. After what seemed like hundreds, this one stood out above all the rest. It was fitted and fell just above the knee in a sleek, form-fitting shape. It was strapless but had a sophisticated neck line. It was gorgeous and Katie was absolutely stunning.

"I think we found the one," Adalynne said excitedly. "Steven is gonna want to get you pregnant all over again."

"He can try." Katie winked. "You're right, I love this dress." Katie admired herself in the mirror. "It's hard to believe there's a little baby in here." She placed her hand on her stomach.

"You'll know it soon when your belly gets bigger," Adalynne teased.

Adalynne decided on a simple pale blue wrap dress with a subtle pattern embossed on the fabric. The details on the fabric were beautiful but only could be appreciated upon close inspection. The simple lines of her dress were complementary to Katie's. They both had a very classic style. As soon as Adalynne stepped out of the changing room, Katie insisted that it be her choice. The soft white of

Katie's dress looked beautiful next to the refreshing blue. Once they found the perfect accessories for their attire and Katie found the perfect heels that made her legs look irresistible, the girls headed out for a late dinner.

"What do you think the guys are up to?" Katie asked thoughtfully.

"Nervous?" Adalynne asked.

"Never, those strippers have nothing on me." Katie smiled mischievously.

"Very true." Adalynne laughed.

"Oh shit!" Katie blurted, suddenly acting strange. "Um...are you excited for pampering tomorrow morning?" Katie tried to distract Adalynne, grabbing Adalynne's hands she pulled her around to face her.

"What are you doing?" Adalynne asked, suspicious of Katie's behavior. Adalynne looked over her shoulder. Behind Katie was a poster for Outcome with concert dates that ran their stay. "Fox is here?" Adalynne said in disbelief. Fate would not let her live down her failed attempts at love.

"I tried to protect you," Katie offered sadly.

"This city is huge. What are the chances that we would even run into each other, anyway?" Adalynne tried to be optimistic.

"Exactly," Katie agreed. "God, he is gorgeous." Katie admired the poster.

"You're not helping." Adalynne sighed.

"I know, I'm sorry. It's just he is extremely hot and it was just an observation. I mean look at the poster—it has lipstick marks all over confirming that." Katie justified her comment.

"I need a drink." Adalynne sighed.

"Have one for me too," Katie suggested playfully. "After all, it is my last night as an unmarried woman."

Katie and Adalynne found a nice restaurant and spent the rest of the evening sharing drinks, non-alcoholic for Katie of course, and laughs. They decided they wouldn't make it a late night because Katie was getting tired and she didn't want to have circles under her eyes for the pictures tomorrow. "I can't believe I ran off to get married. My mother is going to freak."

"Especially when you tell her you got married because you got knocked up," Adalynne teased.

"So true." Katie laughed. "At least I know my parents will come around. Not so sure how Steven's parents are going to react. They're more of the stick in the mud types. Nice enough but they might not like me so much after we break the news."

"They will do nothing but love you, I'm sure. What's not to love? You're absolutely adorable." Adalynne squeezed Katie's cheek jokingly.

***

Once they returned to the hotel Katie spent the night in Adalynne's room watching movies until they both fell asleep. The girls had a full schedule of pampering the next day. They filled their morning with relaxation, starting with a manicure, then a pedicure, and finally a massage in the hotel's spa before they went back to their room to order room service for lunch. "Do you think the guys are up yet?" Adalynne asked curiously when Katie checked her phone repeatedly since they had gotten back to the room.

"I hope they survived last night. We are in Vegas and there's lots of trouble to be had." Katie looked at her nervously.

"Do you want me to go check? He probably has his phone turned off if they were trying to sleep in," Adalynne offered.

"That would be great." Katie brightened. "Tell him if he's hungover for our wedding I'll kill him," she added with an evil smile. Adalynne laughed on her way out of the door. They guys' room was next door to theirs and when Katie knocked, she heard a muffled response from within. A moment later the door opened to reveal their dark room. The suite smelled of stale beer and Adalynne couldn't help but wrinkle her nose.

"Wow, you must have had fun last night," she stated, looking at Steven, whose bloodshot eyes and half-closed lids told all his secrets.

"Fuck yeah, but now I feel like shit on a stick. Katie okay?" he mumbled.

"Of course, she wanted me to tell you if you're hungover, you're in trouble. So I guess I'll let you sleep it off." Adalynne turned to leave.

"Tell her I was a good boy last night even when Matthew tried to convince me otherwise." Steven smiled, rubbing his head.

She heard a moan of protest in the dark room. Apparently Matthew made it back as well.

"I'll tell her. Just don't be late," Adalynne warned.

"Never." He smiled and disappeared back into the room.

In the afternoon Adalynne and Katie returned to the spa for hair and makeup before they came back to their room to dress. The girls were planning on arriving at the service just before it started. Katie didn't want Steven to see her until she walked toward him to take their vows.

"Are you nervous?" Adalynne asked as they walked toward the doors to the small chapel that was the embodiment of a Vegas wedding.

"Hell yes," Katie answered quickly, taking a deep breath. She squeezed Adalynne's arm tightly as they pushed through the doors. Steven and Matthew were standing at the altar with the justice of the peace. They were both dressed in black suits with silver ties and shirts. They did not show the distressed hungover condition that Adalynne had found them in earlier that afternoon. Both were handsome and well-groomed as they turned to acknowledge the girls' entrance with huge smiles on their faces. The justice of the peace was a middle aged man with thin and greying hair. He was stout and short compared to Steven and Matthew who both towered over him. He wore a grey tweed suit with a white shirt and black tie. A woman began playing the organ when the girls entered. Adalynne smiled as she looked around at the over-the-top decorations of fake flowers and endless length of tulle bunched on every available surface.

As Adalynne watched Katie and Steven exchange their vows she couldn't help but admire the affection in their eyes. Nothing else mattered as they made a promise to love each other for the rest of their lives. It was a moment that Adalynne was grateful she had witnessed. It didn't matter to them that they were surrounded by fake flowers and dated wallpaper. This was the beginning of their lives together and it was beautiful. Adalynne couldn't ease the smile on her face as she stood in support of her friend's devotion.

Adalynne noticed Matthew staring at her. She wondered if he was thinking about the wedding they would never share. She pushed those thoughts from her mind and brought her focus back to Katie and Steven who kissed each other passionately as they officially became man and wife.

They posed for pictures and had a good laugh at how quickly things got out of hand. The night was beautiful as they made their way to dinner and then drinks afterwards, with the exception of Katie. They all made it a point to take pictures throughout the evening to capture every moment.

Everywhere they went they were surrounded by people having a good time and it was contagious. Katie was over the moon with the excitement of her wedding night and they danced until the early hours of the morning. They had requested Katie and Steven's song at one of the bars and they obliged, allowing Adalynne to get some beautiful photographs of their first dance as a married couple. The night was magical for them as they hummed with the energy of the city that never sleeps.

"I think I am going to take my wife back to our room now. I need to make sure she still has energy for our private dance." Steven winked at Katie.

"What? Do you think this is our wedding night or something?" Katie teased.

"I can't wait to get that dress off you." Steven wrapped his arm around Katie, causing her to giggle excitedly. "You can keep the shoes on though."

"Adalynne, do you want to hit up the casino?" Matthew asked with a hopeful look upon his face.

"No. I'm not much of a gambler. I think I am going to head back to my room too." Adalynne had a good time tonight with Matthew. They had gotten along very well the entire evening but she didn't want to be alone with him. When they were in Katie and Steven's company he was keeping a respectful distance but she could tell by the looks he had given her during the progression of the evening that things might become awkward if they were left on their own.

"Yeah, you're right, it's late. I'll head back with you guys." Matthew shrugged his shoulders. Adalynne could see the disappointment in his eyes.

They walked through the busy street and Adalynne could not get over how many people still filled the streets at the late hour. The city still pulsed with life and had a way of drawing you into the excitement. It was a seductive escape from the rest of the world and Adalynne thought the atmosphere was perfect for Katie and Steven, who thrived on the pleasures of life.

Adalynne watched the people enter and exit the bars along the strip, a constant flow of people. Adalynne's eyes were drawn to a black limo that pulled up in front of an elite looking bar with a long line stretching down the street. A few screams erupted from the line as someone exited the bar. Adalynne watched the tall, handsome Fox saunter out of the bar. The sight caused her to stop in her tracks. He was flanked by two bleached blondes, barely dressed. They had so much skin exposed it was hard not to stare at them.

The familiar pull tugged at her heart when she looked at him. Even after their last encounter and the words he said to her it did nothing to lessen her need for him. In fact, it felt stronger than ever. She wanted to run away from him and into his arms at the same time. All the drinks she consumed over the course of the evening affected her composure, normally she would be more aware of her actions but she could only openly stare at the man who owned her heart, knowing there was nothing she could do about it. She felt Katie's hand on her shoulder. "Fox." The word left her lips dreamily.

"Fox? Isn't that the guy from the Outcome band? Do you know him?" Matthew asked.

Adalynne was so lost in the memories her drunken mind forced her to revisit, she hadn't noticed Fox noticed her too. They only looked at each other as if the world around them faded away and they were the only two people left. Flashes were going off all around Fox, as people were taking pictures, screaming out to him in adoration. Adalynne shook her mind clear and looked at the surrounding fans all gathering. She wondered if Fox only saw her now as just another fan who desperately clung to the hope that he would acknowledge her. Adalynne wanted to know what he thought when he looked at her.

Adalynne watched the girls at his side become increasingly annoyed from his wavering attention. They wanted Brolan Pierce all to themselves. He had become so famous that people begged for his notice. He had never felt so far away, even as he stood looking back at her. He might as well have been on the other side of the world.

Adalynne stepped back out of view. She couldn't look at him any longer without doing something she would regret. "Fate is the cruelest thing in the world," Adalynne mumbled as Katie's concerned expression met hers.

"I thought I imagined something going on between you two at the concert we went to and now I know. There is no way to deny you two know each other. I saw the way he looked at you. What the fuck, Adalynne?"

Adalynne didn't respond as she started to walk away. "Did you fuck *him*?" Matthew raised his voice to an uncomfortable level. Onlookers turned their heads.

"Matthew, please!" Katie scolded. "She doesn't need to answer to you. Let's go." Katie grabbed Adalynne's arm. She looked back and noticed Fox climbing into his waiting car. Adalynne turned her focus on Katie, who led her across the street and headed toward their hotel. She could tell that Matthew stayed close on her heels. She could feel his hot stare on her back as she walked.

After Adalynne said goodnight to Katie and assured her she was fine, insisting they go enjoy their night, she collapsed on her bed. When they had arrived at their rooms, Matthew was no longer behind her. She was grateful he didn't ask any more questions. Adalynne kicked off her shoes with a sigh, looking up at the white ceiling overhead. A knock on Adalynne's door caused her to complain as she dragged herself up off the bed. "Katie, I told you I'm fine." She opened the door to see Matthew standing in front of her.

"What, Matthew? It's really late and I'm tired." Adalynne took a deep breath. All she wanted to do was crawl into bed and sleep off the liquor that still made her head spin.

"I'm sorry for earlier. Can I come in?" Matthew pleaded. His hair was disheveled and he did look genuinely regretful.

"It's fine. I'm just going to go to sleep. Can we talk about it tomorrow?" Adalynne sighed.

"It will just be a moment." They both turned to see a group of people stumble down the hallway as they noisily returned to their rooms.

"Fine, but just a second." Adalynne warned.

Matthew walked in behind her as she led him into her room. When she turned around Matthew was closer than she expected, taking her by surprise. He leaned down to kiss her before she could even register his next move. Adalynne protested against his lips. "Matthew, this is not what I meant when I let you in," she gasped.

"Addie please, I can't think of anything else," Matthew said, pushing her back toward the bed. Adalynne couldn't help but fall back when the bed pressed against the back of her legs. He pinned her on the bed and looked down at her.

"I don't want this. Please stop," Adalynne

pleaded.

"I messed up, Addie, but I can make it up to you. We were good together."

"I'm in love with someone else." Adalynne knew it was not the time to make the confession when she was in a vulnerable position. She could not think clearly as the words escaped from her thoughts. "I have always been in love with someone else. It would never have worked between us."

"Who? The Outcome guy?" Matthew breathed angrily. "He doesn't look like he feels the same about you from what I could see. He's probably fucking those girls right now," Matthew said cruelly. Adalynne pushed Matthew's chest but he wouldn't move. "Just give us a chance."

Matthew smothered her mouth with his and his hands greedily sought out her flesh as he pulled at her dress. "Please Addie. I need you."

Adalynne's struggles became more frantic as she felt the material of her dress rip. "Get off, Matthew!" She managed to get her knee to connect with his groin. It was enough to alleviate his hold on her. Adalynne rolled off the bed. "Get out now!" Adalynne pointed a shaky finger towards the door.

Matthew keeled over from the pain of impact. "Fuck that hurt! Addie listen, I'm sorry. I don't know what got into me. I drank too much."

"Leave. Now."

Matthew stormed out of the room, slamming the door behind him. The tears started to fall as soon as the sound of the door clicked shut. Adalynne sat on her bed and reached for her phone. She couldn't call Katie so she called another number that she had always kept on her phone, unable to bring herself to erase it.

Chapter Twenty-Three

Adalynne called Fox. She only wanted to feel close to him for a moment. She wanted to be back in their camp when he would sing and play his guitar and she could pretend that all they needed was each other. It was doubtful he even had the same number now that so much time had passed. They lived in two different worlds now. Adalynne was surprised when his smooth voice answered. "Hello?"

Adalynne couldn't form words on her uncooperative tongue. "Bee? Are you okay?" All she could manage were quiet tears. "Where are you?" he asked.

"Is the Fox I know still in you somewhere because I really need him right now," she admitted.

"Where are you?"

Taking a deep breath, she whispered the name of the hotel and he was gone. "Fox?" Adalynne dropped her phone down and curled up on her bed. She wasn't sure how much time had passed before a knock on her door stirred her. She peered cautiously through the peep hole. Relief washed over her when Matthew did not come into view. Instead, her heart began to pulse wildly as she opened the door to Fox.

"I'm sorry," Adalynne apologized, opening the door. He looked more like a dream standing before her. He was impossibly beautiful with his vibrant eyes that practically glowed under his disheveled dark hair. He embodied the sexy image that sold his music like food to starving people. She was suddenly showered with guilt for pulling him back to her when he made it very clear it was not what he wanted. It was an act of instinct to reach out to him when she was upset. "I shouldn't have called you. It wasn't fair."

"To you or me?" Fox picked her up and held her against him, kicking the door closed behind him. She let her body melt into his as he walked them over to the bed. Lying her down gently, he moved to sit beside her. Adalynne wrapped her arm around his waist, pulling herself close against his chest and breathed in his comforting smell. She pressed her body into his as he rubbed her back. "What happened?" He ran his fingers gently over her cheek and then down to the rip in her dress. The bodice was torn, the material barely held onto the last remaining stitches.

"I don't want to talk about it right now," she whispered. "I just needed you. I just wanted to remember what this felt like."

"Did he hurt you?" Fox asked, leaning down to look into her eyes.

"No. He's just drunk and so am I," Adalynne

murmured into his shirt. He smelled so delicious her mouth watered.

Adalynne reached up and rubbed her hand gently over Fox's chest. His body felt hard and radiated a powerful energy. She listened to his heart beat respond to her caresses, it quickened until it matched her own elevated pace. She closed her eyes and imagined this was her place. She tried to pretend that she was the only one he held close, the one he loved.

A smile spread across her lips when he began to sing. It was what she used to do for him to make him feel better when they were younger. His voice was beautiful and flowed around her, sending a heat through her that took over her body. A need so strong it refused to be controlled by logic.

Adalynne sat up and looked into his endless eyes that she missed so profoundly. He was so far from the scared little boy that came into her life. He was a man, powerful, strong and she was a woman whose desires were personified by him in every sense. She straddled his waist, not taking her eyes from his. The words died away on his lips. His breathing became heavy as he looked back at her. She wanted to lose herself in this moment forever and never let him go again.

Adalynne's gaze dropped to his mouth and she leaned in closer, feeling his hands upon her back, drawing her in. Adalynne slowly pressed her lips against his, remembering their last kiss. Excitement flared to life and she demanded more. He met her kisses with the same heated urgency. Adalynne couldn't get close enough as she ran her hands over his body, her head swam and her body practically fell apart with the unfurling pleasures driving her. He sat up straighter, pulling his shirt up over his head. A smile broke across his beautiful face when Adalynne realized he had already unzipped her dress. He began pulling it down to expose her naked flesh. She matched his smile. Giving herself to him was the most natural thing in the world, her body craved it and her heart desired everything that was him. She could feel her skin tighten with anticipation of his touch.

Adalynne slid off the bed and let the dress fall to the floor. Fox sat up and came to stand tall before her, refusing to let space separate them. He pulled her up to meet his body, wrapping her legs around his waist. She was incapable of thinking of anything else while she let her body greedily enjoy him. His strength was rousing—he held her as if she weighed nothing. A moan of pleasure slipped from his lips as she rubbed her soft skin against his hard body. He was food to her starving desire as they indulged in the pleasures of each other. His entire body was hard except for his lips as they teased her mercilessly.

He laid her back on the bed, kissing her more gently as he gazed down at her. Adalynne trailed her fingers along his cheek and he turned into her hand to kiss it before leaning into her kiss her lips. He continued to savor her as he moved down her neck to the sensitive skin of her breasts before his mouth covered her taut nipple. Her body screamed out in excitement as his lips stirred pleasure wherever they touched. She wanted to stay in this moment forever, in the illusion of love between them. It wasn't fair that she could love someone so completely when he didn't share the same feelings. She was living half of a perfect love story that could never have its happy ending.

Adalynne lost herself in the beauty they shared, a wonderful dance flowing gracefully from one moment to the next. It couldn't have been more perfect if she had fantasized it. Even the affection expressed in his touch and his gaze seemed genuine. She could almost believe the depths of her love were reflected in him.

Adalynne's body thrummed with need, deep and intense as it pulled at her core. Her anticipation became unbearable until he finally slid deep inside her. She was primed to the point of release already from his slow sensual teasing. She came undone in his arms with only a few thrusts.

Fox wrapped his arms around her, holding her tight as he followed soon after. He spilled deep inside her and she felt all the tension melt from his body. He collapsed beside her and held her close. It was beautiful.

The next morning Adalynne awoke to find Fox still by her side, his arm thrown over her waist as she faced him. He was her favorite person in this world and she loved having him in her bed. His breathing was slow and steady as she watched his chest rise and fall. His skin begged to be touched, but fear of waking him caused her to remain perfectly still. She knew their time together was drawing to a close. Adalynne looked up at his face and noticed his eyes were open, watching her.

"Morning," Adalynne whispered.

"Morning," Fox said with a raspy voice

"I thought you would have changed your number by now since you're now a famous rock star."

"I do have a new number but I kept that one too, just in case." Fox smiled. "Did he hurt you last night?"

"He had too much to drink," Adalynne said thoughtfully. "It was just a misunderstanding."

"Don't excuse what he did," Fox said, taking her hand and bringing it to his lips.

"It was selfish of me to call you away from your life last night."

"It was selfish of me to come." It was torture as she felt his lips on her hand. It would be over soon, any moment he would come up with an excuse why they couldn't be together. She didn't know how much longer she would have him.

"I miss you…"

Fox placed his finger over her lips silencing her. "Don't," he whispered. They looked at each other in silence. Adalynne became lost in his sad eyes, wondering why fate pulled them so far apart.

Adalynne's phone rang, pulling her from her thoughts. "Hello? Kent?" Adalynne was surprised to see his number on her display. He was a guitar instructor at the Music House and although they spoke every day, he had never called her before. She listened as Kent told her about a fire last night at the Music House. Elizabeth had been taken to the hospital. Devastation settled over her.

"What's wrong, Bee?"

"I have to go." Adalynne started grabbing her

belongings and throwing them in her suitcase.

"What happened?" Fox grabbed her arm and pulled her toward him.

Adalynne looked up into his eyes. "There was a fire at the Music House. Elizabeth was taken to the hospital. I have to go."

"Is she going to be all right?"

"I don't know." Truthfully, she was unsure and didn't want to think about the possibilities. She needed to keep her emotions in check if she was going to hold herself together to make it home.

"Fox, I appreciate you coming over last night. It was a moment of weakness and I needed you but I'm not naïve enough to think this will change anything. I know how this works. I will save you from having to spell it out for me again."

"Bee?" He reached for her but Adalynne stepped back.

"I really have to go and you have a tour to get back to." Adalynne tried to keep her calm. She couldn't afford to get emotional right now. She needed to hold herself together until she got home and made sure Elizabeth was all right. His expression was defeated as he stepped back, letting her pass.

Adalynne packed quickly, throwing all her belongings in her bag. She dressed in a state of panic, unable to process simple thoughts as she threw on whatever clothes were sitting on top of her suitcase. When she came out of the bathroom Fox was already gone. She tried to keep her mind distracted from the news Kent had given her, trying not to process it until she got home and knew all the details.

Adalynne scribbled a note to Katie, sliding it under her door. Her plan was to take the next possible flight back home when she arrived at the airport. She felt bad leaving a vague note but she didn't want to alarm her on the morning after the wedding. She didn't want to ruin their bliss.

The journey home was surreal as Adalynne let numbness and denial settled over her. She turned on her iPod and let the music drown any thoughts that tried to enter her mind. She kept reminding herself that she needed to hold it together until she got home. When the plane finally landed, Adalynne called Kent to find out what hospital Elizabeth was in. Instead, of relinquishing the information, Kent insisted she meet him at the Music House. She could detect sorrow in his tone and it terrified her. She suspected the truth she would soon face.

During the drive Adalynne felt the tears overcome her on more than one occasion, having to pull over and allow herself time before resuming her drive. When she pulled up she could see his car there in front of the remains of the building. It was devastating to see the scorched remnants of the place Elizabeth and she had spent so much time trying to build up. A few vehicles were parked in the lot but Adalynne could not register who they were.

Adalynne stepped out of her car, her eyes finding his as Kent approached. His expression told her the truth before he even spoke. "She didn't make it, Addie."

Kent wrapped his arms around Adalynne as she

fell, catching her. "Elizabeth…" she cried. She wasn't sure how much time had passed as she held onto Kent. She let him console her as they stood in the parking lot, both completely devastated from the loss. Adalynne heard her name called by an unfamiliar male voice.

"Adalynne Fairweather?" She turned to see a police officer standing behind her.

"Yes." Adalynne wiped her eyes.

"Mrs. Elizabeth Martin had you listed as her next of kin. I need to talk to you about the details regarding her death."

"Can Kent come?" She clung to his arm, knowing he was the only reason she was still standing. It was strange how the dynamics of their relationship had changed dramatically under the circumstances. Kent was a guitarist who had worked on and off with the Music House. Until today Adalynne had never discussed anything with him other than work related topics but they both had a great appreciation for Elizabeth. Kent had been a former student of Elizabeth's and he was also inspired by her passion. Now, he was Adalynne's support in this tragedy.

The police officer told Adalynne they believed the cause of the fire was faulty wiring. An investigation was being conducted to confirm their suspicions. The fire spread quickly because of the age and condition of the building. They believed after Elizabeth had called to alert the authorities she did not exit the building. Instead, she tried to gather some personal belongings before ultimately surrendering to smoke inhalation.

Over the next few days Adalynne dealt with the raw emotion of the loss of her close friend. Unfortunately, it was not a feeling she was unfamiliar with. Old feelings were stirred and soon the grief felt suffocating. Adalynne felt she suffered more loss than one heart was capable of enduring in one lifetime.

By the time Adalynne had checked her phone that day, Katie had already left countless messages. She called Katie back as soon as she could manage. Like always, Katie was her emotional support. She stayed on the phone with her for hours, even when all Adalynne could do was cry.

Katie told Adalynne when Matthew met them to leave for the airport he was sporting a black eye and a fat lip he refused to talk about. He also refused to let Katie listen to Outcome on the drive home, saying that the lead singer was crazy. Adalynne didn't tell Katie, but she had her suspicions that Fox had paid Matthew a visit.

Adalynne called and told her mother what happened to Elizabeth but their relationship was still strained. Adalynne could not bring herself to face her mother. She needed time to deal with her loss in her own way. She spent most of her time over the days that followed at John's house. Being around John and Meredith made everything more bearable. Even though Fox was a topic they avoided, their hearts were both invested in him, giving them a bond.

John had not spoken with his son since he had left home before the end of high school. Adalynne knew Fox had sent money home regularly to his father but it had been their only contact in years.

Adalynne told John she had seen Fox in Vegas, telling him about the concerts, his fame, and success. She could see the pride in John's eyes. Although it pained him not be in his son's life, he was proud of what Fox achieved.

Adalynne avoided telling John anything that had happened between Fox and her, only the information that seemed important to pass on. He seemed grateful she had told him. Adalynne was proud of John for turning his life around, he was a completely different man now that he was learning to shake off the demons of his past.

John worked hard every day to get his life back in order, and Adalynne was proud of his success. She knew John had to be the one to decide when to reach out to his son. It was his decision alone when he felt ready.

The day of Elizabeth's funeral arrived before Adalynne was ready for it. Luckily, Elizabeth had prearranged all of her funeral arrangements leaving no guess work. A public ceremony was prepared so the community was able to show its respect for her. The church was packed with so many faces that frequented the Music House. It warmed Adalynne's heart to know even though Elizabeth did not have any blood relatives, the service was full of people that loved her.

Adalynne stood in front of the large crowd, looking at all the faces directed at her. She saw Katie and Steven smiling encouragingly. Molly and Brooke were sitting together close by. John and Meredith were sitting front and center. Everyone she knew would be there to show their respects to a wonderful woman. The only unexpected face among the crowd was her mother, who had seated herself next to John and Meredith. She didn't think her mother's presence would affect her as much as it did, especially since she had avoided her lately. Seeing her mother among her closest friends gave her the encouragement she needed to speak in front of the awaiting crowd. Her mother had come to show her support and in that moment she realized just how much she needed her.

"We are gathered here today to show our love for Elizabeth Martin. She was a beautiful woman with inspirational dreams she brought to life for the people of this community. It was her vision to bring music into the lives of the children and people who desired to learn the 'language of the soul,' as she used to refer to it." Adalynne paused to take a deep breath. Kent was at her side and he placed a comforting hand on her back. She looked up and met his eyes. He had become a reassuring presence in her grieving. They both shared a love for Elizabeth and now they had turned to each other in support. It was nice to be able to speak to someone who knew Elizabeth as closely as she did.

"I remember the first time I met Elizabeth. It was the day she purchased the Music House, it was just an abandoned building at the time but Elizabeth saw potential. She saw all the possibilities she could create through music. It was then, looking into her bigger than life heart, I was convinced I would do what was in my power to help her dream come to life. That was the way Elizabeth was, she inspired everyone. She inspired me to carry on her dream because it has become my own. I will rebuild the Music House in Elizabeth's name and continue to bring music into people's lives." Adalynne smiled through her tears as the crowd met her with smiles and applause. "She will never truly be gone because she will live on in the music that we create in her name."

Adalynne loved hearing everyone's stories of Elizabeth, some made her laugh and some made her cry, but they all made Elizabeth seem closer. Talking about her with all the people who loved her helped the healing process. So many of the people were delighted Adalynne was planning to rebuild the school, extending their gratitude and help should she need anything. Adalynne knew Elizabeth was loved but was still overwhelmed with how many people were touched by her.

"I've known Elizabeth for many years. She was one of the best. She spoke of you often. You said she was your inspiration but you should know that you were also hers. She loved you, Adalynne, and she would be so proud to know that you're going to rebuild the school and carry on."

"Thank you, Mrs. Steinberg, for your kind words." Adalynne smiled. Mrs. Steinberg was a tiny woman with gray hair she always pulled back into a bun on the base of her neck. She had stopped by on occasion to share a tea with Elizabeth. Elizabeth had told her they taught at the elementary school together years ago and remained friends.

Adalynne turned with a soft touch on her shoulder. "Mother." Adalynne smiled. Most of the guests had already left, leaving only small groups still sharing words.

"Do you have a moment?" She could tell her mother had been recently crying. Everyone was feeling the loss, even those who didn't know her well. Adalynne glanced over at Katie and Steven, who were waiting for her to join them for dinner before they returned home. Katie gave her an encouraging wave, letting Adalynne know they would give her a few minutes with her mother. Katie was aware of the tension that Adalynne had with her mother lately and was supportive of her mending the rift between them.

"Of course." Adalynne led her mother to sit in privacy.

"I haven't been as supportive as I should have been in your music career. I believed it was merely a temporary endeavor, something you would eventually grow tired of, but now I see I was wrong. I want you to let me be a part of your life." She took her hand and held it in hers.

"I would like that very much. I missed you, Mom." Adalynne wrapped her arms around her mother. "Thanks for coming."

"I missed you too. You have suffered too much for someone so young, losing your father and now your close friend. " She squeezed Adalynne tight. "I don't want to waste any more time on frivolous things. We need to be able to be a family, Addie. I want to be the mother you need. Your father left big shoes to fill and I need to start."

Chapter Twenty-Four

Over the next few months Adalynne focused on rebuilding the Music House. Adalynne received the money the insurance company issued, giving her the funds needed to initiate the plan. Elizabeth had also left her house to Adalynne.

Adalynne used the three bedroom house as a temporary music school to offer classes while the new school was being built. It was cramped and didn't allow them to resume all the classes they would have liked but they made do. None of the musicians complained, arriving every day to their cramped quarters. Adalynne appreciated everyone's optimism and patience. Once all the initial groundwork for the new school was laid and the construction could begin, Adalynne sought out John's help to give her guidance on how to begin the process. Even though John had removed himself from the construction industry years ago, he still had connections and was familiar with the methods.

John got in touch with a contractor he had been good friends with when he was younger. Luckily, he was eager to help with the project. Before long everything was coming together. Adalynne stood on the lot cleared of the debris from the fire and watched the beginning of the rebuilding process. Kent was by her side and they both smiled at the new beginning. They knew Elizabeth would be proud.

"We should go to dinner to celebrate." Kent nudged her shoulder.

"Sure, sounds great." Adalynne smiled. She hadn't thought much of her relationship with Kent at first, other than that they were there for each other in their time of need, but lately his subtle touches and comments told that his intent was not a platonic relationship. At first she chose to dismiss his advances as her imagination but now there was no denying his meaning as he wrapped his arm around her shoulder and left a kiss upon her forehead, leaving his lips to linger against her skin.

Since Adalynne lost Elizabeth, she needed someone to distract her from her pain and Kent became just that. She knew it was selfish of her to lead him on but she told herself that he needed her as much as she needed him. He was tall, fit, and he took care with his appearance. His hair was long and his rugged features gave him handsome charm, although Adalynne couldn't help the disappointment she always felt when she looked into his eyes and was not met with the beautiful sea of green that she loved so much. Kent had deep brown eyes and as handsome and amiable as he was, he was not Fox. She couldn't stop herself from making comparisons—a habit she was doomed to repeat.

Even though Adalynne wanted to run to Fox, she couldn't. It wasn't fair to either one of them. She began turning to Kent more and more. Their relationship began to shift in a new direction, one that promised intimacy. She knew going to dinner meant that they would be officially taking the next step; the truth hung in the air between them. After her failed attempt with Matthew she was in no rush to try again any time soon, even though she had physical needs she wanted to satisfy. Her body craved touch and affection. Adalynne wanted to feel desired and Kent seemed more than willing to comply. If she set the tone of their relationship as sexual in nature it might make it easier to walk away. She didn't want expectations or promises.

"Actually, why don't you come to my place." She smiled nervously at Kent. "No date, just two people looking to see what happens behind closed doors."

Kent's features lit up. "I can live with that."

"Seven?" she confirmed, hopping into her car to head to her classes. She was finishing out the spring semester. She would soon be freed up to commit herself to teaching classes full time during the summer months. She didn't know if it was wise to start something with Kent because they worked with each other but she was tired of thinking about every small detail. Being a little reckless seemed very appealing right now.

Katie and Steven had finally broken the news to their parents. Steven had been right when he assumed his parents would take the news with some difficulty but it didn't take too long for them to recover. Steven's mother insisted once the baby was born they have a proper wedding ceremony. Steven and Katie had anticipated his mother would insist and willingly accepted the request.

Adalynne laughed when Katie replayed how her mother shuffled through every possible emotion before she laughed through her tears and hugged Katie while she congratulated her. It was the first grandchild for both sets of parents, so excitement was bound to win over the initial shock of the news.

Katie called Adalynne every day on video chat so she could show Adalynne her growing belly and cute maternity clothes. Also, since Adalynne was not there she had to inform her of her morning sickness that wouldn't subside and how she couldn't get through the day without having a nap. Adalynne loved the detailed renderings of her days because Adalynne didn't feel so guilty missing out too much on Katie's life.

Their time together soon became just their daily video chats when Steven didn't want Katie traveling on her own while pregnant. His protectiveness had increased when Katie began showing. Adalynne was committed to her music lessons. They consumed her free time but they did not let it deter them. Their friendship was just as strong as ever. It was something Adalynne could always count on.

When Katie called her, screaming excitedly that Steven was taking a job offer close to where Adalynne lives, Adalynne couldn't help but scream back in the phone. Katie said Steven was tired of Katie sulking about not being about to see her.

When he was offered the job he decided to take it for his sanity. They were currently trying to find a place and make the move. Katie had finished out her year but was going to take some time off to have the baby and adjust to life as a mom while Steven began his career.

***

At 6:55 Adalynne's buzzer rang, indicating Kent had arrived. Adalynne had flipped back and forth between fearing she was making a big mistake, to wanting to throw caution to the wind. Eventually she pulled on her sexy black dress, committing herself to letting her wild side out for the evening. Adalynne pulled open the door to reveal Kent with a bouquet of flowers. He was dressed in a freshly pressed bold shirt that looked like a painting, putting the beautiful flowers to shame. Adalynne smiled to herself. The fact that he was an artist was written all over him.

"Too much?" he asked, looking down at his shirt.

"No, it's very you." She laughed. "I like it." Kent was definitely the thinking out side of the box type and had his own set of rules to live by. It was refreshing.

"I know it's not a date but it didn't feel right coming empty handed. And might I say that dress is sinful and I am suddenly very, very nervous." He stepped over the threshold, passing the flowers to Adalynne. His hands shook slightly affirming his statement.

"Thank you, they are beautiful."

"I really like your place." He looked around as Adalynne placed the flowers in a vase, setting them on the counter.

"Thanks." Adalynne bit her lip. She gave Kent a mischievous look and took his hand. "Let me show you around." She led him through her small apartment, ending in her bedroom, standing next to her bed. "And this is my bedroom." She motioned toward her bed. Kent swallowed exaggeratedly. She had never seen him so quiet before.

Adalynne didn't allow herself time to think her actions through. She knew she would talk herself out of what she had planned. Adalynne ran her hand along Kent's chest, feeling his racing heart under her touch. Bringing herself up on her toes, she gently caressed her lips to his, quickly deepening the kiss with Kent's insistence. It lacked excitement for Adalynne, she found herself just going through the motions. She tried to feed off his enthusiastic pace but she was unable to stir real passion of her own. Her reluctant mind refused to shut down and let the physical need drive her. She wanted to let go and let instinct take over. She hoped if the pressure of a relationship was off the table then somehow she could bring herself to enjoy the moment for what it was, to fill the void.

Adalynne pulled back and met his brown eyes. They hungrily returned her gaze but he was allowing her to take the lead. Adalynne pushed him back onto the bed and climbed on top of him. She was desperate to ignite some desire. She found Kent attractive but she could not get her body to heat with need. Adalynne slowly unbuttoned his shirt, leaving a trail of kisses down his chest. Kent's breathing became heavy as she teased him. Kent pulled the straps off her shoulders, revealing her black lacy bra. His hands roamed keenly over her body.

A knock at her door startled them both. Adalynne climbed off the bed quickly, righting her dress. "Don't answer it," Kent pleaded, leaning up on his elbows.

"I want to see who it is. Just a moment." She peeked through the door to see Fox standing on the other side.

"Who is it?" Kent asked, standing up from the bed, fixing his hair. The color drained from Adalynne's face. "Are you all right?" Kent's voice trailed off as she unlatched the lock.

Taking a deep breath, Adalynne swung the door open. Her heart felt like it fell to the floor as she was left shocked by his arrival. "Fox? What are you doing here? How did you get in the building?"

"I took a few pointers from you," he stated casually with a shrug. His eyes roamed her body. Her dress hugged her figure shamelessly with a plunging neckline that left little to the imagination. Adalynne's hands moved self-consciously to her hair under the heat of his gaze.

When Fox walked in the room, his eyes darted toward Kent, straightening his shirt. The air became very thick in the room as the realization of what had been taking place hit Fox. Adalynne tried not to wear a look of guilt. He had no claim over her. She was free to do as she pleased. Adalynne tried to regain her composure as Fox's eyes settled back on her.

"Kent...Damon." Adalynne awkwardly introduced them. Fox didn't respond when Kent held out his hand toward him. Fox's eyes followed Kent's other arm as he wrapped it around Adalynne's waist. The tension in the room was unbearable as Fox ignored Kent.

"Why are you here, Fox?" Adalynne asked, searching his expression.

"I came to thank you for what you did for my father. I have never seen him so happy. He's a different person." He looked into Adalynne's eyes and Kent's hand on her back was the only thing that kept her from falling into Fox's beautiful embrace.

"I'm glad you saw your father. He's turned his life around and is now in a better place, but don't thank me. He was the one who decided to make the change. He has become a good friend," Adalynne said tentatively. She had invited herself into his father's life when Fox didn't want her to be in his. She couldn't help but feel embarrassed with his realization. She wasn't sure if Fox would feel like she overstepped her place but John had become an important part of her life and she had no regrets.

A scowl formed on Fox's face when Kent persisted in touching Adalynne possessively. "Do you have to fucking touch her right now?" he snapped at Kent. Adalynne could feel Kent's body grow taut and the tension in the room sky rocket.

"Yes, actually," Kent responded tightly. Adalynne wanted to squirm away from Kent but she had invited him here after all and led him on.

"Kent, please." She smiled at Kent as sweetly as she could manage. She didn't want him encouraging Fox's erratic behavior.

"You heard her. Get your fucking hands off her," Fox commanded.

"She wasn't complaining about my hands a moment ago," Kent stated angrily. She could feel Kent's hand shake as he held her stubbornly. Adalynne was embarrassed at Kent's admittance, even though she knew that it was obvious when Fox arrived. Her cheeks flamed red and she wanted to run away from the showdown unfolding before her.

Adalynne's thoughts betrayed her when she noticed how breathtaking Fox was as he stood before them, exuding enough power to pull all the air from the room Every time she found herself in Fox's presence it became increasingly more difficult to motivate herself to move on without him. It would be so easy to throw herself at him and beg him to love her. She knew the thought was completely ridiculous but that was exactly what was in her heart. It wanted her to rip it out of her chest and hand it over, knowing he would walk away again.

Adalynne gasped when Fox's fist hit Kent in the face. It happened so quickly there was no time to react before the deed was done. "Jesus!" Kent cried out as he brought his hand up to meet his bloodied nose. Adalynne grabbed for her kitchen hand towel to give to Kent in a panic.

"Fox! What are you doing?" She glowered at him. "I don't get it. You don't want to be with me but you also don't want me to be with anyone else.

Why don't you want me to be happy?" Adalynne couldn't stop the pleading tone that took over her voice.

"I want you to be happy, that's why I'm living this shit life." Fox turned and stormed out of the apartment.

"News flash, Fox!" She followed him out into the hall. He turned back and looked at her without saying anything, his intense green eyes wound so tight they took her breath away. "I'm not happy!" she screamed at him, then stormed back to her apartment and slammed the door. Adalynne leaned against the door trying to calm her nerves.

"Wait...was that the singer from Outcome?" Kent asked with sudden awe in his voice.

"Seriously, Kent, he just punched you," she reminded him.

"Yeah, but that guy is amazing on the guitar." His sudden upbeat mood was irritating. "Can you get me an autograph?"

"I think you need to leave." Adalynne opened the door and motioned for him to go.

"What about..." Kent walked toward her, his hand finding her waist.

"Out, please. I need to be alone right now. I'm sorry." She felt bad for kicking him out but she had no patience for company right now. "And keep the towel."

Chapter Twenty-Five

The next afternoon, Adalynne made her way to her mother's house. It had been awhile since she had spent time with Carmen, she missed her greatly. She needed Carmen's wisdom and guidance now more than ever. Adalynne spent most of the night lying in bed trying to figure out the puzzle that was Fox. She was tired, confused, and completely unsettled. He had sauntered into apartment last night like he owned the place. She wanted to be furious with him for how he could so casually come in and out of her life, only to leave her mourning the loss of him every time. No other man could ignite such an intense reaction. She was pulled in so many directions her head spun.

"Yum, new recipe?" Adalynne asked when Carmen pulled a fresh batch of cookies out of the oven. The scent of vanilla wrapped around her as Carmen set them on the counter.

"You haven't been around much. My plan was to entice you with new sweets." Carmen smiled deviously.

"I missed you too, Carmen. I have been so busy with the Music House and finishing classes. Do you forgive me?" Adalynne smiled guiltily.

"Always." Carmen chuckled. "Is there something you want to talk about, Addie girl? I can see you're troubled." Carmen leaned on the counter, bringing her full attention to Adalynne.

"My heart won't forget him. I can't love someone else. I can't be with anyone else…what am I supposed to do?" Adalynne sighed in defeat. She knew Carmen would know exactly who she was talking about. Her warm brown eyes softened as she looked at her sympathetically.

Carmen wrapped her arms around Adalynne's shoulders. Her scent was so familiar it reminded her of her childhood. When Adalynne was small it had always been Carmen to soothe her injury or nurse her cold. Carmen was the one who showed her how to love when her own mother could not. Carmen had raised Adalynne since she was a small girl and she would always have a strong emotional bond with her. She had always made Adalynne feel special even when her parents were never around.

"Matters of the heart can be very complicated but what I don't understand is why you keep letting him walk out of your life. You didn't give John the option and now he has turned his life around. You made him see the truth with your persistent love. They had been through hell and back. Those two are cut from the same cloth and sometimes people cannot see their path until someone shines a light on it. You, my dear, are the light for those men."

"But he doesn't want me in his life," Adalynne

whispered.

"Sometimes when we're so close to something, we cannot see the truth when it is right in front of us." Carmen smoothed Adalynne's long hair down her back.

Adalynne was surprised when her mother walked into the kitchen. "Mom? I thought you would be working. Why are you home so early?" Adalynne straightened in her seat. Adalynne watched the exchange Carmen and her mother made. It surprised Adalynne because her whole life her mother avoided creating a bond with Carmen, treating her as an employee and nothing more, but their look told of something deeper they had created. An understanding was reached between them without words.

"Those cookies smell delicious, Carmen," her mother commented, picking one up off the plate. It was like those few days after her mother had finally dealt with her father's loss. She knew her mother was making more of an effort when she had spoken to her at Elizabeth's funeral but it still surprised her to see her mother with her guard down. It was nice to look at her mother and not the façade she always wore. This was how she had always wished her mother was like when she was growing up. "It looks like I have interrupted an important conversation." Her mother broke a small piece off a cookie and popped it in her mouth.

"I was just unloading all my frustrations on Carmen in regards to my pathetic love life," Adalynne confessed. She tried to smile past the emotional turmoil within her but it felt awkward.

She wasn't sure what her mother would say about the topic. She was nervous Matthew's name would surface and that was a topic she couldn't handle right now.

"Love is a very complicated thing, isn't it?" her mother said thoughtfully. Adalynne couldn't help but smile at the word they both used when they spoke of the topic of love—complicated, it definitely applied. Everything about love to Adalynne seemed extremely complicated. "What has you so troubled?"

Adalynne took a deep, thoughtful breath before she broached the topic of truth with her mother. "I have been in love with someone for a long time and they have never loved me back." Adalynne was surprised by her confession to her mother. She had never spoken to her about Fox before. Not even to mention his name. "I know nothing else but to love him with everything I have and I feel so lost and alone. I can't breathe." Adalynne sighed.

"A heart loves who a heart loves," her mother said softly as she rubbed Adalynne's back. Adalynne looked up to see Carmen sharing a supportive smile to her mother.

Adalynne's eyes watered as her mother spoke the words her father said to her once when she had asked him why he loved her mother. "Yes, it does," Adalynne agreed sadly. Her mother pulled her close and Adalynne leaned against her shoulder.

"Your father was a wise man, he knew how to love. It's why I fell in love with him. You're like him, you know. I see it in your eyes. I feel like I have stood in your way. I kept telling myself I was doing what was best for you but I think I was doing more harm than good. I made a promise to your father before he died I would make sure you were happy and I have only caused you pain..." Adalynne listened as her mother's words broke off with a soft sob. She looked up and saw the tears in her mother's eyes. "I have advanced in my career with ease, gained the respect in the field I sought, and became what I set out to achieve but I have failed at the most important thing. I have failed time after time to be the mother you needed."

"Mom, you—" Adalynne started but her mother cut her off.

"There is something I have tried to show you many times but I couldn't bring myself to do it." She reached into her purse and pulled out a worn envelope and passed it to Adalynne.

Adalynne looked down at the envelope that had her father's handwriting on it.

Damon Knight

I was strange to see his name written across the front of the white envelope. Adalynne was overcome with confusion as she looked up at her mother. "You know who Damon is?" Her mother only nodded, looking away to avoid the tears that were about to fall. "I don't understand."

"Just read it, dear," Carmen encouraged. Adalynne realized Carmen knew about the letter as she looked up into her eyes. She didn't know what to make of the situation.

Adalynne opened the letter and read her father's

written words.

Dear Damon,

I remember the first time you showed up on my doorstep, no more than six years old, with the most determined look in your eye when you asked for my permission to be Adalynne's friend, only to be turned away with my rejection. You would not have believed my shock when you showed up the very next week to go through the motions again with the same result.

It never failed to amaze me the dedication you held for my daughter when you insisted on visiting every week to ask a question you knew I would not approve. I would never admit it at the time but I came to enjoy your weekly visits, especially when you changed the game plan and we battled it out with the chess board when you discovered my love of the game. Even when I told you there was no way you could possibly beat me, you were determined to learn the game to eventually win the upper hand.

As the years went by and your dedication proved deeper than anything I could have ever imagined, I discovered the makings of a great man in you. I admired your heart and your devotion to my Adalynne. You proved to me it is not where a man comes from but what he makes of himself in his lifetime that really matters. I remember on one of your visits, I believe it was when you were asking for permission to take her to the prom, I asked you why you needed my approval and you said because Adalynne was the greatest part of your life and you never wanted to put her in a position she would have to choose between her family and you. My permission meant that I believed you were worthy of her.

My reasons for denying you my consent changed over the years but when I saw the love you had for her I became scared you would take her away from me because like you, Adalynne was the greatest part of my life. There would have been no man I would have permitted to be with her, for I believed there was no one good enough for my baby girl. I am her father and I will fight for her until the end to protect her heart from any pain that might come her way. Though, I have come to learn over my many years that pain is unavoidable when it comes to love and what is life without love? No one deserves the joys of love more than my Adalynne.

This is not an easy thing for me to do because as you know I am a very stubborn man. Much to my dismay my time on this earth is limited. Lying in this hospital bed has reminded me of that, so I need to make right the happiness I denied my daughter in my attempt to protect her. So if I do not have the opportunity in the future, I would like to officially change my answer to all the questions you have asked me over the years. After you left here today, I realized I no longer have a valid reason to deny you your request and maybe I never did have a good reason and for that I am sorry.

I give you my permission to befriend my daughter, to date my daughter, and to love my daughter. As for the question I know that eventually you would want to ask, I give you my permission to marry my daughter, should it be her heart's desire. I will leave this life knowing you will continue to protect her when I no longer can. I know with all my heart you will do a better job

*than I have because the love you have
for her is unselfish and true. It is one of
the most remarkable things that I have
experienced in my lifetime. I am
grateful that I had the chance to know
you.*

Please forgive me,
Thomas

Adalynne could hardly see the words through her tears as she read every word her father had written. She looked up at her mother's sorrowful expression. "Dad wanted you to give this to him?" Adalynne struggled to speak.

"Yes, I'm sorry." Her mother sobbed.

"When did you know about Damon?" Adalynne asked with widened eyes. She was completely bewildered by this new development.

"The first time he showed up on our doorstep when you were at your piano lessons and every Sunday after that," she confessed guiltily.

"I have loved him my whole life. Did you know that?" Adalynne asked her mother. Unsure of what emotion was controlling her at the moment. She was confused by the realization that her parents knew Fox the entire time, unable to process it.

"I suspected. Adalynne, I thought he was going to cause you to lose your way. He didn't have the future you had before you. I thought he would be a distraction. I told your father we could never let him be with you, even when your father grew to love that boy I refused to let him entertain the idea. I thought I was doing what was best for you. Can you forgive me?"

Adalynne hugged her mother tightly. "I have to go." She kissed her mother's cheek and then Carmen's before she left, flying from the kitchen and out the front door.

Adalynne hopped into her car and drove straight toward Fox's place. She wasn't sure if he would be there but she needed to find him and that was a place to start. Her heart was overwhelmed with hope that she could have her happy ending she thought she could never have. She just hoped it wasn't too late.

***

When she arrived at Fox's condo there was no one holding the door open so she couldn't sneak into the building. She looked at the names on the list of the apartments until she saw the name Knight, apartment 402. She pressed in the numbers and the number rang on speaker but no one picked up. She tried one more time but there was still no answer.

Adalynne waited for fifteen minutes before deciding to leave. She pulled out her cell phone to send Fox a message when movement on the other side of the glass door captured her attention. It was Fox's girlfriend. She stumbled toward the door and pushed it open, causing it to slam against the wall. A deafening sound pulsed through the enclosed space of the entrance. Surprisingly, the glass door did not shatter.

Adalynne stepped back, hoping to go unnoticed,

but the girl's red, dark circled eyes looked up at Adalynne and sneered. "You can have that fucking asshole, bitch," she slurred. Her hair was a mess and her mascara ran down her cheeks. "I'm done putting up with his shit." Adalynne didn't bother responding to her, from the looks of her Adalynne doubted she would remember this encounter anyway. Adalynne grabbed hold of the door to stop it from closing. "What? You think you're too good to talk to the likes of me with your expensive clothes and the...whatever the fuck else you have. Life must be so easy for you walking around with...looking like you. And guys will write all kinds of songs talking about how fucking perfect you are. Eat my shit!" She screamed in Adalynne's face. "He's crazy anyway. He always wakes up screaming for a bee...a fucking bee!"

She was so close to Adalynne that she breathed her foul breath in her face. Adalynne couldn't help but turn away. "Is that your cab?" Adalynne asked. The girl spun on her heel and marched out of the building without another word.

Adalynne knocked on Fox's door but there was no answer. She tried the handle and it was unlocked. She walked in. "Fox?" Adalynne was met with silence when she called into the dimly lit interior. Adalynne closed the door behind her and looked around. She had been in Fox's place before but she was too distracted to take in the surroundings. The décor was minimal, only the necessities were laid out so it could function as a living space. Adalynne walked into the main living room. Framed posters and pictures of the band were stacked against the wall, along with some unpacked boxes that had never opened since he moved.

Adalynne's attention was drawn when she heard a faint noise down the hall. "Fox?" She called heading toward the direction of the sound. When she came to the entrance of Fox's room she could see him sprawled out on the bottom of his bed, his arm thrown over his face. A pained moan escaped his lips as he seemed to be slipping in and out of consciousness. Adalynne approached him tentatively. His shirt was ripped and long red scratches spanned across his chest. Adalynne figured it must have been the work of his girlfriend, judging from her mood when she had left.

Adalynne touched his arm. He jerked away from her touch and turned his back toward her. "Fuck, Trisha…I told you to leave me alone."

"Fox? It's Bee," she whispered, unsure of how he would react to her being in his apartment uninvited.

He pulled his arm away from his face and turned back towards Adalynne. "Shit, I'm fucking tripping." He grabbed her wrist, pulling her down on top of him. He rolled them over so she was pinned under his weight.

"Fox!"

"You feel so fucking real," Fox said, staring down at her with a lazy hunger. Adalynne looked into his bloodshot eyes. She touched his face and he leaned into her. She was concerned for him. He looked as if he hadn't slept in days. His normally vibrant green eyes were darkened and strange. The smell of liquor was heavy on his breath. He kissed her neck, melting her. "You even smell just like her," he whispered against her skin, causing goose bumps to rise on her flesh.

"Fox." She pushed back on his chest. "It *is* me. It's Bee." She watched him focus on her. His expression changed from the playful smile she wanted to kiss from his lips, to a scowl.

"Bee? What are you doing here?" He pushed off her, stepping away from the bed. He stumbled and had to lean against the wall for support. Adalynne immediately felt the loss of his touch. She stood up to help him but he refused her assistance. "Don't help...I'm fine."

"I'm worried about you." She moved toward him, touching his shoulder. He flinched away from her as if the contact caused him pain. The sting of his rejection hurt worse than if he had slapped her across the face.

"I don't want you to worry about me. I don't want you here," he spat out, barely able to raise his eyes to her.

"It didn't seem like that a moment ago when you thought I was a figment of your drug-induced state." Adalynne let the anger slip into her voice. She was trying to remain composed but he always ignited intense feelings, making it hard to keep her calm and objective mind set. "Besides, who else is going to take care of you? Your girlfriend ran off and you can barely stand."

"I don't need anyone to take care of me. I'm doing fine on my own."

"Fox...everyone needs help sometimes. Let me help you."

"What? You want to clean me up like you did my father? What good would that do? It won't fucking change anything." Fox slid down the wall, rubbing the palms of his hands into his eyes. "I like not being able to think about shit. I just want to be numb."

"Why, Fox? Why are you doing this?" Adalynne placed her hand on his knee as she sat down next to him. He looked at her hand before reaching up to touch it gently like he was not completely convinced she was actually there.

"Because…" He looked up into her eyes. "I miss you." She watched his eyes tear up. He seemed so broken in front of her, so beautiful and broken.

"You don't have to miss me." She took his hand in hers and brought it against her heart. "I'm here with you." Fox laced his fingers in hers and pulled her toward him, holding her tightly like he thought she was going to disappear. Adalynne lay against his chest, listening to his accelerated heartbeat and feeling the comfort of his embrace.

Chapter Twenty-Six

Fox gently traced his fingers on the bare skin of Adalynne's lower back where her shirt rode up. "Fox?" she whispered against his shirt.

"Yeah?" His tone was lazy as he spoke. Adalynne looked up to see his eyes closed. His long dark lashes fanned out over his high cheek bones. His full lips looked irresistible, so close to her.

"Can I kiss you?" she said softly, her hunger building to taste him.

His eyes opened, looking down at her. "You have a boyfriend," He stated. "I met him, remember? The skinny fuck with the weird shirt. Why would you want to kiss me?"

"He's not my boyfriend." Adalynne looked away guiltily. "He was supposed to be a distraction. I wanted to know if someone else could make me feel the way you do so maybe I could stop thinking about how it felt when you touched me or how your lips felt on mine." Her face heated at her admission but the truth always surfaced when she spoke to Fox. "I don't know how to *want* anyone else."

301

"You should *want* someone else." He sighed.

Adalynne sat up despite his protesting grip on her, trying to keep her close. His actions didn't match his words. He was giving mixed signals like he always did. "I don't. I never have. You're the only person I want to be with. There has never been a day that I have not thought about you, Fox. I'm tired of living without my heart. That's what it feels like without you. I need you in my life even if it's just as friends." She looked at Fox staring back at her with an unreadable expression. After a silent moment a tear slipped down his cheek, he wiped away roughly with the palm of his hand.

"Yes."

"Yes, we can be friends?" Adalynne asked softly, looking for clarification.

"Yes, you can kiss me."

Adalynne didn't know who initiated the kiss but before she knew it they were crushed together as if they were starving and this was their reprieve. "I want you, Bee," he whispered against her mouth.

Adalynne pulled back from the kiss. "I like the sound of that, say it again." She smiled.

"I want you more than anything." He looked at her longingly before he pulled away. He leaned against the wall with his intense eyes trained on her.

Adalynne was confused by his sudden withdrawal despite the need that was heavy in his eyes. He was always running hot and cold around her, it was confusing. Adalynne reached down and started to unbutton her shirt, slowly fingering each button. She watched his eyes follow her every movement. "It's just a little hot in here." Adalynne bit her bottom lip playfully. She watched his reaction with anticipation as she slowly slipped her shirt off her shoulders. "That's better." The shirt slipped from her fingers and met the floor.

"Yeah that's better." He swallowed.

"Do you find it hot?" Adalynne asked, running her finger flirtatiously down his arm. She wanted to bring up the letter with Fox but she knew he was too drunk to have a serious conversation but he was too enticing to leave.

"Yep, now that you mention it." He reached back behind him and pulled his shirt off over his head. His body was hard and steely, with sinful lines that made her mouth water. Her hands were immediately drawn to him. Running her fingers over his body, she remembered every curve. She knew she should ask about his girlfriend, ask about what this meant, but she selfishly wanted all his affections. She wanted to feel his need for her before she brought up the words that could cause him to pull away again. She didn't know what the letter would mean to Fox, if it would change anything or if it was too late. She knew what it meant to her and that was renewed hope.

"I like this." She ran her fingers over the letters on his chest that spelled Bee, over his heart. "Why did you get it?"

He took her hand that was pressed against his tattoo. "Because you are my heart," he whispered and kissed her fingers. She felt overwhelmed with happiness, her heart swelled with joy.

Adalynne stood up and unbuttoned her jeans, sliding them down her legs. Fox followed her every movement, drinking in all of her. "Would this be considered taking advantage of you, since you are clearly drunk?"

"Fuck no." Fox stood up, pushing off the wall. He shuffled through his playlist and turned on his stereo. Adalynne smiled at his sudden playful mood. He wrapped his arms around her and Adalynne melted against his solid body. They both moved to the music, getting lost in the moment. His hands followed her every curve, leaving her skin heated and wanting more.

Fox always knew how to move, drawing the eye of anyone that could see his tall gorgeous form. He moved in a tantalizing manner that spoke of sex and promises. He sang along with the words playing through the speakers, his voice more alluring than the vocals from the original song.

"I love monkeys." He chuckled.

"What?" Adalynne looked down where his attention was drawn and noticed her underwear. Heat bloomed in her cheeks as she noticed she was wearing underwear with little monkeys holding hearts and blowing kisses. "Oops…I wasn't planning on seducing anyone today." Adalynne's face flamed red as she buried it in his shirt.

"I am very seduced. I have never seen monkeys look so appealing. In fact, I think I would like to sit down and get a better view." Fox sat on the edge of his bed with a crooked smile.

"Monkeys do it for you, huh? Well what about dancing monkeys?" Adalynne teased. She swayed her hips to the music, turning around so that she could entice him with her round bottom as she moved with the music.

"*Especially* dancing monkeys." He grabbed Adalynne by the waist, pulling her against him as he rolled her onto the bed. Adalynne screamed in excitement until he kissed away the sound that left her lips before he began trailing down her neck. She didn't know why his lips made her skin explode with pleasure but everywhere he touched was left tingling with delight. Adalynne unclasped her bra and threw it down to the floor with the rest of her clothes. He leaned up on his arms to explore her body with his intense eyes, as if he was remembering every detail. His lips sought the soft flesh of her breast before they teased her taut nipples. Adalynne couldn't stifle the moan of pleasure that escaped her lips as an intense heat pooled in her core. His eyes had never looked as dark as they did when he stood up and kicked off his pants. "Sorry monkeys, but it's time to go." Fox pulled them off.

Fox knew the secrets of her body like he was playing a beautiful song on his guitar, hitting all the right notes. They both moved in a slow, lovely dance. She had never felt as beautiful as she did when she was in his arms. There was no denying his attraction for her as he cherished every part of her body and she celebrated the thought that in this moment he was hers.

Fox grabbed hold of her hands and pinned them on the bed over her head. His other hand grabbed hold of her hip as he plunged deep inside her. His eyes never left hers as he pushed and pulled at her core until she came undone in his hold, melting upon the bed. Her head swam with pleasure, the rest of the world completely forgotten.

***

Adalynne awoke in Fox's bed. She was surrounded by darkness from the late hour. She roused when she noticed Fox was no longer in bed with her. She sat up and slipped her feet off, her foot grazing something that was sticking out from under his bed. She turned on the lamp beside the bed. Looking down, she noticed a shoebox. She planned to slide it back into its place when she noticed a music sheet sticking out of the top. Curiosity got the better of her. She pulled off the cover to reveal a stack of notebooks and music sheets all in Fox's handwriting.

They were all songs Fox had written. She looked at the words and was taken aback by the beauty of his words and the fact that her name was written in some of the lyrics. He had written songs about her. Excitement bubbled deep within her with the realization that Fox cared for her more than she realized, first with the letter and now his music. A noise startled her, she quickly put away the box so she wouldn't be caught looking in his private things.

She noticed a light in the kitchen as she walked down the hall. Fox was leaning against the counter, his chest was bare and his jeans rode low on his narrow hips. The sight of him was breathtaking but the smile immediately fell from her face when she noticed what was in his hand. He was drinking in the middle of the night. His hair was mussed like he had run his fingers through it countless times. He was obviously not in the same blissful state that Adalynne was in.

"Fox? What are you doing?" Adalynne couldn't stop her hand from covering her mouth in shock. She didn't realize until now how lost he was. He looked up at her with dull eyes. Liquor bottles and various pills spread out over the counter, along with bags of suspicious looking substances. He had already taken whatever it was that he decided he needed. She could tell he was already experiencing a new high along with the buzz of alcohol. He leaned against the counter, not even fazed by the fact that she found him amongst a sea of drugs decorating his kitchen counter.

"Why do you keep coming into my fucking life and showing me everything I want but can never fucking have?"

Adalynne reached for him but he pulled away like he was disgusted with her. "Why can't we be together?"

"Because I am no fucking good for you, Bee. You won't be happy with me, I will ruin you. We are not supposed to be together. We were never fucking supposed to be together. Why can't you fucking understand that?"

"You're wrong, Fox. You are all I ever wanted. I have loved you since you found me when we were six years old. How can everything I have ever felt be wrong?"

"I should never have been there that day." He turned away from her. His words tore at her, threatening to break her.

"What are you saying, Fox…that you wished you never met me?"

"Yes." He was cold. "That's exactly what I'm saying. Why did you even come here?"

"To give you this." She grabbed her purse off the floor and retrieved the letter. She thrust it into his chest, pushing him back against the counter. She was mad, the anger pulsed through her. She watched him open the letter and read it while she stood there and watched. Her heart beat was the only sound she could hear as it echoed through her body. She didn't even know if he could make out the words in his state.

"This doesn't change anything," he said after he read the letter. She could see the tears in his eyes and his hands shook when he held the paper. "It's too late."

"Is it because of your girlfriend?" Adalynne fumed.

"What? Fuck no. I don't give a shit about her."

"Then why?"

"Look at me, Bee." He hit a bottle of liquor off the counter, causing Adalynne to flinch. It shattered on the floor. "I can't get through the fucking day without getting high. You were the only good thing in my life and I have done nothing but try to stay away from you so I wouldn't take you down with me when I fell. Everyone knew I was going to fucking fall on my face."

"Fox…"

"Get the fuck out of here. Do me a favor and just forget about me." He leaned his elbows on the counter, raking his hands through his hair.

"I can't forget about you," Adalynne cried.

"Get the fuck out!" he yelled, rubbing the heels of his hands into his eyes.

"I still see the Fox I fell in love with," Adalynne pleaded, moving closer to him. "Let me help you."

He held up his hand to stop her from coming any closer. "You can't help me. Do me a favor and don't waste one more minute on me."

"I will wait for as long as it takes," she said stubbornly.

He held the paper up for her to take it back, the paper shook in his grasp. Adalynne refused to take it. "It was meant for you," Adalynne whispered sadly.

***

Adalynne sat in her car and cried. A crushing weight felt heavy against her chest. When she finally pulled herself together enough that her tears were under control, she pulled out her phone and dialed John's number.

"Adalynne, are you okay?" John's voice was urgent, fearing what Adalynne would say.

"It's late. I'm sorry." Adalynne's distress was still apparent in her words, despite trying to control herself.

"What's wrong?" John asked.

"It's Damon. He needs help but he won't let me," Adalynne sobbed. "He always pushes me away. I don't know what he's taking...I'm so worried about him."

"Where is he?"

"I just left him at his place...he was drinking heavily and taking pills."

"I'll head over now. I'll do whatever I can to help," John assured her.

"What about all the liquor? Is it going to be hard for you?" Adalynne wiped her eyes, taking a deep calming breath.

"Not as hard as it will be for me to see my son following in my footsteps."

"He's strong like you," Adalynne said encouragingly.

"He's stronger than me..." John's words trailed off.

"John?" Adalynne asked quietly to see if he was still on the line.

"When Damon was a small boy, I heard him talking in his room. I suppose it was not too long after he had met you. He spoke to his mother a lot back then when he thought no one could hear him. He told his mother he met an angel and she was the most beautiful girl he had ever seen. He asked her if she had sent the girl from heaven to love him because she couldn't anymore." John's voice broke off as he could no longer speak through his emotions. "I walked into his room and I told him there is no such thing as angels. I still remember the look on his face when I told him that his mother didn't love us enough to stay..." John broke off in tears. "I was wrong, Adalynne. You are an angel and you are the best thing that happened to my son and me. We owe you so much."

"You don't owe me anything. I am so grateful

that you both came into my life. I wish I could help Damon but I think he needs you." Adalynne struggled to keep her words calm. The emotion in their conversation was overwhelming.

"I will do everything in my power and then some, I assure you." When John spoke she knew without a doubt he was telling the truth. "I do love my son, you know."

"I know."

Chapter Twenty-Seven

John informed Adalynne that Fox refused to speak to her. Even though his rejection hurt, knowing Fox was taking steps in the right direction gave her great peace of mind. John was rebuilding his relationship with his son and helping him down the difficult path to recovery.

Her thoughts never strayed too far from Fox and when John informed her that Fox had entered a rehab facility, she was torn between relief and sadness. He was taking the time to heal but it meant that she wouldn't see him for an extended period of time. Things were left unfinished between them but she pushed her selfish thoughts aside and began focusing on her life as it unfolded in front of her. He would have no contact with her while he stayed in the rehab facility and she didn't know what would happen upon his release. The uncertainty haunted her.

Katie and Steven made the move, buying a house within walking distance to Adalynne. It was a beautiful property with a large fenced backyard. It gave them a luscious oasis in the middle of the city. Steven's job had begun immediately after he graduated and now they were frantically trying to settle into their new place around his busy schedule. Adalynne spent most of her free time with Katie, helping her unpack and making sure she didn't do any heavy lifting on Steven's orders. Their time together was a perfect distraction for her.

Katie was in full swing preparing for the baby and decorating their new home. She insisted Adalynne help her with every detail, which Adalynne delightfully welcomed. They bought every decorating magazine and narrowed the style preferences down enough to take action. The house was newly renovated when they bought it. Luckily, the only room that needed to be painted was the nursery. They decided to decorate it in various tones of greens and yellows because the sex of the baby was going to be a surprise.

"Whose idea was the stripes again?" Adalynne jokingly complained as they painted the walls.

"You showed me the picture," Katie defended herself. She was currently taking a break, sitting next to the window so she could feel the breeze blow through her hair. "It is so hot!" she complained, fanning herself. "We have to get this done so we can air this place out and get the air conditioner working again."

"Yeah, it's actually hotter for those of us who are working. Did you give up? I think you have taken more breaks than you have actually worked." Adalynne laughed.

"The baby is tired," Katie whined. She patted the

spot next to her. "Come take a break with me and tell me about hot Brolan Pierce, aka Damon, or what you like to call him by, Fabulous Fox. Did you hear anything yet?"

Adalynne sighed and placed the paint brush down before situating herself beside Katie. "No, he's still at the rehab place and that's all I know. Even John doesn't have contact with him until he checks out."

"I heard them saying on the radio he was admitted, so I guess it's not top secret anymore. They said he overdosed and almost died. I guess they're trying to make it sound more tragic. He's so famous you know, like girls throwing their panties on the stage and tattooing his name on their bodies famous."

"I know." Adalynne nudged her playfully. "He's always been so talented, it's about time the world saw how great he is." Adalynne smiled sadly.

"I'm sure you'll hear from him once he gets better," Katie said encouragingly. "You share a beautiful history together and the most amazing connection. You guys are meant to be together and of course there is the fact that there is no one more gorgeous than you. Why would he want to be with anyone else?" Katie laid it on thick.

Adalynne shook her head at Katie's relentless optimism and laughed. "Thanks for trying to make me feel better. I would like to think that was true, Katie, but I have no idea what's going to happen when he gets out."

"But it's so romantic he asked your father for permission for years. That's why he was at the

314

hospital that day, wasn't it...to speak to your father."

"Yeah maybe, but he never needed my father's permission because he always had mine," Adalynne added with a shrug.

"He thought he needed it. He had honorable intentions, Addie. In his mind he needed to be seen as good enough to be with you and that's why he wanted your father's permission."

"The letter may have come too late," Adalynne's breathed.

"You love with a love that is more than love. How can it not work out? It's fate." Katie smiled at her own logic.

"I wish everyone could see the world like you do. Life would be so much easier." Adalynne smiled.

"And crazier." Katie laughed.

"That too. But at least it would be good crazy." Adalynne laughed.

"Ooh, baby kicked." Katie ran her hand over her stomach. Adalynne placed her hand on her stomach. There was no mistaking Katie was pregnant anymore, her belly was round and growing so fast. Adalynne found it amazing watching the baby grow inside her. It truly was a miracle to watch the beginning of a new life, especially with someone she loved as much as Katie.

Everything in Adalynne's life was coming together harmoniously other than her love life. Adalynne's mother became a regular presence in her life, making an effort to become familiar with her musical career. Their relationship had developed into more of a friendship, something they never had before. She found she could open up with her mother and discuss the things she previously avoided around her, like music and her plans for the future with the Music House. She also spoke of her concern for Fox and the depths of her love for him, something she thought she would never be able to divulge with her mother for fear of the repercussions.

Adalynne's mother even shared with her the stories of Fox's visits and how her father grew to enjoy their weekly chess games and how angry she had become with her father when he had grown fond of Fox. Adalynne even laughed at some of the happenings her mother retold because there were no hard feelings left between them where Fox was concerned. Adalynne understood her mother's belief that she was doing what was best. Adalynne didn't want to hold onto anything negative, she no longer wanted to live in the past. After all, Adalynne's mother didn't know Fox like she did. She had only heard the stories of a troubled boy from a broken home. Adalynne never did tell her mother of their secret meetings in the woods, or how he spent so many nights in her bed when they were younger. She created a bond with him that would always claim her heart. She had only shared those memories with Katie and she wanted to keep those close to her heart.

Her mother developed a new appreciation for Carmen. Her rigid view of Carmen's position blurred. When Adalynne visited her mother always insisted Carmen join her and Adalynne for tea. Her mother's change of heart shed great light for Adalynne's peace of mind. They were the two women who raised her in this life and it brought her so much joy to see the relationship grow warm and friendly between them. Her mother was making a wonderful effort for Adalynne's benefit, she knew the change could not have been easy for her and she appreciated the depths of her mother's love. It was the first time she saw how strong and beautiful her mother really was and understood the vast depths of her father's love that he had held for her. She was every bit of the woman he claimed her to be.

The construction of the Music House was running as smoothly as possible. There was so much outreach from the community, it made Adalynne push even harder. John was there as often as he could to lend a hand to the workers and doing more than his share of work to contribute to the cause. She loved having him close, his company was comforting. Adalynne considered him family. The relationship they had formed was easy and natural. She valued his strength to turn his life around for his son.

Adalynne remembered the afternoon when they had sorted through the remains of his wife's belongings that did not perish in the fire. She had arrived early that day to check on him, she stayed close those couple of weeks because they had been especially hard on him. The call to drink dug at his very being and Adalynne watched him go through a full range of emotion. She and Meredith both encouraged him to remember why he was doing this when his mind became so rattled he could not see the light.

"We can do it together." Adalynne gave him a comforting squeeze on his shoulder as he hesitated at the entrance to the shed. The scorch marks still scarred the side of the structure. Adalynne walked in the dark space. Most of the boxes had significant fire damage but there were some boxes that seemed relatively unharmed. Adalynne struggled to lift a plastic container. Although the exterior looked slightly melted it still held its shape which gave hope to the survival of the contents inside. John lifted the box for her and walked out of the shed. She followed him into his living room as he dropped the box on the floor. They both sorted through the contents. They did this for the remainder of the day, box after box, salvaging everything that was not burned.

"You shouldn't try to forget her. She was your wife, and the mother of your son. She should be remembered as the woman you loved, not for the pain that she caused."

"She was a beautiful woman. I loved her so much. I hated her for leaving us," John said softly as he looked at the photographs of her.

"This is how she should be remembered." Adalynne set a picture up on the mantle in the living room. It was a framed picture of Fox's mother. She wore a beautiful smile as she cradled her swollen stomach. John looked at the picture Adalynne had placed in the bare room. He was lost in thought as he studied the picture. "I took that picture, you know," he said after a few moments in silence. "I

was so happy then…and so was she."

"Then that's a good picture to have there."
Adalynne smiled.

"She would have loved you, Addie," John said
warmly as he wrapped his arm around her shoulder
and placed another picture beside it on the mantle.
It was a picture of their wedding day.

Things with Kent were awkward at first, but his admiration of Fox made things easier. He had almost seemed proud he had sported a black eye from the lead singer of Outcome. She owed him an explanation after what happened. She told him about her history with Fox in a brief and need to know basis. He seemed to take the news in stride and Adalynne was glad when their relationship seemed to fall back into its normal working state shortly after. Adalynne was relieved things did not go further between them. She knew she would never feel anything more than friendship for him. In her desperation she had almost tried to make it something that it could never have been, ultimately leading to the possible loss of his friendship. Luckily it seemed that they had not crossed the line of no return. Kent eventually even began innocently flirting with her again, like he had always done before. It felt normal and that was exactly what she needed.

Adalynne was on site for the Music House, talking to John about some interior details when Adalynne's phone rang.

"Hey Katie," Adalynne answered.

"It's Steven, the baby is coming," Steven blurted

in the phone. "I'm fucking freaking out!"

"Give me the phone," Katie hollered from the background before she came on. "Addie, I need you. This baby is ripping me apart. Oww…" Katie started moaning in the phone.

"I'm on my way," Adalynne informed her. She gave John a quick heads up before running toward her car. John waved goodbye excitedly as she pulled out of the lot. Adalynne had been over the moon excited Katie's baby was due to come any day now. It was all she was talking about to poor John and Meredith. Now the time had arrived she could barely contain her excitement.

Adalynne drove to Katie's as quickly as she could without breaking any laws. Steven was too panicked to drive so Adalynne insisted she pick them up. Adalynne couldn't help but laugh when she pulled up in front of their house and saw the two of them. Katie was still in her slippers and a shirt that didn't cover her large stomach. Her hair was in a knot on the top of her head. She was holding onto her stomach like she was afraid the baby would fall out and Steven looked as freaked as he sounded on the phone. He threw the bags in the trunk and then helped Katie in the car like he was nervous she would explode.

Katie was in a Dr. Jeckle and Mr. Hyde state of mind. With every contraction she seethed anger and screamed profanities but as soon as it passed she would be overwhelmed with excitement for the arrival of their baby.

"How is it even possible to flip through emotions like that?" Adalynne commented nervously. Katie sat beside her smiling, only seconds after she threated to do bodily harm to Steven.

"I don't know. I can't believe this is finally happening," Katie said breathlessly. "It feels like I was pregnant forever and now we finally get to meet our baby." She looked back at Steven, who only managed a very awkward smile. He was so quiet in the backseat. Adalynne wondered how he was going to make it through the delivery when he looked like he was going to pass out already.

"God dammit this hurts like a motherfucker!" Katie screamed as Adalynne pulled up in front of the hospital. Steven jumped out and grabbed a wheelchair from the front door and brought it over.

Katie's labor progressed quickly and the doctors were surprised how far along she was already when they arrived. It was only an hour after they arrived at the hospital when Katie started pushing. Katie tried to leave and give Steven and Katie privacy to welcome their baby into the world but Steven refused to let her go. He needed the emotional support, while Katie threatened to take his life. With Steven and Adalynne by Katie's side, she delivered a beautiful healthy baby girl. Much to everyone's surprise, Steven stayed conscious the entire time.

"She is so beautiful, Katie." Adalynne held Katie's daughter who was swaddled and sleeping peacefully in her arms. "What is her name?"

"We are naming her Taylor Bee Holston." Katie beamed happily from her hospital bed. Steven held her hand; they were both still overwhelmed with emotion from the birth of their daughter. Katie's murderous words were long forgotten as they gazed at each other with boundless love.

"I like it very much." Adalynne smiled. She was honored.

"We thought you would."

Soon the delivery room filled with family. Katie's parents arrived, followed by Steven's, and then it continued until the room was full of people welcoming Taylor. It was a perfect way to enter the world surrounded by the love of family.

Chapter Twenty-Eight

It had been twenty-four days since Fox was released from rehab. Adalynne had seen the pictures in the gossip magazines lining the shelves on the street corner when she picked up her tea every morning since. The first title read "Brolan Pierce leaves rehab." There was a picture on the cover with his favorite leather jacket wrapped around his broad muscled shoulders. He was so handsome she couldn't help running her fingers over the glossy pages.

"Will the band get back together?" So many questions about his future printed on the pages. "What was the reason for Brolan's downfall?" She didn't know any of the answers. He hadn't contacted her since his release. She had thought of every possible reason why he did not seek her out and none of them meant a happy ending for her. The only title that came to her mind was "Fox doesn't love Bee after all."

As hard as it was when he was in rehab not knowing how he was doing, it was worse knowing that he was out, recovered, and still didn't want to see her. So many times she sat in her car with the intention of driving to his place and demanding to know why he continued to shut her out, but it wasn't fair to him when he was getting his life back together. She was proud of him and wouldn't get in his way.

Adalynne felt like she was the victim of some sick cosmic joke. Her whole life she had convinced herself Fox felt something more for her when he did not, stringing herself along in this twisted one-sided love affair since she was a little girl. After all that happened, after what she discovered about Fox, he still chose to stay away from her.

John remained elusive when it came to her questions about Fox. She knew he was in contact with Fox on a regular basis and it pained her when she realized John was avoiding her questions, only letting her know that he was doing well and figuring things out. As much as it relieved her to know that rehab had been a positive experience and he was now able to move forward with his life, she was sad to realize his plan did not involve her. Luckily, she had the grand opening of the Music House to distract her. She knew Katie was worried for her. She could see it every time she looked into her eyes.

She felt like she was in mourning again, she was grieving the hope she had held onto for her entire life. The hope that Fox would one day be hers to love felt as if it were drifting further and further away. She had promised she would wait for him the last time she had seen him and she intended to keep that promise even if it meant that she would be alone for the rest of her life. She had already tried to love another and failed miserably, this was her life and she would have to learn to accept it. She had played all her cards and lost her hand and now all she could do is sit out of the game of love.

***

The construction of the Music House had been completed a few weeks ago. Adalynne started music classes immediately in the new facility. The building was larger than the original, allowing much more space and flexibility. The concert room was large enough to host all of the families of the children, and the acoustics were optimal for music. More classrooms meant more opportunities to teach and she was already receiving resumes for music instructors wanting to join their reputable new school. News of their school spread and people were requesting classes from outside the community, making the commute to join their establishment.

They were praised for the quality of music they were exposing to their students. Adalynne ensured standards Elizabeth had established were carried on in her memory. Adalynne sold Elizabeth's old house once they moved the classes back to the Music House. She used the funds to build a new playground for the children and also built an amphitheatre on the large property. It was exciting to think they could now host outside performances in the warm months. John had taken responsibility to build the amphitheatre. He did a beautiful job and

Adalynne was overwhelmed with his workmanship. He could create anything from raw materials. It was always so impressive to see what he was capable of producing. The future of the Music House was bright and the crowd that was forming on the grounds for the grand opening was in support of this.

"Well done," Molly praised, giving Adalynne a hug.

"Thanks Molly, and thank you for your help," Adalynne said gratefully. Molly had been a wonderful help in preparation for the celebration. She had arranged for local bands to play on the new stage and advertised on the website about the official opening celebration.

People were gathering as the first band set up. Adalynne just finished setting up the BBQ that Molly and Brooke offered to run during the event. Brooke had recently toned down her appearance and was going for a more natural look. She had decided to try a more professional career path of real estate and was now trying to fit the profile. "Who's the one with the long hair and wild shirt?" Brooke narrowed her gaze on Kent, who was currently helping John with something by the stage.

"Oh Kent, he's a good guy. You would like him," Adalynne encouraged.

"I do. I *like*. Is he single?" Brooke asked with bright eyes.

"Like it matters to you," Molly scoffed.

"Yes, he is." Adalynne laughed as Molly and Brooke playfully quarreled about Brooke's morals. "I'll see you guys later. I'm going to see what John is up to." Adalynne wasn't even sure if the girls heard her as they continued their banter.

Adalynne walked up to the stage. John was putting a plaque up on the front of the wooden structure. "Oh hey, Addie. What do you think?" Adalynne read the words on the metal plaque now secured on the front of the stage. It read:

In memory of Elizabeth Martin. She will live on in our hearts and in the music we play.

Tears immediately came to Adalynne's eyes.

"It's wonderful, John." She wrapped her arms around him. He squeezed her back in a warm hug.

"I thought you would like it," he said proudly.

It wasn't long before the large property was filled with people. The band played and people enjoyed the atmosphere and the food. Children played with balloons, danced to the music, and tried out the new playground.

"Addie!" Katie called excitedly as she walked toward Adalynne. Taylor was in her arms and Steven was a few steps behind her weighed down by all the bags Katie had brought. "Wow, girl. This is quite the gathering. You must be proud," Katie said as she swayed Taylor to the music, now in full swing onstage.

"Yes, it's wonderful to see so many people come." Adalynne smiled. She leaned in to kiss Taylor's round cheeks. "I can't wait to teach these little fingers to play music," she said, kissing her little hands, making her beautiful little face break out into a smile. Every time she saw Taylor she looked bigger, she was growing so fast.

Everyone praised Adalynne for the work she did, commenting on the beautiful new Music House. It was nice to be surrounded by so many appreciative people. Adalynne quickly forgot all her fussing over all the details and became lost in the excitement. She was enjoying the company of her friends here to show their support.

Meredith arrived and Adalynne was elated when she noticed that John took her hand when they stood side by side. John met Adalynne's gaze and winked. She was glad he was finally moving on and exploring the relationship they had developed between them. She knew they cared for each other. She could see it in the way they looked at one another and now that John no longer needed her as a sponsor, their relationship took its natural course.

The conversation in their group died away. "Why didn't you tell me?" Katie hollered wide eyed at Adalynne, who looked back at her in confusion.

Adalynne turned to see why the crowd started cheering loudly. Her eyes found Fox onstage and she was immediately overcome with shock. The crowd cried out in excitement, people were amazed to see Outcome walk onstage to play for the small community gathering. It was funny that no one recognized him as the troubled little boy that grew up here, the very one they warned their children to say away from. They only saw the star he had become but Adalynne saw the boy who found her in her backyard so many years ago. The boy who crawled into her window at night and learned how to play the most beautiful music she had ever heard.

He was her Fox, the boy she had fallen in love with. Adalynne's mouth dropped open. John squeezed her shoulder but she could not take her eyes from Fox or even bring herself to move.

"Good afternoon, everyone." His velvety voice floated over the crowd, he looked around at all the people until his eyes settled on Adalynne. "I have a new song I would like to play for you today. I wrote it for someone who means very much to me." The crowd shouted out in anticipation. His eyes stayed with Adalynne as the band began to play, the song was captivating and everyone became entranced in the music.

He sang of his love for a girl, the most beautiful girl in the world who was always out of his reach. He dreamed to make that girl his and to love her like she deserved to be loved. It made Adalynne ache for him as he sang directly to her, his eyes never leaving hers. Katie grabbed her hand and stood beside her as they listened to his song. She didn't even realize she was crying until Katie passed her a tissue.

"I would like everyone to know that Adalynne Fairweather is the love of my life. I have loved her from the first time I saw her and I will love her for the rest of my life." The entire crowd turned to look at her.

"I knew it!" Katie whispered excitedly beside her. Fox jumped off the stage and the crowd parted as he walked toward her. So many people were taking pictures and videos and she couldn't bring herself to move. She felt like she was dreaming as he approached her. When he neared her, he wrapped his arms around her waist and pulled her close to his body. Everyone around them melted away and she could only focus on him as he looked down at her. She was lost in his beautiful green eyes, her favorite place in the world. "I love you, Bee."

"You don't know how long I have waited to hear those words," she breathed. Her words sounded funny to her, she was ready to fall apart in his arms.

"You don't know how long I have waited to say them." He smiled before he leaned down and brought his mouth against hers. His lips molded perfectly to hers and they both savored the kiss. When he pulled back from her, she touched her lips, still tingling from his touch. That was how a kiss was supposed to feel like.

"Sorry it took me so long. Rock bottom is a hard place to climb out of," Fox said softly, tucking her hair behind her ear and trailing his fingers along her cheek. The sensual touch made her body crave more of him.

"I told you I would wait no matter how long it took." Adalynne smiled brightly. The force that drew her to him was strong and undeniable. It flowed through her body like an electrical current. Every part of her wanted to be closer to him, to touch him, to love him.

"I want you so bad," he whispered wickedly into her ear and it caused heat to pool in her as her body responded to his words. She felt like she could not contain herself being so close to him.

Adalynne's surroundings slowly came back into focus as everyone cheered for them. They were surrounded by all the people she loved. The promise in his eyes spoke of what was in store for her and her body reeled with anticipation of the fact Fox loved her.

She caught her mother's gaze. She hadn't even noticed her arrival amongst the commotion. Adalynne broke out into a ridiculous smile as her mother beamed back at her.

Chapter Twenty-Nine

"Don't peek," Fox warned. The excitement in his voice was evident in his words. Adalynne could picture the smile spread across his handsome face.

"I'm not looking. I can't see a thing with your hands over my eyes anyway." Adalynne let out a nervous laugh as he led her through their house.

It had been a month since Fox and Adalynne had moved in together. Fox insisted on buying a new place to share together so the only memories they had of their place would be the ones they shared together as a couple. They walked through their living room and Adalynne's fingers skimmed the wall, nearly knocking a picture down. She quickly righted it. She knew the pictures from memory, every frame to touch. She had practically covered the entire wall with pictures of people that were close to their hearts. There were pictures of her parents and her favorite ones of her father that showed his beautiful smile that she missed every day. There was the only family picture Fox had before his mother had died. He was only a baby cradled in his mother's arms while John stood proudly behind them with his arm around her shoulder. Fox had his mother's unbelievable green eyes, but the masculine features of his father's handsome face.

There was also her favorite moment with Elizabeth when they first opened the original Music House. They both had ridiculous smiles on their faces and it was a moment she would always remember. Her favorite photos of Katie's wedding always made her smile because the joy captured in those few stills spoke volumes of the love that they had for one another. The most recent addition to the wall were the photos of John and Meredith's wedding. They had traveled south for a beautiful beach ceremony, a trip that was still fresh in their minds. Fox's skin was still irresistibly tanned, reminding her of all the wonderful moments they shared under the sun.

Fox and Adalynne were having so much fun making their house specific to their tastes, deciding on furniture and decorations usually resulted in trying to mesh different styles and unusual things together. Adalynne was painting a huge mural around their fireplace that tied all the varied colors of the items that encompassed the room. The result was comfortable craziness they called it and they loved their space.

"We can't be late for Taylor's birthday party. A little girl turns one only once, after all." Adalynne said as Fox continued to guide her. "Where are you taking me anyway?" She squeaked nervously as they continued forward, unsure of what Fox had planned.

"Trust me," he whispered in her ear. His nearness caused her body to heat and she could feel the familiar pull toward him. After all the years she knew him it never faded.

"Always." She smiled. He pulled his hands off her eyes and kissed the smile from her face. "Umm…is this my surprise?" she asked, running her hands up through his soft hair, always begging to be touched. She was greedily accepting his kiss, demanding more.

"Keep it up and we'll never make it to Taylor's party." His voice was breathy as he pulled away from her with a smile. "This is your surprise." He stepped back and motioned toward the backyard. Adalynne looked over to see their camp, the place they had built together so many years ago in their secret hideaway in the woods. It was strange to see it in their backyard and she couldn't help the shock that took over her features.

"How did you get it here?" Adalynne recovered, her open mouth was replaced with an excited smile. She looked up at Fox's beautiful smile lighting up his endless green eyes.

"Not without difficulty but completely worth it to see your reaction."

Adalynne screamed with excitement and jumped into his arms. She kissed him as he walked toward the camp and ducked into the door, bringing them inside. He set her down and Adalynne looked around, it felt like it had been such a long time since she had been inside but it was exactly how she remembered it. She reached up and touched the painting and smiled. "I love that you did this. I missed this place." Adalynne spun around while he watched her. "Do you know that this was the first place we kissed and umm…" She looked mischievously at him.

"Oh, I remember very well what happened in these walls." Fox gave her his sexy smile before grabbing his guitar, leaning against the wall, pulling the strap over his head. He sat down on a wooden crate and Adalynne did the same, wanting to listen to his beautiful music. Looking around, she noticed everything they had kept inside was still in its place. Their stash of supplies still sat in a box in the corner.

"Any requests?" He smiled while looking over at her.

"Surprise me." Adalynne smiled excitedly.

Fox began strumming his guitar. He always took her breath away. He affected her on every level and she was completely captivated by him. It was more than love.

Adalynne looked into his eyes as he began to sing to her. He was playing a song new to her and she listened as he sang the words.

"There once was a fox that fell in love with a bee
The most beautiful creature that he ever did see."

Adalynne listened with tears of joy in her eyes. He continued to sing the most beautiful lyrics she had ever heard. His words spoke of them, his love for her and his desire to spend his life with her.

"Oh Bee...marry me."

The realization of what was taking place hit her as he sang on and she was left crying before him. He slid the guitar off his lap and knelt down before her, retrieving a small box from his pocket.

"Adalynne Fairweather, will you make me the happiest man in this world and be my wife?"

Adalynne looked at the ring he presented to her. It was a form of a bee designed in diamonds. The sight of it made her gasp. "Yes, a thousand times, yes! I will marry you!" Adalynne cried. She climbed into his lap and kissed him through her tears and he held her like she was the most precious thing in the world.

"You know, I wrote that song when I was twelve years old. I've waited a long time to sing it to you," He said softly, stroking her cheek and tracing her swollen lips with his thumb.

"You knew you wanted to marry me when you were twelve?" Adalynne looked up at him, through her tear soaked lashes.

"No, I never thought I would be lucky enough but I wanted to."

"I love you, Fox." Adalynne pressed her lips against his.

"I love you too, Bee. More than you could ever possibly know."

Epilogue

Ten Years Later…

Fox

Fox looked down at his guitar as he strummed. He had been trying to find the right melody for a song he was working on. He closed his eyes and let the sound consume him as his fingers moved over the strings. Music was his language and he loved the process of creating, putting different combinations of chords together to create something that could pull the emotions out of listeners. He loved the raw reaction of fans as he stood on stage and played music they could connect with, sing along to, and dance to until exhaustion claimed them and they were emotionally spent.

He pulled his small, chewed pencil from his mouth and scribbled notes on the sheets of paper on his music stand. Movement caught his attention and he looked down. A set of big green eyes looked up at him. Fox pulled his headphones off his head and set his guitar down.

A deep smile captivated his face as he looked down at his beautiful little boy. He wore his favorite monster truck pajamas and had his toy guitar slung over his shoulder. "Shouldn't you be asleep, little man?"

"I 'ave a new song to show'd you." Quinlan looked up with his adorable crooked smile and it melted Fox's heart.

"Let's hear it then." Fox moved his music stand to give his son room to perform.

Quinlan swung his guitar around and positioned his tiny little hands on the frets. Adalynne had been teaching him the basics and he absorbed it all with his hungry little mind. He shared his parents' love of music deep in his bones.

Quinlan widened his stance and ran his fingers through his hair before he started playing. Some of the strings protested and screamed in pain as he played but the intensity on his little face was priceless. He was in his zone and in his little world he was a rock star.

Pride swelled deep and true in Fox's chest. He had learned long ago what was important in life and the little man standing in front of him with fierce determination to conquer music meant the world to him.

When Quinlan ended with his signature guitar shake and head nod, Fox stood and clapped before tapping his fist against his chest.

"Could you feel it?" Quinlan asked with wide eyes.

"I felt it all." Fox beamed at his son before

leaning down to kiss him on the top of his golden hair.

"How come you 'ave that picture wit your others?"

Fox turned in the direction Quinlan was pointing. A row of platinum records lined his wall in his home studio, displaying his musical accomplishments.

Quinlan was pointing to the frame with a worn letter inside. It was the letter that Adalynne's father had written before he died.

"That letter is very important to Daddy because it made me realize that I didn't need someone else to tell me I was good enough. I just needed to believe in myself."

"Why?"

"Because I wanted to love Mommy."

"That's funny. You do love Mommy."

"Always."

When I grow up can I be a rock 'tar like you?"

"Come here." Fox picked Quinlan up and walked over to the window. They both looked out at the dark night sky. "See all those stars?"

"Yeah."

"Daddy loves Mommy so much that it shifted the stars and one came loose and fell down to earth. Do you know where it landed?"

Quinlan shook his head.

"It landed in Mommy's tummy and then you were born. You are already a star. You shine every time you smile."

"Someone snuck out of bed, I see."

Fox turned around to see Adalynne walk into the

room. It never ceased to amaze him how breathtaking she was. She had owned him since the moment he walked into her life. "Hi babe, we were just looking at the stars."

"Daddy said I'm a 'tar."

Adalynne smiled brightly at her son, the kind of smile that only a mother can give to her child. "You are," she whispered before kissing his cheek. "Just like your daddy."

Acknowledgements

A huge thank you to:

My family—who are always my biggest fans.

Limitless Publishing—for giving me the opportunity to share this book with the world.

My editor, Toni Rakestraw—for polishing my words and her wonderful advice.

Readers—these were only words upon the pages until you brought them to life.

About the Author

Aimee McNeil was born and raised in Nova Scotia, Canada, where she continues to live today with her husband and three children. She is a stay-at-home mother that loves every colorful moment with her family.

Aimee spends most of her free time indulging in her love of writing. You can also find her lost in the pages of a good book, or making a mess with her paints. Aimee loves to explore anything that promotes creativity. It is one of the many reason she enjoys writing.

Facebook:
https://www.facebook.com/aimeemcneilswriting

Twitter:
https://twitter.com/aimeeswriting

Blog:
http://aimeemcneilswriting.blogspot.ca/

www.ingramcontent.com/pod-product-compliance
Lightning Source LLC
Chambersburg PA
CBHW051948240626
47153CB00005B/1674